THE CELLAR

JOHN NICHOLL

Boldwood

First published in Great Britain in 2022 by Boldwood Books Ltd.

Cover Design by Head Design

Cover Photography: Shutterstock

A CIP catalogue record for this book is available from the British Library.

Paperback ISBN 978-1-80426-368-6

Large Print ISBN 978-1-80426-369-3

Hardback ISBN 978-1-80426-370-9

Ebook ISBN 978-1-80426-367-9

Kindle ISBN 978-1-80426-366-2

Audio CD ISBN 978-1-80426-375-4

MP3 CD ISBN 978-1-80426-374-7

Digital audio download ISBN 978-1-80426-372-3

Boldwood Books Ltd
23 Bowerdean Street
London SW6 3TN
www.boldwoodbooks.com

1

Marcus Gove stared at the wall clock high above the psychologist's head, willing the hands to move a little faster. He raised an open hand to his mouth, yawning at full volume and then rubbing his eyes, as if struggling to stay awake. It was all part of his show. The persona he'd decided in advance to present that particular morning – anything to make his mundane existence just that little bit more interesting.

'Is this going to take much longer, Doc? It's getting boring.'

The secure hospital's most experienced expert, Dr Sally Barton, looked back at Gove, her senior nursing colleague, with a disdain it seemed she could no longer hide. Her professional identity was slowly disintegrating before Gove's eyes. Growing contempt was written all over her face.

'This assessment is part of the disciplinary process, Marcus. My report will inform the clinical director's decision regarding your future employment here at the hospital. You're an intelligent man, therefore you must realise your predicament. You need to take the process seriously. You're working with some of the country's most dangerous patients. As of now, I have serious doubts as to your suitability for the role.'

Gove's arrogant smirk became a full-blown belly laugh, head back, Adam's apple bouncing, dark mercury fillings in full view. There was much about working in a hospital for the criminally insane that amused him.

And this experience was no different. He began picking his nose, knuckle deep, flicking the snot over her right shoulder, as if aiming at the wall. His manic laughter suddenly morphed into a smile, replaced seconds later by a frown, the toothy grin disappearing as quickly as it had appeared. The appointment was progressing much as he'd hoped. He'd anticipated her seeking to retain a professional persona despite his antics, and now it was happening, making it all the more delicious.

'So, I need to take this shit seriously, do I? Do I really? Is that so? Dr Know-It-All has serious doubts about my therapeutic abilities. It would be funny if it weren't so pathetic. You are so full of crap, lady. The director is a bitch, and so are you.'

Gove watched as the psychologist slowed her breathing, steadying herself, sucking in the air before releasing it. The strain was getting to her. She was usually so calm, self-assured, and composed, but not now. There was a sheen of sweat on her brow, which pleased him. He'd liked to have licked it away. He considered it briefly but decided against it. He wasn't ready to bring the interaction to a close. Everything was going his way. The bitch was squirming. Ha! There was more fun to be had.

Gove silently acknowledged that he was starting to enjoy himself. He studied the psychologist closely as she prepared to speak, her lip trembling ever so slightly, her facial muscles tense. The second hand on the clock was moving a little faster now, time passing more quickly.

'Your behaviour has become extremely concerning, Marcus. You're alleged to have had an overly familiar relationship with a patient, a man with paranoid schizophrenia, a predator who killed seven women before disposing of their bodies. It doesn't get any more serious than that.'

Gove began rocking in his seat, his eyes wide, popping.

'You said "alleged". It was alleged, alleged, *alleged*! Doesn't that suggest an element of doubt on your part? It seems you're not nearly as clever as you like to think you are, Doc.' He repeatedly jabbed out a finger, pointing towards the three framed academic certificates on the wall to his left. 'Maybe all those flashy paper qualifications aren't worth shit. All those years of study were a complete waste of time and effort. You're a bad joke, Doc. How much good do you do? Fuck all, that's the truth of it. You come here, day after day, spouting your mindless nonsense to no good effect.

Surely you must have realised that by now. Anyone with even half a brain would understand that reality. You're a non-person, an irrelevance. Such a sorry sight to witness. How very sad to behold. Maybe you should crawl off and die somewhere in a dark hole where others wouldn't have to suffer your vile attentions. I'm sure I would in your place. I couldn't stand the shame of it all. To have wasted one's life as you have, deluded by an unjustified sense of self-importance. You're no more than a wallflower with your expensive clothes, permed hair and make-up. You're a decoration for the amusement of males starved of female attention. And you're not even very good at that.'

The psychologist somehow held it together despite Gove upping the pressure, but he felt confident her resolve was weakening. He was getting to her. Something he was good at, something he'd rehearsed and practised, sitting in front of a mirror, picturing her face, choosing his words, even his expressions, anything to make her twitch. He saw her stoic determination as a challenge to be overcome as he sat listening intently, searching for weaknesses, throwing one verbal grenade after another into the mix, simply because it amused him to do so. He waited with interest to hear what she said next, already deciding to dismiss it, preparing to go on the attack.

'This isn't a criminal court of law, Marcus. We're not talking about proving the allegations against you beyond a reasonable doubt. I think we both know what happened. You agreed to cooperate with this process. At the very least, you developed an excessive interest in the patient concerned. Your fascination with his crimes went *well* beyond the professional. If anything, you fed his fantasies. We need to address that openly and honestly if we're to make any progress. It seems that, yet again, I need to remind you that I'll be making a recommendation as to whether you should keep your job at the end of this assessment process. There are issues you need to address.'

He tilted his head at an angle, leaning towards her with his open hands held wide.

'Were they crimes?'

Her eyes narrowed.

'Sorry, what are you talking about?'

'Isn't it obvious? It would be to anyone with even the slightest degree of insight. I'm referring to my new friend. The Hunter, as he was so appropriately referred to in the press. The gentleman you so flagrantly dismiss with your tired moral judgements and labels. Think about it. All he did was kill a few worthless vagrants, homeless trash, hardly a great loss to society. Is he insane? Should he even be locked up like some caged animal for idiots like you to irritate with your endless nonsense? I'm really not sure he should. So, he didn't live by your rules. So what? Who are you to judge?'

She screwed up her face, and he knew he was winning. For a fleeting moment, he thought she might start crying.

'Those women had a right to live like everybody else.'

He couldn't reply until he stopped laughing. And even then, he giggled as he spoke, stopping between sentences to draw breath. He thought her contention utterly ridiculous. One of the most ludicrous things he'd ever heard. And that was saying something, given her lunacy, the moral straight jacket within which she lived her life: such misplaced principles, such unfortunate limitations.

'You claim they had a right to life, these dregs of society, the filth that lives in the gutters. Did they? Did they really? Who are you to decide? Governments kill with impunity, as does nature, wars, famines, earthquakes, disease. It seems it's the way of the world, survival of the fittest.'

'Please think very carefully before saying anything else, Marcus. Some of the things you've shared are extremely concerning. Are you trying to be provocative? Is that what's happening here?'

He spoke more quietly now, his body language relaxed as he sat back in his chair, legs crossed, a single finger raised to his chin below his bottom lip.

'I'm told you have a strong religious faith. The Bible on your bookcase hasn't gone unnoticed. You're one of those do-gooder, God-botherer types who think they are oh so very special. But you're just a big bag of shit, blood and intestines like everybody else. The Good Book is full of death and destruction, plagues, pestilence and genocide. Where is your God in all that? Surely, He must be the architect of it all if your belief system is accurate. Or is all that the work of the Devil? Is evil the dominant force in our universe? Let me know your thoughts. Are you as confused as it seems?'

Dr Barton shuffled a sheaf of papers, the colour draining from her face. It seemed she didn't know what to do with her hands.

'We're here to talk about *you*.'

'You flatter me, Doc. Am I that fascinating? Don't answer that. I must be, or we wouldn't be sitting here now. It's all about me, my interests, desires and thoughts. I bet you wish you were more like me. You're so uptight, so restricted in your ways.

'I've actually developed a growing admiration for the man in question. Harrison approached his activities with a passion. He killed because such things gave him pleasure. He sucked the juice out of life. He explored the very limits of human behaviour and got away with it for six long years before the interfering police finally caught up with him and a judge sent him here. Isn't that something to celebrate? I was keen to congratulate him. I wish I had even an ounce of his courage. I'd pin a medal on his chest if I could. He has so much more to offer the world than you.'

The psychologist spoke more slowly now, as if she thought her tone might calm him, eliciting a different response.

'Fredrick Harrison has a serious, chronic mental health condition, Marcus. He hears intrusive voices. His paranoid schizophrenia drove him to kill. He's ill, Marcus. And I'm beginning to think you may be too.'

Gove jumped to his feet, spinning in a circle on the ball of one foot before standing to face her.

'Well, isn't that just fine and dandy? The oh-so-clever Dr Full-Of-Shit thinks I'm ill. Maybe I should take an aspirin. Or perhaps eat an apple. Doesn't one a day keep the doctor away? I'm sure either option would be a lot more beneficial than talking to the likes of you.'

She pressed herself against the back of her seat. To Gove, it seemed she'd had enough. She'd soon bring the meeting to an end. Too soon for his liking, but he was determined to make the best use of whatever little time he had left. He decided to let her say her piece before pouncing. Whatever mindless bullshit she came up with was a mere preamble to his dramatic climax, no more than that.

'I'm going to recommend to the director that you take an extended period of sick leave. I've seen a significant deterioration in your mental health in the time you've worked here. That now appears to have reached crisis point. I implore you to listen to me. You need help, Marcus. I need you to understand that. I plan to refer you for an urgent psychiatric assessment. Please take what I've told you on board.'

Gove bent easily at the waist, placing his face only inches from hers. And then he opened his mouth wide and licked her, poking out his tongue, leaving warm saliva smeared across one cheek and eye as she flinched back in apparent fear. The look of total shock on her face amused him immensely as she urgently reached for her panic alarm. She almost succeeded but not quite, as he moved quickly, with agility and grace, and pulled her arm away, holding it tight by the wrist, digging in his fingers, not letting go.

'Oh no you don't, bitch. Don't ever make the mistake of thinking you're in control. It's always "Marcus this" or "Marcus that" with you. Do you think I might forget who I am without the endless reminders, you ridiculous woman? I don't like you very much. You may have realised that by now. You remind me of my mother. That vile skank was a bitch too. And as for my job, you can stick it where the sun don't shine. I've won the lottery, Doc, almost twelve million quid. I'll be moving across the country. A big flash house, a new car and new interests in which I'll have ample time to indulge. I won't be your problem any more. I hope you've enjoyed my company as much as I have yours. Looking at you cowering there like some pathetic, powerless victim is quite a turn-on.'

The psychologist wiped her face with a hand, blinking repeatedly, her voice faltering. 'What m-makes you think I w-won't go to the police?'

Gove laughed, genuinely amused. He'd never heard anything funnier.

'The police? Because of a lick and a little grab? Don't be so fucking ridiculous. We both know the system. It's your word against mine. There's only you and me here. Where's your corroboration? The CPS would drop it like a stone.'

She shouted now, close to tears. 'Go, and close the door behind you. I want you gone!'

'Oh, dear, so not very professional after all. You can go fuck yourself. I'll leave my uniform in the bin on my way out.'

2

FIVE YEARS LATER

Gove wiped himself with a tissue as his erection slowly subsided and he let out a long, audible groan that reverberated around the room, echoing off the walls. His exhilaration slowly faded now, feelings of great happiness replaced by the familiar sad regret that inevitably followed each killing. Not because a life was lost, not because he'd murdered again, robbing another young woman of her promise, but because it was over. He'd lived out his imaginings in what he considered a glorious frenzy of uncontrolled violence – visceral, explosive and orgasmic – with none of the self-imposed limitations indulged by weaker men who would never understand what was truly possible if one embraced one's darkest desires without restriction. Frederick Harrison had known that, and he knew it too. But for now, the pleasure was at an end for another day, nothing but a memory. The worthless bitch was dead, her torment in the past. She was free of him, and that hurt. It ate away at his peace of mind, engulfing him mercilessly, threatening the black shadow of depression as her blood began to slowly coagulate, forming semi-solid stains on his hair and clothing.

Gove reached down to touch her broken hand – three fingers missing, the nails torn out – and lamented the fact her suffering was no more. If only he could go back, do it all over again and slow down time. The killing was a wondrous experience, but it passed all too quickly. As enjoyable as it was, there was only so long the final act could last once he lost control, cutting her throat from ear to ear while simultaneously shooting his load. It all happened so fast, in a heartbeat, as the endorphins flooded his system.

Gove looked around the room now, taking in the details: the total lack of furniture, the high ceiling, the bare floorboards stained with various body fluids, and he felt another deep pang of regret as the remains of his latest victim caught his eye. There was always the intention to take it slowly, inflict as much pain as possible before death, take pleasure in the victim's suffering, and savour the terror in her eyes, her desperation as she pleaded for her worthless life. But the excitement always got the better of him. The desire to inflict that final blow, driving the life force from her body, tearing her apart, became utterly irresistible in the end, as predictable as night and day. Whether he used a blade, his hands or some other implement of execution, the outcome was always the same. And the blood, he so loved the blood. He was erect again now as he thought of it, his penis standing to attention, throbbing. Blood seduced him. The colour of it, the way it flowed, its scent, the taste, the metallic tang on his tongue as he sank in his teeth and tore his victim's flesh from the bone. Yes, he loved everything about death, killing, the suffering of others, but not his own. It was his needs that mattered, his and his alone. He was a man devoid of a moral compass, that moronic sense of right and wrong that lesser men indulged. He felt no guilt, no remorse. Not for her, not for any of them. The girls who'd suffered at his hand, who breathed their last breath as he loomed over them, appreciating their final moments on Earth as the light faded in their eyes.

And that was a good thing, that lack of conscience. He thought it and believed it. It was a wonder; he was proud of it. His victims didn't matter as he did. They were inferior creatures, unimportant, disposable, fertiliser, no more than food for the worms. It was all about him, meeting *his* needs, feeding *his* desires in the only way that was even remotely satisfying. He was an artist. There was a beauty to death as he created one glorious masterpiece after another. If a few more mindless females had to die to achieve that end, so be it. It was his mission in life. He felt the hand of providence guiding him. And so he'd keep killing in one way or another, one after another. Such things made his life worth living. Murder would happen time and again.

But for now, it was over as he slumped to the wooden floor, still panting slightly, his chest rising and falling in rhythmic movement as he lay next to her naked torso, various body parts scattered around the room. He was weeping, warm tears running down his angular face as he whispered his goodbyes into what was left of her ear. If only he could bring her back to life to kill her again. But that wasn't possible, not in this life. It seemed there were limitations after all.

Gove rose to his feet, shivering slightly as he raised an arm high above his head, punching the air, howling like a demented banshee as a full moon, now free of clouds, lit the killing room with a pale-yellow light. Yes, it really was over, and, for a time, like it or not, the memories would have to sustain him. But only until the next time, until he captured his next target. He held his hands together now as if in prayer, linking his fingers, his mind racing. May the waiting pass quickly! It was getting harder. He had to admit that. The waiting was agonising, more so than ever before. There was no denying that reality. The time between killings had reduced, going from years to months and then weeks. And now it was time for the next one, probably the best yet. And she had no idea of the raging storm coming her way.

Gove took his smartphone from a trouser pocket and flicked through the photos with repeated swipes of two bloodstained fingers, left to right. Yes, there she was. Lucy, lovely Lucy. Outside her flat, shopping in town, leaving her workplace, sunbathing at the beach in that skimpy red bikini he'd found so attractive, the colour of blood. He'd never targeted a local girl, living and working no more than half an hour's drive from his large Georgian home. He hadn't even hunted within Wales – no zone of comfort for him. The hunting grounds of the far-flung English industrial cities offered a much safer option. In the poorer areas, the red-light districts where poverty ruled and the vulnerable plied their trade, selling themselves to anyone who'd pay, slaves to their addiction. So, why was this time so very different? He wasn't merely targeting a local girl, but a girl who was loved, with a successful, influential family, a boyfriend, an impressive social-media profile and a well-paid job. A girl who'd be missed. A girl they'd look for, the snooping authorities with their misguided morality. Why take the risk?

He turned slowly in a circle and pondered his silent response, shifting his slight eleven-stone frame from one foot to the other, as if the floor was too hot to stand on. Because she was special, that was why! He'd known it the first time he saw her on the Welsh evening news. An award-winning artist and lecturer, no less. Stunningly beautiful with her long flame-red hair, sea-blue eyes and flawless pale skin, so white it looked almost translucent, like the finest porcelain. That skin was aching for a blade, his blade. He'd never been more sure of anything in his life. He'd create a masterpiece of red, white and gore. She should appreciate that, being a fellow artist and all. They had that in common. It would be so delicious to get his hands on her. And maybe he'd keep her alive for a week or two this time to appreciate the company, build the tension, and anticipate the inevitable final climax as he tore her limb from limb.

Gove laughed out loud on considering the apparent contradiction, jumping up and down on the spot as he anticipated what was to come. Keeping a guest alive for a time was something he'd never done before, something he'd never even considered, not for a moment. The killing always proved too tempting once his prey entered his lair. But maybe Lucy would appreciate his genius; perhaps she'd understand the things that drove him to do what he did. If he gave her time, there might be some satisfaction in that. But could he stand to wait that long before watching her die? It would take some determination, however pleasing their interaction. Maybe it was possible to hold himself back, just maybe, if he tried hard enough, and if she tried too. If she said and did all the right things in the face of adversity. She'd have to suffer for his art and do it willingly. Nothing less was acceptable.

He placed his phone aside and began ambling towards the far right-hand corner of the room, where the decomposing body of a prior victim was propped up in a seated position close to the open door to the hall. He had no real objection to the company of corpses. There was no fear in them. They weren't as much fun as the living, but he could still find some satisfaction in the dead's total compliance as they acceded to his every whim and desire. But things had gone too far now, even for him. The body was stiff, the flesh rotting, her bony face more a skull than a person. It was time for burial in a garden grave, deep in the Welsh countryside, far from prying eyes where no one else would see.

He pictured Lucy's pretty face as he dragged the nameless young woman's remains away from the wall. Now, where was that meat cleaver? And the bone saw. Where the hell was the saw? The shed, yes, that was it, the shed. He'd cleaned and oiled them before putting them away. It was essential to look after the tools that served him so well.

He continued his thought process as he strolled out into his overgrown garden to where a small wooden shed that looked well past its best was located among several mature apple trees, which always provided a good crop. Once the bitch was buried, he could continue planning, focusing on lovely Lucy and her alone. As he opened the shed door, he paused and licked his lips, first the top and then the bottom as he pictured events, making them real in his mind. Yes, he'd capture her when the time was right, lure her in and pounce before she realised her uncertain fate. It was something he was good at, a skill he'd practised, inspired by his time at the hospital. He could be Mr Nice or Mr Nasty, whichever was needed. He'd play the game, hooking Lucy in one way or another, whatever worked best in the particular situation. But he had to be careful. He couldn't grab her off the street as he had some of the others. He couldn't just shove her into the back of a van or lure her in with the offer of cash for one sexual favour or another. This one was different; the circumstances were different, her lifestyle, the location, the dangers. This time there was a need for caution. He'd been watching her closely for weeks, something he'd never done before. And it seemed she was a creature of habit, which would help him snare her.

Gove picked up his butcher's tools, closed the shed door with a grin, and began giggling uncontrollably as he walked back towards the back door of his spacious detached home. Yes, Lucy, lovely Lucy would soon be his to do with whatever he wished. A plaything caught in his spider's web. He'd never been more sure of anything before. It was destined to be and written in the stars. And that was a cause for celebration.

He stopped in the kitchen, placing his tools aside on the polished black granite worktop, having decided on a little light refreshment before continuing his night's work. Dismembering a corpse could be exhausting. He needed fuel, sustenance to keep up his energy levels. It may be an excellent time to open a bottle of sparkling mineral water. And maybe a sandwich too – prawn with garlic mayo, or lean beef with English mustard, either would fill a gap very nicely. A man had to eat.

He smiled, full of self-praise as he approached the larder fridge, opening the door and looking in. He was evolving, becoming a better, more considered killer: a predator at the top of his game. He looked to the future with a significant element of glee, like a loved child anticipating a birthday treat. Yes, lovely Lucy would be his. It was just a matter of time.

3

Lucy felt a deep sense of regret and frustration – not the best way to start her day. Andrew Baker glared at her with an angry, sour expression, spitting out his words as if the very taste of them was disgusting to him. It had all become too depressingly familiar. It seemed he was witnessing one of the worst sights he'd ever seen, an abomination, right there in front of him. 'Why the short skirt?'

More disappointed than surprised, Lucy turned to face her boyfriend as she prepared to leave their ground-floor flat for work at eight fifteen on an unusually warm Welsh May morning. She glanced down, pointing at her hemline before meeting his angry gaze one more time. She noticed his left eye was twitching ever so slightly. It seemed the tension was getting to him too. It was all becoming so very regular. Every day, she was forced to appease him in one way or another. This ever more hostile man-child was becoming harder to like, even slightly, let alone love. He was so very different to the boy she'd met at college, the one with a relaxed, non-judgemental demeanour and friendly smile. Happiness, it now seemed, was well beyond them. It was all so regrettable. Where oh where had that boy gone? Was it just a nice-guy act? A mirage, an illusion? Sometimes she wished she'd never met him at all.

'What on earth are you talking about, Andy? It's just above the knee.'

He walked towards her, one step, two steps, as she went to open the front door. She waited for him to say something, as she knew he inevitably would. And when he did speak, it wouldn't be good. She felt sure of that; these days, it rarely was.

'And that blouse, you need to fasten the top button. Have you even got a bra on? It's a little revealing, don't you think? Have some respect for yourself. Be a lady. I can see through the material when it catches the light. Other men will notice that. They'll think you're a tart. It won't just be me.'

She took a backwards step as he stood in front of her, their noses only a few inches apart. She could feel his hot breath on her face, the stink of last night's beer filling her nostrils.

'Don't stand so close. Please, Andy, you're making me feel uncomfortable. Back off.'

She raised a hand to his chest when he didn't move, gently pushing him back, forcing an unconvincing smile that felt so out of place in circumstances that were anything but amusing. The smile was impossible to maintain despite her best efforts. What she'd like to have done would be to tell him to fuck off. To say it to him right there and then to his face, loud and proud, leaving him in no doubt about her feelings. It would have felt so good, so very satisfying. But it wasn't in her nature. She thought of herself as a lover, not a fighter. The words would stick in her throat.

'For goodness' sake, Andy, why this again? I'm dressed for work, and I'm dressed professionally. My outfit is entirely appropriate. It's almost the end of May. It's going to be hot. Did you see the weather forecast? It'll be boiling by this afternoon. One of the hottest days on record for the time of year.'

'A bit of hot weather shouldn't stop you covering up.'

Lucy gritted her teeth, frowning hard and thinking this was the final straw, ready to say what was on her mind.

'Please, Andy, you've said enough. It's every single day, and you never let up. It's always the same thing. It's time to stop. You're wrecking what's left of our relationship. And for no good reason at all. What part of that don't you understand?'

His overly muscular shoulders slumped over his chest as his voice lowered in pitch and tone; melancholy, bordering on the pleading, a change of strategy she'd seen before. 'Please, change your clothes for me. It's not much to ask. I'd do it for you if you asked.'

She sometimes thought that his earnest emotional appeals were even worse than his anger. She knew she'd have to listen as she always did, feeling she didn't have a choice. Once again, she wished that she did.

'Put on something more modest,' he continued. 'A pair of loose trousers – maybe the pair I bought you on Saturday, the green ones, something less attention-grabbing. You said you liked them, so why not wear them? I could fetch them now. They're hanging in your wardrobe. I cut the labels off. You weren't lying about liking them, were you?'

Lucy felt her entire body tense. She looked down at her watch, holding her arm out in front of her, making it obvious, and for a moment, she feared he might start weeping again. He did that sometimes, and she hated it more than almost anything else. It was either anger or tears, always one or the other, and sometimes both. She wondered again what had happened to the man she fell in love with, the fun Andy, the confident Andy who could be a pleasure to be with, the man who contributed. It seemed he was long gone, never to return.

She reached for the door handle and he finally stepped aside. She turned it, pulling the open door towards her, keen to get out of there and on her way. Her college workplace beckoned as a means of escape, a sanctuary. There'd been far too much recent drama in their lives. Andy had changed so very much and not for the better. Maybe he was showing his true colours, or perhaps they just weren't right for each other any more. She'd grown as a person, developed, matured, moved on with her life, and he hadn't. In fact, he'd gone backwards. The entire situation had become toxic, more destructive than she could ever have imagined. 'I haven't got time for this. I've got a job to go to, and I'm going to be late. I need to get going.'

'Just change – you can do it quickly. It won't take you long. You don't want men drooling over you when you're walking down the street. It makes me feel like puking just thinking about it.'

Lucy's expression hardened as she resisted the impulse to scream out a string of heartfelt insults, something that was becoming harder by the day.

She silently swore that she'd tell him exactly what she thought of him one day. But today was not that day.

'Have I ever cheated on you, even once?'

He chose not to answer, looking away.

'I'm wearing what I'm wearing. It would be best if you accepted you're not the boss of me. You can't try to dictate to me like this. If you want to drive me away, you're doing a damned good job. There's only so much I can take.'

He followed her on his bare feet, wearing only jockey shorts and an overly tight vest, as she rushed towards her faded red two-seater convertible sports car, parked in the street about thirty yards from the flat.

'Will you be home for lunch?'

Lucy couldn't quite believe he'd asked the question. It seemed so unreasonable, so demanding, so very needy. As if he thought all that had been said before was of little, if any, consequence. She unlocked the car, threw her tan faux-leather handbag onto the passenger seat and climbed in, slamming the door more forcibly than she intended before winding down the window with an electric buzz.

'I'll see you sometime after five. Lunchtime isn't an option. I can't come rushing back here and then go straight back to work again. I've got a full day of commitments. You're going to have to sort out your own lunch. I haven't got the time.'

'Oh, you've got more important things to do, have you? But then, of course, you have – everything's more important than me.'

Lucy had a sinking feeling deep in the pit of her stomach. She bit her tongue hard, wincing, rather than say something she may later regret.

'I'm going now, Andy. You've said enough. Please, please, please, try to do something constructive with your day.'

Even in the fresh morning air, she could smell the reek of his stale body odour as he placed the palms of both hands on the car's black canvas roof.

'What's that supposed to mean?'

Lucy considered driving off without saying anything more, but she decided against it. Some things needed to be said. It had to be worth one more try. Maybe this time, her words wouldn't fall on deaf ears.

'Take a shower and take some time going through the online job adverts. We can't keep borrowing from my parents. It would help if you started earning some money again. My salary isn't enough to cover all the bills.'

He snarled his reply, anger now his dominant feature as it contorted his unshaven face – another side of him she'd seen before.

'Oh, you'd like that, wouldn't you? Me doing some shit job while you swan around being the oh-so-successful artist I was meant to be. I suppose you think one day you'll win the Turner Prize. You're so full of big ideas.'

Lucy sighed deeply. She'd heard enough. She could have responded again, but there was little, if any point. She felt sure he'd spend his entire day playing pointless computer games and lifting ridiculously heavy weights again. It's what he did every day, either that or spying on her, snooping, going through her phone when he got the chance, asking questions, making judgemental comments, trying to control.

She started her car's petrol engine with two key turns, signalled, and pulled out into the road, taking full advantage of a sudden gap in the morning traffic. The car was almost ten years old, not worth very much, but still drove well. It felt so good to be driving away, a small victory of sorts. She could still see Andy standing on the pavement, ranting at her in the rear-view mirror, before negotiating the first bend in the road, losing sight of him. She reminded herself that if things didn't change for the better very soon, she'd have to end it. She'd thought the same thing many times before. But she told herself that this time she meant it. There was only so much she could deal with, however much she loved him. And did she even love him any more? Maybe it was all just memories of a better past keeping them together. In some ways, the relationship had already died. At best, it was wallowing in its death throes. She had to face that truth.

As Lucy pressed her foot down hard on the accelerator pedal, driving a lot faster than was sensible, she decided it was a time for change. But maybe she'd talk things through with her mother first. That always helped. Mum was the one person in life she could truly rely on in times of adversity.

4

Lucy sat on the edge of her old wooden desk in her small, cluttered art-college office, picked up her mobile and tried to decide whether or not to ring her mother. Should she or shouldn't she? Yes or no? She still had half an hour or so before giving her first lecture. Time wasn't a problem. And she'd already prepared. Oh, what the hell, why not ring? Mum wouldn't mind. She never did.

The decision to reach out to her mum wasn't easy. A part of her still hated placing any kind of emotional stress on her, particularly since the breast cancer diagnosis. There was always an element of guilt when she finally made an emotionally charged call. But she always made it. Her need to chat with the one person who loved her unconditionally and wouldn't ever sit in judgement whatever she shared inevitably overrode her reticence. Lucy touched the phone's screen with her finger and only had to wait a few brief seconds before the call was answered.

'Hi, Mum, have you got time for a chat?'

'Of course, I have. I've always got time for you. You should know that by now. Nobody is more important than my girl.'

She felt relief and pleasure on hearing her mother's familiar musical West Wales tones on the other end of the line. There was comfort in her mother's voice. Like the cool side of a pillow in summer, or a roaring log fire on a cold winter evening. It took Lucy back to a happy childhood.

Lucy smiled, a thin smile but a smile nonetheless. Just talking to her mum made her feel better. 'Andy has been at it again.'

Myra Williams let out a contemptuous snort.

'Oh, for goodness' sake no. What has he done this time? He hasn't hit you, has he?'

Lucy closed her eyes tight shut, shaking her head slowly before opening them again. Weeping without words, her salty tears soiled her face, smudging her mascara. How much should she say? Should she mention the intimidation, Andy's use of steroids, the money he was wasting, the jealousy, the anger, the scary tantrums? She laughed despite herself. Living with Andy was like parenting a giant toddler, the terrible twos but in his twenties.

'No, it's nothing like that. Andy's not a violent man. He can be intimidating and he sometimes frightens me, particularly when he's drunk – he's a big guy – but I don't think he'd ever hurt me, not really. It's the jealousy thing that truly gets me down. I've never given him even the slightest reason to doubt me, not since we first met at college. He never used to be like this. It's like he's paranoid.'

Lucy pictured her mother's frowning face before she heard her response.

'What about that time you had the bruising on your face? The slap marks. That's something I'm not going to forget in a hurry. I can see it now as if it was yesterday. You should have dumped him then.'

'I've told you, they weren't slap marks. Andy reached out to grab me when I tripped and fell. It was an accident. I thought I'd made that perfectly clear. I don't know how many times I need to repeat myself.'

'Men don't change, Lucy, not fundamentally. They are what they are. They do what they do. Your father's not perfect – nobody is – but he's never laid a finger on me in anger, not once in over thirty years of marriage. If Andrew did slap you, he will do it again one day. And next time, he may even do something worse. You've just told me you're scared of him. You said it in your own words. I've told you what I think. It would be best if you told him to move out. It's you paying the bills. It's your flat, not his. You deserve a lot better. He's not the man for you.'

'How's Dad?'

Myra laughed humourlessly. Lucy knew that sound. It was a conversation they'd had before.

'Are you changing the subject?'

'Yes, I suppose I am now the lecture's over. So, how is Dad? I don't think I've seen him for weeks.'

Myra emitted a long, deep audible breath.

'Oh, you know what your father is like. Always working, rushing from one commitment to the next. What with his trips back and forth to London, the constituency surgeries, social events, the media work and everything that goes with it, it sometimes feels like I hardly ever see him myself. But I wouldn't want him any other way. I knew what he was like when I married him. He's a go-getter, a dynamo. He was no different back then to now. I suppose I've got used to it over the years.'

'It's not like you've had a choice.'

'Well, there's some truth in that, but I've no complaints. We've had a long and happy marriage. We still love each other after all the years. And he's never let me down, not even once. That's more than many can claim.'

Lucy was silent for a few seconds before speaking again.

'And how are *you*, Mum?'

Myra was quick to reply, as if she wanted to get this part of the conversation over with as fast as possible. 'Oh, you know me, getting on with life as best I can, always looking on the positive side. I'm a glass-half-full sort of girl. I've got a roof over my head, good friends and a family who love me. There are a lot of people coping with a good deal worse. It's important to be grateful for your blessings.'

'No, really, how are you? How are you feeling? No more avoiding the subject, I want to know.'

There was a short silence followed by a series of muffled sobs and then the sound of her mother blowing her nose before she finally spoke again. 'Do you really want to know?'

'I asked, didn't I?'

'Well, the chemo's a drag, being sick's no fun at all, and losing my hair isn't the best look in the world. I won't be winning any beauty contests anytime soon. And the wig is just too hot and itchy. I only wear it if I've got company. But other than that, I'm doing fine.'

'You're so strong, always making light of it all. I think you're amazing. I don't tell you that often enough.'

Myra inhaled so loudly that Lucy could hear.

'I'm tired, love. I didn't get a great night's sleep. It's lovely talking to you, but I need to lie down.'

There was one other concern Lucy had considered mentioning, but she decided to let it go. It could wait for another time when her mum felt stronger.

'I'm sending you a big hug.'

'Right back at you. Tell me some good news before we end the call, something positive. Say something to make me smile. I could do with cheering up. It would give me something to meditate on. You know, I just can't concentrate on a book. I so used to love reading. Hopefully, I will again. I think it must be something to do with the medication.'

Lucy thought for a second or two, searching her busy mind. Her mother made the same request regularly, but coming up with something positive to say every time could sometimes prove a challenge.

'There is one thing. I wouldn't exactly call it good news, but I find it intriguing.'

'Oh, that sounds interesting. I'm all ears. Tell me more.'

'I've received a letter. All written on high-quality, watermarked, ivory-coloured paper in a beautiful flowing red script, with a pen and ink, not a biro. It's like a work of art in itself. It's the proposal of a commission. The writer said he saw me on the Welsh evening news after I won the award and was impressed by my work. He wants me to paint a large original oil painting of his home and extensive grounds. And he says he's willing to pay me well above my usual rate, no expense spared. The quality of the work is more important to him than the cash. That's not something I ever expected anyone to say. He's even offered to put me up at his home as his guest while I complete the painting. I'm not sure I'd want that, but I do like the idea of the work. It's the kind of thing I love doing.'

'Is it somewhere local?'

'I assume so, but that's the strange thing. The letter doesn't include a full name or any postal address. There's not even a phone number or email, no way of me contacting him at all. It's just signed with a single name at the end: Moloch. He said he's a man who appreciates the arts. And that if I'm interested, as he seems certain I will be, I'm to meet him at that nice vegetarian café in Merlin's Lane at one o'clock on Monday lunchtime. You know the place.'

'Yes, of course I do. We all used to go there when you were younger. You loved the banana milkshake.'

Lucy smiled warmly as the memories flooded back.

'Whoever wrote that letter said it's meant to be, written in the stars. Can you believe that? It's, um, it's not like anything I've encountered before. But I have to admit, I'm finding it all rather exciting. I like to think the author must be romantic, a poet, maybe, an artist or an actor – a creative type like me. It should be interesting if nothing else. It's the sort of thing Andy may have done years ago in his student days but not any more.'

There was a harder edge to Myra's voice when she spoke again.

'I hate to rain on your parade when you seem so very enthusiastic, but I don't like the sound of it. Why no address? Why no contact details? You're a beautiful young woman, Lucy. That comes with risks. It shouldn't do, but it does. Be careful, love. Don't you think you're getting rather carried away with all this?'

Lucy made a face, a little disappointed by her mother's reaction. She'd been hoping for wholehearted parental encouragement. She was beginning to regret mentioning the letter at all.

'Oh, come on, you're being a little overdramatic, don't you think? It would do me good to have some fun. And it's well-paid work. My car's due for a service, and the tax runs out in a few weeks. It's too good an opportunity to miss. Andy hasn't earned a penny for months. I could do with the cash.'

'Some things are too good to be true. Isn't Moloch the name of an Old Testament devil? Something to do with human sacrifice. I'm sure I saw something on *University Challenge*.'

Lucy chuckled to herself, not a belly laugh, but close.

'No, of course not, don't be so ridiculous. It's a Welsh thing. I looked it up online. *Moloch* means, "please praise". I admit it's a tad unusual. What were his parents thinking?'

If anything, Myra sounded even more alarmed.

'Surely you're not planning on actually meeting this man?'

'Um, yeah, I think I very probably will. What harm could it possibly do to find out more over lunch? I may even enjoy myself.'

There was a growing tension in Myra's voice. 'In that case, why don't you take your sister with you? It wouldn't be a bad idea to have a bit of support.'

'I'm a big girl now, Mum. I don't need Cerys holding my hand.'

Myra emitted a loud yawn.

'Okay, you know best. I've said my piece. I know when I'm beaten. You can tell me more about it when we next speak. My bed is calling.'

'I love you. Say hello to Dad for me.'

'I love you too. And please think carefully before going to that meeting – it might not be such a good idea as you think. There are a lot of strange people in this world of ours. Not everyone is like you and me. It's a mistake to assume they are. You only have to watch the news to know that. It all sounds a little bit too weird to me.'

'Oh, I don't know. He can't be any weirder than some of the people I know at the college.'

'Think on it, that's all I'm saying. Better safe than sorry.'

'Bye, Mum!'

Myra yawned for a second time.

'Bye, love, see you soon.'

By the time Lucy ended her call, she was even more determined to meet the man who'd written the letter with such a creative and artistic hand. She briefly pondered her mother's cautionary words but quickly decided they were an unnecessary and misplaced overreaction. The style of Moloch's writing appealed to her. There was a creative flow to it that impressed. Even the dark-red ink she found interesting. Some might say it was the colour of life, the colour of blood. Okay, so it did all seem a little bit strange, but what did that matter? The artistic people of the world were prone to eccentricity of one kind or another. Some of life's most fascinating people were somewhat peculiar. Like Dali, who was stranger than him?

Didn't they say there was a thin line between genius and madness? She
needed some adventure in her life, some excitement. What harm could
meeting with the man for a bit of lunch possibly do? As long as Andy
didn't find out. He'd never understand. He'd corrupt it, making it into
something it wasn't. The lunch was something to look forward to, a chat
with a like-minded creative and a potential payday, no more than that.

5

Gove was dizzy with excitement. The 1 June had finally arrived, the day of days, when he'd meet the special one of his dreams for the very first time. He could not wait to look lovely Lucy in the eye.

As he leapt naked from his emperor-size bed, hurrying to the direction of the palatial black-and-gold-tiled en suite, he told himself that everything that had gone before had been leading to this. His terrible childhood, his disinterested drug-addled bitch of a mother, one abusive stepfather after another, the beatings, the sexual assaults, his time working at the secure hospital, meeting other killers, learning of their skills, sharing their passions, had all been a preparation for this glorious day. His life experience had been an apprenticeship of sorts, a transformation process. And lovely Lucy would be the reward for his dedication. All of his other victims now seemed unimportant by comparison. They'd been mere appetisers, something to whet his appetite, and no more than that. He could not wait to welcome Lucy to her new home.

Gove was salivating now, his fantasy-driven anticipation heightened almost to ecstasy, saliva dribbling from one side of his mouth, wetting his chin and neck. He lowered himself to the bathroom floor, masturbating, frantically stimulating his engorged penis, moving his hand up and down with ever-increasing speed as he pictured future events in his mind's eye, bright, large and loud. Moving pictures played behind his eyes like a dark cinematic film he'd scripted and directed. Yes, entertaining Lucy would be the high point of his life, the main course, delicious, fulfilling and so much more than that. He was sure of it. The very thought was almost orgasmic. He was getting harder, harder than ever before. It felt almost as if his penis might burst. He could see Lucy at his mercy, fearful, bleeding, as she collapsed to her knees and praised him. He could hear her chants of deep love and respect and see the dark-red blood running from her wounded eyes, nose and mouth. He could see the warm scarlet liquid contrasting dramatically against her pale white skin. He could almost taste her blood, almost touch it, raising his spirits to a new and dramatic high as he happily indulged his fantasy, fully intending to make it real.

Gove gripped his penis a little tighter and ejaculated, sticky semen spraying over his flat belly as he yelled out in delight. Ah, yes, lovely Lucy would so appreciate his genius, his work as a rare and exceptional executioner. How could she not praise him? How could she not worship him as the most remarkable man on Earth, almost godlike, greater than all others, those killers who lived in his shadow? Maybe he would become a god in time. Yes, yes, that was his journey, his ultimate destination as an arbiter of life and death. He had that power. The power to decide who lived and who died. And how they died too as they screamed in a sea of searing pain. He and he alone was worthy of her adoration. Lucy would understand that; she'd act on that wisdom. He was sure of it. It would become a momentous reality, one of the most extraordinary and significant events in human history.

After showering, Gove sang along to his favourite country music CD as he ate a light breakfast, just a bowl of sugar-free cereal and a cup of strong coffee with a dribble of skimmed milk taken from the fridge, cautious of calories. He placed the dirty dishes in the dishwasher, brushed his teeth for a full three minutes in the small ground-floor bathroom, then entered his killing room, where he sat next to the one remaining corpse he still hadn't buried in his private garden cemetery. He was keen to tell the dead girl of his plans. And eager to remind himself of all that had led to what he considered this sacred moment in time. He held the girl's decapitated head up in front of him by her long bottle-blonde hair, looked into the one remaining blue eye and began telling her his story with unbridled enthusiasm.

He'd been watching lovely Lucy for several weeks now, always in one disguise or another; travelling by train, paying in cash, tracking her movements, taking photos of the girl with flame-red hair who promised so much. And now the day had finally come, the day he'd meet her, speak to her, study her features up close at a glorious touching distance. It would be so delicious as he groomed her, built a relationship, trapping her and sinking in his claws. He looked forward to introducing Lucy to his killing room, sharing his interests, achievements, methods of torture and ambitions for the future. There would be ever more fascinating ways of inflicting pain, new recipes, cannibalism – something he hadn't yet embraced – cooking at its creative best. And records, he'd create records, committing more murders than anyone else in human history. That was the aim; not just the numbers but the most dramatic and imaginative methods of killing. One day, he'd be celebrated in the annals of true-crime history, recognised for his greatness when a misguided and confused world would finally see him as the master he was.

Gove decided on another garden burial as the morning progressed. Anything to help the minutes pass more quickly until the time came to leave the house to meet his special new love. He carried his young victim's head out into the overgrown garden, appreciating the sun's warmth on his face as he approached an area of ground adorned with a kaleidoscope of multi-coloured early-summer flowers surrounded by high, mature trees that seemed to reach up to touch the sky. There was a large oval pond, six to seven feet deep, where ducks and other waterfowl paddled among tall, slender reeds, and the old wooden shed, where he kept the various butcher's tools of his trade and a petrol lawnmower he rarely used. He looked around his expansive garden with a feeling of deep pleasure and satisfaction, congratulating himself on his inspired wisdom. It really couldn't be better. The nearest inhabited dwelling was over half a mile away – a large dairy farm surrounded by green fields and hedgerows. He'd chosen his home for the privacy it offered, with no nosy neighbours, no potentially interfering curtain-twitchers to spoil his day. He lived in wonderful isolation, just him and his involuntary guests; one young woman after another, brought there to die. There was no one to witness his activities, no one to hear his victims' cries, and that had suited him just fine. But now, everything would change. Lucy would be the first to see and admire, a potential partner in crime until her turn to die.

Gove threw the young woman's head to the ground with speed and force, rolling it in the style of a bowling ball, watching it tumble over and over until it came to an eventual halt next to a terracotta flowerpot planted with camomile. He thought he saw the head's one remaining eye wink at him just a fraction of a second before turning away, which amused and pleased him. It seemed the young woman supported his activities in death in a way she never had in life, when she'd bled and screamed and pleaded right to the end, testing his patience. He decided to bury his victim's body parts together in the one shallow grave rather than scatter them as food for nature's scavengers, the birds, the rats and the flies, which ate away the flesh, leaving nothing but bones; an act of kindness on his part. Sometimes, he chuckled to himself; he was too generous of spirit for his own good.

Gove sang a favoured operatic exit aria as he approached the shed, considering his eclectic taste in music a laudable aspect of a sophisticated personality. He'd listened to the recording in Italian but had translated the lyrics to English to better understand the words and sentiments. The impressive female soprano was singing about death, burial and loss, which he decided was eminently suitable given the task at hand. He opened the shed door with a self-satisfied smile. He'd use the wheelbarrow to transport the various body parts from his killing room to the burial spot rather than carry each in turn as he'd initially intended.

The victim's torso was surprisingly heavy as he lifted it from the wooden floor with both hands, wrapping his arms around it, struggling to hold it to his chest. She was of a bigger build than any of his previous guests, bigger boned and fleshy, which posed problems. Removing the limbs had been a surprisingly demanding process, even with the sharpest of saws, and now the lifting was challenging too. Maybe he should opt for slighter victims in future, ten stone at most – unless there were exceptional circumstances, of course. Yes, that made sense.

It took Gove at least five minutes to wrestle the torso into the barrow.

He lifted and dropped it three times before finally succeeding, bending his knees, keeping his back straight, and using his leg strength to take the strain. He was utterly exhausted, his chest rising and falling with the effort of it all as he added the young woman's legs and arms to the load. His earlier positive mood was fading fast as he wheeled the barrow from his killing room, through the kitchen and back out into the garden, where he noted the birds were no longer singing. An arm fell to the ground twice as he made his weary way. He cursed loudly and crudely. It now seemed his victim was mocking him, taking advantage of his kindness in the way women so often did with their dismissive ways. He hated her for that sneering, scornful attitude and lack of respect. Just like his mother. His victim's wink had been a sham. That seemed obvious now. The bitch, the total and utter bitch! He'd never hated anyone more. He screamed out his rage. If only he could kill her again. If only he could make her suffer as she'd never suffered before.

Gove discarded the barrow, ran towards the woman's head, drew his right leg back, and kicked it with all the force he could muster, launching it into the pond, where it slowly sank, making him feel a little better almost immediately. He returned to the barrow, threw the remainder of the body parts into an old steel oil drum he sometimes used for the disposal of rubbish, and doused the entire contents in petrol poured from a red plastic container that had originally been intended for the lawnmower. He stood a few feet from the drum, struck a match, tossed it skilfully into the air with a deft flick of his wrist and watched, mesmerised, as yellow-blue flames leapt and danced, exploding into vibrant life for his entertainment. He spent the next few minutes dancing energetically around the drum, issuing repeated yelps of triumph as his victim's flesh gradually burned away, leaving only blackened bones. The air filled with acrid smoke and the smell of barbecued meat as he continued to dance, his melancholy mood quickly forgotten. All was well with the world once more, and that was down to him. He was the master of all creation – the lord of all he surveyed.

Another five minutes passed before Gove eventually slumped to the ground, panting hard, gradually regaining his strength before finally returning to the house. He looked up at the kitchen clock: black Roman numerals on a white face. The minutes were ticking by. He was pleased with his morning's efforts. He'd achieved something worthwhile. But such things were no more than a mere distraction. The time had come to prepare for his meeting. Lovely Lucy would be wet and waiting, keenly anticipating his arrival just as he'd planned. Being late was utterly unthinkable. Killing was one thing. But there was no need for unnecessary rudeness. Not where Lucy was concerned. He smiled, recognising the apparent contradiction, but shrugging it off as of no real consequence. It was, he told himself, simply one of his charming quirks. An engaging eccentricity to be embraced and celebrated. No doubt Lucy would think the same.

Gove showered, careful to clean every inch of his slim muscular body with fragrant, white sandalwood soap, taking sensual pleasure in the piping-hot water warming his skin. He dried with a large fluffy white bath towel taken from the heated stainless steel rail to the left of the shower cubicle, applied an aluminium-free natural antiperspirant under both arms, and checked his high-end Swiss sports watch three times in under a minute. He felt a growing sense of urgency as he stood at the sink, shaving his head and face, studying his features in a brightly illuminated circular mirror secured to the black-and-gold-tiled wall. There were only fifty-seven short minutes before he'd need to catch the train. It was time to get a move on. Time to don one disguise or another. Something he was good at. Each character he'd created had its charms. He was fond of them all; they were friends, never critical, always supportive, and enthusiastically shared his interests without negative judgement. But which character to choose today?

Gove decided on an older persona for his special day; a middle-aged man in his late fifties or early sixties, with a short grey wig and neatly trimmed matching beard, both of which he'd bought from an online theatrical store for what he considered a reasonable cost. Both items were made from human hair – the best on the market. Nothing less was acceptable. He thought this particular disguise eminently sensible due to the character's unthreatening demeanour. Disguises had to be both convincing and appropriate to the circumstances.

He'd practised this means of concealing his true identity many times before, and as he sat in front of a dressing-table mirror in his spacious bedroom at the back of the house, he was confident of convincing results. He ran the palm of his right hand slowly over his head and face, confirming both were completely free of hair with the exception of his eyebrows, shaved to perfection. He reminded himself that such attention to detail was crucial to success as he gradually transformed his appearance. There was no room for complacency, no room for mistakes. There was too much to lose. Getting caught was never a part of the plan.

Gove applied generous amounts of spirit gum to his scalp and face with a top-quality vegan make-up brush, ensuring to use sufficient quantity of the clear sticky liquid before securing the hairpieces in place, adjusting their position carefully and quickly before the glue began to dry. He made one final adjustment to the wig and smiled broadly, delighted with the results to the point of joy. Once again, he was filled with a sense of invincibility. He really was a man of genius and outstanding accomplishments. Even without the blue-tinted non-prescription glasses he'd already chosen from a large and growing collection, he looked like a very different man, older and even more distinguished than his true self, if such a thing was possible. This character of his was a triumph of creative ingenuity, one to be roundly applauded, another example of his inventive genius. Even his vile bitch of a mother would struggle to recognise him if she was alive and there in the room. He bared his teeth, snarling. If she were, he'd kill her too. Tear her to fucking pieces, cut out her tongue, scalp her, poke out her eyes and then burn what was left of her, destroying her memory, until there was nothing left but bone. Nothing to taunt him. Nothing to haunt his dreams.

Gove decided on a smart but casual outfit for the big day: black straight jeans, a crisp white Egyptian cotton shirt, not too tight but not too loose either, a light-brown Savile Row cord jacket with leather elbow patches, and highly polished twin-tone English brogues, in which he could see his reflection when he glanced down towards his feet. As he stood admiring himself in front of a full-length mirror on the back of a wardrobe door, he felt confident that Lucy would appreciate his sartorial elegance too. He was a man of style and unparalleled discernment who enjoyed the better things in life. Lovely Lucy would know that as soon as she saw him. How could she not? She was a lucky lady, so fortunate to be chosen. It was meant to be.

Gove smiled as he entered his top-of-the-range luxury German SUV, appreciating the supple black leather upholstery and well-equipped cabin. He laughed as the powerful engine roared into life with the press of a button. What a fantastic sound, what glorious opulence – it was no more than a man of his abilities and accomplishments deserved. Fate had smiled on him because he was special, picking his lottery numbers, showering him with riches beyond most men's imagination. Good fortune defined him, and there was nothing wrong with that.

He drove the fifteen miles from his home to the nearby industrial town with caution, careful to adhere to the speed limits and not to do anything that could draw any unwanted attention to his car. It was essential to keep a low profile, to appear unremarkable but affluent to all those who saw him; hidden in plain sight. The interfering authorities, he reminded himself, tended to focus on a lesser class of person, not someone of his social standing with all the trappings of success.

Gove used his SUV's automatic parking-assist feature before leaving the vehicle securely locked in an unassuming side street close to the station. He sat alone on a metal bench in a quiet spot on the platform and then caught the next available train, only waiting a short time before boarding one of three pleasingly quiet carriages. A group of four casually dressed girls he assumed to be students got on a short time after him, happily chatting as they sat a few feet away; two on either side of a table, on the opposite side of the aisle. Gove looked at each young woman as they began their journey, his mind racing as it so often did, one thought after another tumbling in his mind. He felt like a child in a sweet shop, contemplating the various forms of torture he'd so like to inflict. He'd want to kill them all if the opportunity arose at some future date.

The half-hour rail journey to Lucy's home town passed relatively quickly. He indulged his fantasies, picturing one method of murder after another, raising his spirits, hardening his penis, making himself smile. He was disappointed and angered, silently swearing revenge, when the girls disembarked one station before him. He so wanted to make them suffer for their lack of respect. But their leaving wasn't such a bad thing. Any form of distraction, however pleasurable, couldn't be seen as a positive. He could always find the girls one fine day if he chose to. It was Lucy who truly mattered. Everyone else could wait.

Gove took a taxi to the area of town in which the café was located; a choice of eatery he considered likely to put almost any young woman at her ease. Planning was everything, and nothing was left to chance. He prided himself on the attention to detail with which he approached his endeavours. He paid in cash, telling the driver to keep the change. Not because he was feeling generous or because he could spare the money, which he certainly could, but because any delay was unwelcome. There was still over an hour before he and lovely Lucy were due to meet. But he wanted to be hidden and waiting, watching as she entered the café first. He'd allow her to settle, and then he'd follow soon afterwards, not wanting to appear too keen. He'd make an entrance and smile. That smile was important. It had to be warm; it had to be right. Convincing, that's what it had to be; utterly persuasive, drawing her in. There couldn't be even the slightest clue as to his true intentions. Not at that stage, that would come later. It really was that simple. Soon, he surmised, she'd be eating from the palm of his hand.

Gove walked along King Street, down Merlin's Lane, and finally onto a small square, where he sat on a wooden bench under the green bows of a large mature oak tree, from where he had an unrestricted view of the café's yellow-painted door. The anticipation was almost unbearable as he sat there, repeatedly pushing up his jacket sleeve to check his watch, resisting the temptation to tap a foot against the ground with a rhythmic beat for fear of drawing attention to himself. A small part of him was concerned that the lovely Lucy might not arrive at all. That all of his glorious plans would come to nothing. But he reassured himself that she almost certainly would come.

He'd see her soon, an unparalleled vision of beauty, walking towards the café door, striding with purpose towards her new life of bondage. Yes, she'd come. He had to be patient. It was just a matter of time.

6

Four days had passed since Lucy's telephone conversation with her mother and she was still hoping the contents of the letter would come to something. She had a free hour from twelve until one that afternoon and then another hour for lunch after that, so it seemed an ideal opportunity to leave the art college and head into town, with plenty of time to spare before she met with Moloch at the café. Of course, that's if he turned up – maybe the whole thing was someone's idea of a joke.

Lucy drove the short distance from the college to the centre of the pleasant market town she called home with the car's canvas top down, enjoying the wind in her hair and the warmth of the early-summer sun on her face. She parked in her usual car park, struggled with the ridiculously overcomplicated ticket machine, locked the convertible, took her glasses off due to vanity and then strode quickly in the direction of the nearest chemist shop, about a five-minute walk away, opposite the town's public library in King Street. She stood at the counter, filled with feelings of trepidation. She wasn't surprised to notice that her hand was trembling uncontrollably as she handed over the cash to pay for two pregnancy test kits, both of which she intended to use to be sure of the result. She'd been feeling nauseous in the mornings and had missed a period. One way or the other, she needed to know the reality. The entire situation felt almost surreal, life potentially changing forever in the most unexpected way at what felt like the most inconvenient time just as her relationship with Andy plummeted to an all-time low.

Lucy left the chemist shop, rushed across the quiet one-way street with the test kits clutched tightly in one hand, entered the library and then quickly descended a flight of steps, which she knew led to the toilets. She'd been to the lower floor several times before, attending a weekly yoga class that had now moved to an alternative venue she hadn't yet visited. She checked the corridor, glancing to left and right before opening the toilet door, checking the ladies was empty and then locking herself in one of two cubicles. Lucy opened a box, read the simple instructions, took the test and then waited, praying it would be negative. She did want children at some point in her life, but not now, and certainly not with Andy. The possibility of parenthood had brought the reality of her relationship into sharp and unrelenting focus. He couldn't look after himself properly, let alone a baby. Please, God, let it be negative, please God!

Lucy feared her legs might buckle as she saw two blue lines appear in the result window. It was positive. Oh, God, no, it was positive. She quickly took the second test, praying for a different outcome, but it showed the same positive result. She turned towards the toilet, bent at the waist and vomited, her mind racing, a part of her desperately wanting to deny the truth. How on earth was she pregnant? It seemed crazy. She and Andy had had sex once in almost five months. Once! And only then because she'd drunk nearly half a bottle of red wine before heading unsteadily to bed. They'd argued earlier that evening, a shouting match with him the primary aggressor – no surprises there. And then he'd apologised and pleaded and begged her forgiveness as he so often did when in the wrong. Make-up sex, wasn't that what they called it? She'd read about it online or perhaps in a women's magazine. Brief, fumbled, unsatisfying drunken intercourse following yet another pointless quarrel she could well have done without. Why, oh why hadn't she said no? Why hadn't she refused, just slept alone? Once, fucking, once! And now, look at the consequences. It didn't seem fair; it didn't seem right. It felt like God was laughing at her plans. Everything had changed, possibly forever.

Lucy spat into the toilet bowl one final time, flushed, then adjusted her clothing before swilling her mouth out with cold water for a full thirty seconds at the sink. She discarded both test kits in a convenient litter bin and then left the library building, walking back out into the warm Welsh sunshine with one thought after another tumbling in her mind. She'd been hoping for the best but fearing the worst. And now it seemed the worst had happened. Her new reality felt like a body blow. What on earth to do?

Lucy sat herself down on a nearby bench, located on a wide section of pavement outside a charity shop and took her smartphone from a pocket. She considered ringing her mother, then her sister, but ultimately she decided that she needed more time to process the information herself before sharing it with others, even close family. She was close to tears as she tried to decide if Andy had the right to know the news. Yes, no, yes, no? God, it was difficult. He had to know sometime, didn't he?

After a good deal of quiet emotional thought, Lucy finally decided it wasn't a question she could answer right there and then. She'd need time to consider her options, limited as they were. After all, it was the early days. Bite-sized chunks, that was best. Don't rush into things. It was her body, her future. Surely, at least for a time, she had the right to keep the news to herself.

Lucy looked down at her watch – white ceramic with a fashionably large face. Time was getting on. If she was going to make the meeting with Moloch, she had twenty minutes to get there. But was she really in the mood? Could she face meeting with a stranger, even one who admired her work as much as he claimed? She was inclined to forget it, walk away, miss lunch and head back to work as if she'd never received the letter. But she told herself the meeting was an opportunity that was perhaps too good to miss. The bills were mounting, and maybe now more than ever, the chance to earn a hefty commission for doing something she loved was a potential blessing she shouldn't turn down.

She began strolling in the direction of the café, still deep in thought, along King Street and down Merlin's Lane, arriving at its pleasant, welcoming door almost ten minutes before the allotted time. Even then, as she reached for the door handle, she almost turned to walk away back in the direction of her car. But she encouraged herself on. Life had dealt her a curveball. It was, she concluded, time to re-establish a semblance of control.

When Lucy opened the café door, entering the orange-painted room with eclectic paintings by various talented local artists covering three of the four walls, she saw her sister almost immediately. Cerys was sitting alone on a two-seater black leather sofa at the back of the room close to the serving counter, half-hidden behind a broadsheet right-wing-leaning newspaper of the type she'd never usually read. There was a fresh cup of black coffee and a half-eaten chocolate brownie on the low table in front of her. Lucy glanced from table to table, confirming no men were sitting alone, before approaching her sister with a frown. Cerys lowered her head at first, as if playing an inept childhood game of hide-and-seek, but then peeped out to one side of the paper with a nervous, mischievous grin, her facial expression conveying a peculiar combination of amusement and embarrassment.

'Hi, Lucy. Fancy seeing you here, small world.'

Lucy placed a hand on each of her hips, leaning back slightly and scowling disapprovingly at her sister.

'Surely you're not going to try to tell me that you being here is a coincidence?'

Cerys lowered the paper, putting it to one side, and then raised both hands in the air as if surrendering at gunpoint.

'Okay, you've got me – it's a fair cop.'

'Mum?'

Cerys lowered her arms and nodded.

'She asked me to keep an eye on you. Be the big sister and make sure you don't get yourself into any trouble. She's worried about you. I didn't feel I could say no.'

Lucy blew out a long breath.

'Oh, for goodness' sake – I've never heard anything so ridiculous.'

'Well, I'm here now, so I may as well stay.'

'I'm assuming Mum told you all about the letter.'

Cerys nodded with a grin, appearing to find the situation highly amusing despite Lucy's dismay, all her earlier embarrassment now gone.

'Yes, I've been fully informed.'

Lucy rechecked the time. There were only five minutes to go before Moloch was due to arrive. She still felt far from confident he would turn up at all, but she increasingly hoped he would. She gave her sister another disapproving look.

'He hasn't arrived yet. We could both be wasting our time. Maybe it was a wind-up. Perhaps he won't turn up at all. It wouldn't be a complete shock to me if I found out one of my students wrote the letter. Stranger things have happened. I'm going to order, and then I will sit over there at the empty table nearest the door. If he does arrive, I don't want you coming over. Just stay where you are, don't even speak to me. I don't want him thinking I'm unprofessional. I don't know what goes on in Mum's head sometimes. She seems to think I'm still ten. I know she's got my best interests at heart, but asking you to spy on me is too much.'

'Oh, you know what she's like.'

'Yes, I do – that's the problem.'

Cerys tried not to laugh with only partial success.

'I'll drink my coffee, eat my brownie and keep a low profile. You won't even know I'm here. We can have a nice chat once he's gone, assuming he turns up at all.'

Suddenly Lucy thought that talking to her sister about the pregnancy may not be such a bad idea after all, despite her earlier reticence.

'Maybe a chat wouldn't be such a bad idea. There is something I wanted to mention.'

'Sounds intriguing.'

'I'll tell you later when we've got more time. It's not something I want to rush.'

'Is it Andy?'

'No, not directly, but I do need to talk.'

Cerys picked up her coffee cup, cradling it with both hands.

'I'll be here when you need me.'

Lucy ordered a light lunch and then sat at the empty table. She only had to wait for about two minutes before a man entered the café alone. She guessed it might be Moloch as soon as she saw him. There was something strangely familiar about him, but she couldn't determine why. She may have seen him somewhere before, but she couldn't be sure. He was a little older than she'd pictured him in her mind's eye, but he looked friendly enough, with a slightly unconventional vibe she found strangely attractive. And he was smiling, a beaming Cheshire cat smile that lit up his face as he waved to her as he approached her table. That, she decided, was a good thing. His pleasant demeanour helped put her at ease, or at least as far as possible in the circumstances.

'Lovely to meet you at last, Lucy. I recognised you from the television report. I'm so very pleased you decided to come. I'm a great admirer of your work and so looking forward to learning more about you. Have you ordered?'

When he spoke, it was with a soft English accent she couldn't identify – the south of England possibly, or the West Country. There was a gentleness to his voice, a warmth Lucy found reassuring and endearing. Her first impressions were largely positive. Had he been a few years younger, she may have fancied him. Perhaps she had made the right decision in coming. As he shook her hand, holding it for a fraction of a second longer than was comfortable, she noticed he didn't blink at all. He was focused only on her.

Lucy was a little taken aback by his gushing approach. It wasn't something she was used to, such flattery. She felt her face flush as she struggled to find the words.

'Yes, er, just a toasted sandwich and a pot of tea.'

He smiled again, revealing slightly uneven teeth that were clearly his own. A slight yellow tint to them made Lucy think he may either be or had been a smoker. She focused on his mouth, watching his lips moving. As he spoke again, she still couldn't identify the origin of his accent.

'Sounds good to me. I think I'll have the same. I'll just pop to the counter and then join you at the table. We have a great deal to discuss, you and me. I've been so looking forward to today.'

Within a matter of minutes, Lucy and Moloch were sitting opposite each other, eating their lunch and making small talk, with her taking the lead right up to the time she asked him to tell her more of his proposal.

'I'm so happy you asked me that. I was hoping we'd get down to business sooner rather than later. As much as I'm enjoying the food and convivial company, that's why we're here, after all.' All of a sudden, his enthusiasm grew exponentially. He became more animated, sitting bolt upright, communicating with repeated sweeping hand gestures and enthusiastic words. 'When I wrote that letter, I felt certain you were the right person for the job. And I still do, even more so now that I've had the opportunity to meet you in the flesh. I've viewed some of your work online – the autumn series. Reds, greens, blacks and browns. You seem to have a great appreciation of nature's decay. Fabulous, absolutely fabulous! Am I correct in thinking the paintings are a comment on death?'

Lucy thought it a strange observation. But such things were so subjective, influenced by personal tastes and feelings. She studied his face, trying to weigh him up. Any talk of art fascinated her, and particularly her own. She was starting to enjoy herself a lot more than she'd expected.

'I've always thought my autumn series is more a comment on the cycle of life than death. Death didn't come to mind at all. I plan to create a series for each of the seasons. I'm just completing the final painting to celebrate winter. There's going to be an exhibition of my works at the Lammas Street Gallery here in town. The launch is on Friday evening, if you're interested?'

Lucy wasn't sure if Moloch was displeased or puzzled by her response. But she was sure it was one or the other. He was sitting there with a sour expression on his face. She wondered if he'd interpreted her contradiction of his hypothesis as a criticism. But most of all, she hoped she hadn't blown it. Just her luck; it seemed she spent her life coping with oversensitive men. He lowered his tone when he finally spoke, breaking a silence that had seemed to go on forever.

'Death is a part of life, an integral element of the cycle. It comes to all of us in the end. All living things must die. Warhol was obsessed with mortality for the whole of his adult life. No clichés, but he realised death was something he could play with; he was a provocateur. Like him, such things inspire me. I see that in your work too. That's why I'm here. That's why we're sitting here having this conversation. I need you to understand that.'

Lucy nodded, keen to please him in the interests of the potential commission. She opened her mouth as if to speak but closed it again when she couldn't find the words. She sat, listening, as Moloch filled the silence for a second time. She was pleased to see his expression change, his earlier enthusiasm again a feature of their conversation.

'I'll look forward to viewing your winter collection. I'm sure it's every bit as good as your other work. I'm a fan, and I'm certain you've realised that by now. It's not often one meets with a true artistic genius.'

Once again, Lucy felt her face redden. She felt her temperature rise as she raised a hand, fanning her face. The compliments were almost too much. But she was pleased the meeting seemed back on track. Things were going her way for once. Her mother and sister's concern had been misplaced.

'Please come along to the exhibition as my guest. At your convenience, of course, it's on for two weeks. You'd be very welcome.'

'Thank you. I will.'

It seemed the perfect time to focus back on work.

'Tell me more about the commission. From what I read, it seems fascinating.'

He moved to the edge of his chair, adjusting the position of his glasses with one manicured finger, pushing them back up his nose as if they were slightly too big for his face.

'So, you're interested?'

'Oh, yes, I wouldn't be here if I wasn't. Your letter really grabbed my attention, such beautiful writing – it's a work of art in itself.'

Moloch beamed and then began conveying his delight, saying all the right things for Lucy to hear. But suddenly he stopped speaking mid-sentence. There was a look of disapproval on his face as he momentarily lapsed into silence as if there was a bad smell.

'I don't know what's going on, but there's a woman sitting behind you who keeps staring at us. She's on the sofa with a newspaper.'

Lucy turned in her seat, glaring at Cerys. She cleared her throat in embarrassment.

'Oh, God, I'm so very sorry – she's my sister.' And then Lucy continued, speaking more loudly, glaring at Cerys again as she said the words. 'I can see she's finished her lunch. I'm sure she's about to leave.'

Cerys stood almost immediately, discarding her newspaper, folding it and placing it on the table next to her cup. She paid at the counter and left the café with a sheepish look. She gestured to Lucy with a nervous smile as she opened the door. Neither sister said anything. If the floor had opened, it seemed Cerys would have jumped right in. Sometimes there wasn't a need for words.

Lucy returned her attention to Moloch. She noticed him forming his hands into tight fists, clicking his knuckles before relaxing them. She didn't read anything into it. She was thinking of other things. She searched for the right thing to say as he looked at her with what seemed pained perplexity. She made a point of looking him in the eye as she spoke.

'Look, this isn't going as I'd hoped. I had no idea my sister would be here – honestly, I didn't. I certainly didn't invite her. I've never felt so embarrassed. All I can do is apologise. But I want to assure you that I found your letter intriguing. I really would like to know more.'

He pressed his lips together; teeth clenched momentarily before relaxing his jaw.

'If you're certain?'

'I'm sure.'

'There won't be any further unfortunate interruptions?'

She shook her head. 'No, there won't be.'

He smiled again, not as broadly this time, but still wide enough to ease the tension.

'Well, in that case, I'll continue. I live in a large Grade two listed Georgian home deep in the countryside, about ten miles away from town. It was built by a successful coal merchant, a man knighted by King George IV. The miners did the work, choking on black dust, and the merchant took the profits, living in luxury while they inhabited hovels. It's the way of the world. It was then, and it is now. And the masses vote for it, that's what amazes me. They keep their masters sitting in parliament, filling their coffers and putting them down. But I'm straying off the point. You don't want to hear my theories. We're not here to talk politics.'

'You were telling me about the house.'

'Ah, yes, the house. I love that you're so focused on what truly matters. It's well off the main road and reached by a half-mile-long private track that leads to the property and nowhere else. I live in glorious isolation, surrounded by green fields and woodlands. There are extensive grounds, including a walled garden with trees, flowers and a pond. It's a monument to the past, where I work, creating art, beauty – much like yourself.'

Her eyes lit up.

'You're an artist?'

He drained his teacup and smiled.

'Yes, of sorts. We have a great deal in common, you and I. I'd love you to witness my work. It's more experimental in style than yours, but I feel sure you'd appreciate it as much as I do yours. You have the rare insight and mature thinking to understand what I'm trying to achieve. I like to explore the extremes of human behaviour and experience in the most imaginative and creative ways possible. One day I'll share it with the world. But I don't think the average person is ready quite yet.'

Lucy had no real understanding of what he was talking about, but she would never admit that, not now, not to him. She was keen to focus back on the proposed commission. It's why she was there, after all.

'I'd love to see your work.'

He smiled without parting his lips, his mouth turning up at the corners.

'Oh, you will, you will, I'm certain. When the universe conspires to make something happen, it can't be resisted.'

Lucy was beginning to think of Moloch as an eccentric: a little unusual, intense, intelligent, oversensitive but interesting. He'd grabbed her attention in a way not many people did. She could sense his enthusiasm. It was in everything about him, as if he was keen to please her. It was flattering, a much-needed boost to her flagging ego after all of Andy's many criticisms. It seemed the debacle with her sister hadn't ruined things. But time was getting on. There was only so long before she'd need to head back to the college. It was now or never. 'Your letter said you'd like me to paint a picture of the house and gardens?'

He nodded twice.

'Yes, that's true, but I don't want a painting on board or canvas. I'm talking about a far more ambitious project. Something marvellous, a work worthy of your creative abilities. I want you to paint an entire room, much as Michelangelo did the Sistine Chapel in the Eternal City. Although, of course, our creation will have nothing to do with God or the Catholic

Church. I have a large cellar below my home. I've installed lighting, a speaker system, movie cameras and soundproofing. It's a production studio of sorts. It's all state of the art – no expense spared. It was only recently completed by a team of experts from London at an exorbitant cost. They provided the technical skills, and you'll provide the art. Both are of equal importance, both crucial for my vision. I want you to transform the space into a thing of beauty, a masterpiece reflecting my passions and desires, much as you did with your autumn series. What do you say? Do you share my enthusiasm? Do you feel as committed to the project as I do?'

Lucy was a little overwhelmed by his excitement.

'Just so I'm clear. You said it's a production studio?'

'Yes, that's right. I may make it available to musicians and filmmakers in the future at an appropriate cost. But for now, I plan to make full use of the facility myself. I'm interested in film as a creative art form. It's something we could explore together.'

Lucy was starting to question her suitability for the role for the first time.

'I'm, er, I'm not sure I'm the person you're looking for. I've got to be honest with you. It's not like anything I've done before, not on that scale. And I've certainly got no experience of filmmaking. Maybe I'm not the best person for the job.'

He placed both elbows on the table, leaning towards her, linking his fingers, knuckles white. He focused on her face with such intensity that it felt as if his eyes were penetrating her very soul.

'Would a twenty-thousand-pound cash payment be enough to convince you?'

Lucy jerked her head back, eyes wide.

'Did you say *twenty-thousand*?'

He confirmed that was indeed the sum offered with two more subtle nods of his head. 'Yes, I'd be happy to pay that. Although, I would be willing to add a five-thousand-pound cash bonus on completion if you could start immediately and stay in situ until the work is complete. It's a big house, not quite a mansion, but not far off. There are three large reception rooms and six bedrooms, all with bathrooms and glorious country views. A room will be available for your personal use for as long as you need it. It's en suite with a free-standing bath, walk-in shower and bidet. You'll eat the best food and drink the finest wine. I'll afford you every possible luxury. Whatever you need will be yours. All you'd have to do is ask.'

Lucy fidgeted with a cuff of her cotton blouse. She so wanted to say yes, but there were complications. Frustrating complications that stared her in the face.

'When you say you'd like me to start *immediately,* what exactly do you mean by that?'

He began striking his foot against the wooden floor. She could hear the tap, tap, tap, despite the sound of customer chatter.

'I would have thought that was blatantly obvious. I want you to start *today*. I'm hoping we can leave here together. We could buy whatever paint, brushes and anything else you require en route.'

Lucy shook her head, incredulous. It seemed so unreasonable, so far from the norm.

'I'm sorry, that's not going to be possible.'

Lucy thought she detected a fleeting coldness to Moloch's eyes she hadn't seen before. It was gone so quickly, she surmised she may have imagined it. 'I hope you're not playing hard to get, Lucy. I've offered you a very handsome payment. I wouldn't like to think you were trying to take advantage of my kindness.'

She shook her head.

'No, no, not at all – your offer is more than generous.'

He held up his hands, palms facing each other, fingers spread.

'Well, what's the problem, if that's the case?'

'It's too soon – I can't just drop everything. There's the exhibition. And I've got college commitments, lectures, tutorials and end-of-term exams. I'm not in a job where I can take leave whenever I want. Academic terms dictate my holidays. That's not something I can do anything about, however much I want to. If you can wait a couple of weeks until the end of term, I'll be free. I could commit then, but not before. Is that something we can agree on?'

Lucy was somewhat taken aback by the look of abject horror on Moloch's otherwise ordinary face. His reaction seemed entirely disproportionate to the situation, wholly over the top. For a fraction of a second, she thought she identified a flash of brooding, underlying anger that reminded her of Andy. In recent months, she'd become hyper-vigilant, often on guard, jumpy, easily startled, and on the defensive. But Moloch wasn't Andy. She thought she must have imagined it as she waited for him to reply.

'I have to say, that is incredibly disappointing, Lucy. I'd need you to be fully committed to the project if we're to work together. It means a great deal to me. I need you to share that passion. Nothing less is acceptable. I thought I'd already made that perfectly clear.'

For the first time, Lucy began to question the wisdom of the meeting. Maybe her mother was right all along. But twenty-five-thousand pounds was a great deal of money. Money she'd need if she separated from Andy and kept the baby.

'I could fully commit to starting on 11 June; that's only ten days away. The term ends on the tenth. I could be with you early the next morning. I don't know about staying – I can't see that being necessary. If it's only a few miles to your house, I could drive back and forth each day with ease. Would that work for you?'

He was swift to reply.

'No, I really can't say it would. I thought I'd made my requirements perfectly clear. Surely you can rearrange your commitments in the circumstances? Is it the money? What if I offered you more? If you can't start today, could you be there tomorrow? That should give you more than enough time to cancel whatever else you have arranged.'

Lucy made a face. She folded her arms across her chest. It was as if Moloch hadn't listened to her at all.

'Look, I'm sorry, I don't want to seem uncooperative. I am keen – honestly, I am. But as I've said, I'm fully committed until 10 June, what with the exhibition and my college commitments. And my mother's unwell – cancer – I like to see her at some point each weekend. I can guarantee I can fully commit from the eleventh, but not before. You could send me digital images of the cellar with measurements and an idea of what you've got in mind. A couple of weeks' planning wouldn't be such a bad thing. If I do this, I want you to be happy with my work. I'd want to give it 100 per cent but I can only do that if the timing's right.'

As Moloch stood, pushing back his chair, there was tension in the air.

'I can't pretend I'm happy with the conclusion of our discussions. Let me give it some thought.'

A part of Lucy was disappointed they hadn't been able to reach an agreement, but only a part. She wanted the work but didn't appreciate the pressure. It was beginning to feel too much like controlling behaviour. Something with which she'd become all too familiar.

'I'm sorry if you feel I've wasted your time. That wasn't my intention.'

Moloch left a ten-pound note on the table to cover the cost of his meal. He looked back on approaching the door.

'I'll be back in touch soon. I still believe we have an affinity. It's incredibly disappointing that you can't see that yet. I very much hope you have a change of heart.'

And with that, he left, leaving Lucy alone with her thoughts. She checked the time, realising she needed to head back to work for a two o'clock lecture on French impressionist art. It had been a strange day.

After paying for her lunch, Lucy left the café, picking up her pace as she approached the car park close to the library. She silently evaluated how the meeting had gone as she lowered herself into her car, appreciating its well-worn comfort and support for her aching back. His was a strange proposal, his conditions so unexpected, so far from the norm. He was such a demanding man and so full of expectations. But the work did sound fascinating. And he was offering a great deal of money – more than she could ever have dreamt of.

As she drove away, Lucy hoped she would see Moloch again despite her earlier concerns. Maybe he'd have a change of heart. If he really appreciated her work as much as he claimed, why wouldn't he? Now that she thought about it, he seemed passionate rather than angry.

As she negotiated the first bend, slowing to allow for other traffic, Lucy wondered what he'd meant by the extremes of human behaviour. Perhaps it was something she should have explored further, showing interest, feeding his male ego. She switched on the car radio, Classic FM, continuing her rumination as Verdi's 'Chorus of the Hebrew Slaves' filled the car's small cabin with inspirational sound.

She thought about Moloch's comments again as she enjoyed the music, but she still wasn't sure of their meaning. Oh, well. He'd said he'd give her counter-offer some thought. Hopefully, one day soon, she'd get the chance to find out exactly what he meant. If it were supposed to happen, it would. Some things she couldn't control; she just had to get on with life, do what she could to facilitate the positives, and hope for the best.

7

Lucy drove straight to her parents' home at the end of her working day rather than return to her flat as she'd initially planned. It had been a stressful day: first the positive pregnancy tests and then the café meeting with Moloch, which hadn't gone as smoothly as she'd hoped. She needed to talk to her mum and do it face to face. Sometimes a telephone conversation just wouldn't suffice. She needed a motherly hug.

Lucy was feeling somewhat conflicted as she negotiated the busy rush-hour traffic in the direction of the pleasant, leafy suburbs on the edge of town. The original shock of her pregnancy had been replaced by nagging uncertainties and the need to make decisions. The more she considered her limited options, the more she thought she might keep the baby, despite all the inevitable complications such a significant life change would bring. As the afternoon had gone on, she'd thought about it more and more, trying to reach conclusions that sat comfortably in her mind. Okay, so motherhood hadn't formed a part of her plans, not so very soon. That was a fact. It wasn't the ideal time to bring a baby into the world. But was there ever a perfect time? It was a situation faced by any number of women the world over. Perhaps being a mother wouldn't be such a bad thing, although juggling parenting with work commitments may prove difficult for a single mum. And Andy. Oh, God, what about Andy?

Telling him wouldn't be easy, and that was putting it mildly. If she kept the baby, it would impact his life too. He'd always be the father, but it really was time to end their relationship. It mattered more now than ever. And Moloch, what on earth to do about his offer? Parenthood would be expensive. The man was offering enough to pay off her overdraft and more, a lot more. But it wasn't as if she could contact him even if she wanted to; she'd failed to get a number or an email. Maybe he'd get in touch as he'd said. All she could do was hope to see him again.

Lucy parked her convertible on her parents' block-paving driveway, glad to see that her father's luxury saloon was nowhere to be seen. She loved her dad and always had; he was always there for her, always ready to help if he could. But talking to her mum was easier, particularly where personal issues were concerned. Lucy opened the ornamental metal gate at the side of the large detached Victorian house and walked around to the rear, where she knocked on the back door before opening it wide. She stood in the spacious, modern kitchen with its red quarry-tiled floor, range cooker, oak worktops and high-quality white units and called out her mother's name above the sound of the early-evening television news coming from the nearby lounge. Lucy was met in the hall by her mum, who looked tired and a little older. Lucy hugged her mother tightly. The cancer hadn't been kind. Her mother was the same lovely woman she always had been, but the spark was gone. It was as if the illness had sucked the energy out of her. Lucy lowered her arms, took a backwards step and looked her mum in the eye.

'It's lovely to see you, Mum.'

'And you too. I wasn't expecting you until the weekend. Is everything okay?'

'How are you doing?'

'I've just taken my medication, the painkillers. My head's a little woozy – one of the unfortunate side effects. Your body gets used to them, that's the trouble. They're a lot stronger than the ones I've had in the past.'

Lucy noticed the dark shadows around her mother's eyes. She was looking thinner; she'd lost weight she couldn't afford to lose.

'Have you eaten?'

Myra Williams shook her head.

'I had a cup of tomato soup at lunchtime. Nothing since.'

'Have you been feeling sick again?'

'Oh, please don't fuss – it's nothing to worry about.'

Lucy reached out to squeeze her mother's hand. It felt cold to the touch despite the ambient warmth.

'Right, I want you to sit in the lounge and put your feet up. I'm going to make us some tea. How does some cheese and tomato on toast sound? And a nice mug of milky coffee with a spoonful of honey? I bet you've got a jar of that nice organic one you like in the cupboard somewhere.'

Myra screwed up her face, allowing the wall to support her weight.

'I'm not really hungry.'

'Please, Mum, you're losing weight. I'm worried about you. Eat something for me.'

'Maybe just a slice of brown toast with blackberry jam and a glass of water with ice. The bread's in the usual place, and the jam's in the fridge next to the yoghurt.'

Lucy walked her mother to the comfortably furnished lounge, encouraging her to sit before she headed to the kitchen. Lucy returned about ten minutes later with a wicker tray laden with two portions of her mother's order: one for each of them. Lucy sat on a sofa close to her mother's recliner chair, placing the tray on an Italian marble coffee table with ornate, gold-coloured metal baroque style legs. Myra took a sip of water and then picked up her plate, nibbling the edge of a crust less than enthusiastically.

'How did your meeting with that strangely named man go? Wasn't that today?'

'You know very well it was today, Mother. Cerys was there, just as you planned. I'd be willing to bet she's already reported back.'

Myra shuffled her feet, looking away.

'You'll always be my little girl. I was worried about you, that's all.'

'It's okay – you're forgiven. Just don't do it again, that's all.'

Myra smiled.

'So, how did it go?'

'Not in any way I expected.'

Myra sipped her water, wetting her mouth, only swallowing a few drops.

'Tell me more.'

'He offered me *twenty-five-thousand pounds* to paint a mural in his cellar.'

'He did what?'

'Yes, that's right, you heard me. *Twenty-five-thousand!* But he wanted me to start straight away.'

'But that's not possible.'

'That's what I told him.'

Myra shifted in her seat, first one way and then another, as if unable to get comfortable.

'So, is that the end of it? What happens now?'

'I offered to do the work as soon as term ends on the tenth, but he wasn't having any of it. He said he'd give it some thought and then left.'

'I know you're a great artist, love, of course, you are, but don't you think it's all a bit strange? It seems like an awful lot of money to me.'

Lucy took a bite of toast, chewed and swallowed, relishing the jam's fruity sweetness on her tongue.

'He said he lives in a big house, akin to a mansion, with extensive grounds and a walled garden. I think he's probably moved to this part of the world from over the border, maybe with a lot of money to spend. That's the only sense I can make of it. It's a hypothesis, no more than that. I think he's probably got so much money, it means very little to him.'

'What was he like?'

'He was, er, he was nice enough, but he did get irritated when I said I couldn't do the work until the end of term.'

'Did he give you his contact details?'

Lucy shook her head.

'No, no, he didn't. But, to be fair, I didn't think to ask.'

'Are you going to say yes if he does come back to you?'

'Yes, I think I very probably am if I get the chance.'

Myra paused before speaking again, switching off the TV with a click of the remote.

'I don't want to sound negative, love. But I'm really not sure you should.

There are all sorts of unanswered questions. Why the strange letter? Why the anonymity? Why does he want you to start immediately? And why so much money? You're a beautiful girl, Lucy. Some would say stunning. There are a lot of strange men out there, predators. Your father is friendly with the chief constable. Why don't I ask him to talk to her? This man may be known to the police. Better safe than sorry, don't you think?'

Lucy's mouth fell open.

'Oh, God, no, Mum, absolutely not. I admit it's all a bit strange, but we've no reason to think Moloch is a risk to me or anybody else. If he got even the slightest hint that Dad had checked him out with the police, that would end any chances I might have of the commission. I want you to promise me you won't mention this to Dad. I shared it with you in strict confidence. If I'd thought even for a second that you'd overreact like this, I wouldn't have said a word.'

Myra adjusted her position again.

'Okay, have it your way, if that's the way you want it. I worry about you, that's all. I don't think that's unreasonable in today's world.'

'I can look after myself.'

'If you're sure?'

Lucy rolled her eyes. 'I'm sure!'

Lucy decided it was time to change the subject. She wished she hadn't mentioned Moloch at all. It seemed there wasn't much her mother and sister didn't worry about.

'I have got some other news.'

'Please tell me it's good news. I could do with cheering up.'

Lucy took a deep breath. It was now or never.

'I'm pregnant.'

Myra raised her eyebrows.

'Wow.'

'Yeah, I know.'

'Are you certain?'

'Two pregnancy tests, both positive. I don't think there's any room for doubt.'

'Is it Andy's?'

Lucy nodded. 'There hasn't been anyone else.'

'Are you pleased? Is it good news?'

'Um, yes, I think so.'

'Does Andy know? Have you told him?'

Lucy took a slurp of water.

'I only found out myself a few hours ago. I've decided me and Andy are over. I'm going to ask him to move out as soon as he can find somewhere else to live. It's something I should have done long ago. I can't put it off any longer. I'll tell him he's got two weeks maximum to make alternative arrangements, no longer than that. And then, I'll tell him about the baby once he's gone. On the phone. I don't want to deal with him face to face.'

Myra's smile said so much. She stood, putting her arms around Lucy, holding her close before letting go and sitting.

'I'm so very glad you're ending it. I'm not going to pretend I'm sorry. It's a relief, to be honest. I've felt that way since that day, well, you know what I'm talking about. You're not tempted to ask him to leave straight away?'

'I think two weeks is fair. I loved him once. He wasn't always the pig he is now. With a bit of luck, he may decide to go sooner. I can't imagine I'd stay in the circumstances. But I want that to be his decision. I want to be reasonable.'

'Do you want Cerys to be there when you tell him? You know what he can be like.'

Lucy shook her head.

'No, I can handle him. This is something I need to do myself. And please don't tell Dad or Cerys about the baby for now. Just keep it to yourself. I'll tell them when I'm ready.'

'My lips are sealed. And I'll be here if you need me.'

Lucy ate the last of her toast, drained her glass, loaded the tray and stood.

'Thanks, Mum, appreciated as always. I'll give you a ring to tell you how it goes with Andy. And I'll see you again at the weekend. Don't bother getting up – I can see myself out. Is there anything you need?'

'All I want is for you to be happy. If Andy gives you any problems, he'll have me to deal with; no one upsets my girl and gets away with it. You tell him that from me.'

8

The holiday had been a long time coming. Laura Kesey had been promising her life partner, Janet, and their young son, Edward, a trip for almost three years. But her work as a busy divisional detective inspector in the West Wales Police Force always got in the way, with one high-profile case or another demanding her attention. But now it was finally happening. She'd made the time, booked the leave, a particularly traumatic court case had finally come to a positive conclusion and they were on the plane. She was happily anticipating three whole weeks of fun and relaxation in sunny Lanzarote, a volcanic Canary Island off the coast of West Africa administered by Spain.

The nearly four-hour mid-morning flight from Cardiff to the island's César Manrique Airport passed surprisingly quickly. By the time the three settled in their extra-legroom seats, fastened their seat belts, listened to the preflight safety advice and ate various sweet treats packed by Janet in her recently purchased bright purple hand luggage, they were already well on their way. It was six-year-old Edward's first time on a plane. Everything about the trip seemed exciting to him. He could hardly contain himself as he sat in his window seat, looking out at the grey-white cotton wool clouds and the miniature world passing far below. Kesey turned in her seat to look at her son with pleasure and pride. She'd always wanted to be a parent, and the reality had been even better than her imaginings. She wasn't always able to give Edward the time she felt he deserved, but she told herself she did her best. It was the way of the modern world. Balancing work and home life wasn't always easy, particularly since her promotion. But she and Janet were a team, each playing to their strengths, and that, she reminded herself, worked pretty damned well most of the time. They were a happy family unit, not without problems, but then what family was? Life could be challenging, and hers more than most, as she dealt with the criminals of this world, managing investigations, supervising officers, making arrests and trying to make the charges stick, sometimes successfully and sometimes not. Such were the vagaries of the criminal justice system, with the mountains of red tape and morale-sapping cuts to police resources.

The detective tried to push police work from her mind as a female flight attendant wearing smart dark-navy livery walked past with a friendly smile. Kesey was glad she'd finally booked a period of leave. A break was long overdue and she should have done it ages ago. She was determined to relax, something with which she often struggled despite her best efforts. Sometimes family had to come first. There were memories to be made. Kesey reached out to squeeze her partner's hand, telling her it would be a wonderful trip. Janet smiled warmly and nodded before turning her attention back to Edward, who was colouring a picture of a passenger jet with various wax crayons Janet always kept handy.

They landed five minutes early at a quarter past two that afternoon, negotiated customs, collected their brightly coloured luggage from the carousel and then searched for their rental-car company. The office was conveniently located in the arrival terminal, and it wasn't long before they were looking for an automatic white Kia in the relatively quiet car park a few minutes' brisk walk away through the airport building. Kesey did the driving while Janet sat with Edward in the back, keeping him amused as he repeatedly asked if they were nearly there. Kesey was glad of her phone's satnav app as she left the airport, driving cautiously in the direction of Nazaret, a small village dominated by white-painted villas, well away from the busy coastal tourist resorts so popular with British travellers. Janet had chosen a large detached villa high on a hillside because of the privacy, comfort and dramatic views it offered. It wasn't cheap, but she'd eventually convinced Kesey it provided good value, given the stunning location and excellent facilities.

Lanzarote wasn't like anywhere the detective had seen before. She was pleased the roads were as impressive as they were, with no potholes, and that the island seemed significantly less developed than she'd expected. There were none of the high-rise hotels she associated with other Spanish islands. Just attractive low-rise white buildings that stood out dramatically against the dark volcanic landscape and azure-blue sky. It felt almost as if they'd landed on another planet. It was so unlike West Wales, with its rolling green fields, woodlands and varied dramatic coastline, but there was a beauty about the place.

Within half an hour or so of leaving the airport, they'd stopped at a small supermarket to buy some basic provisions and were approaching the villa, having taken a wrong turn only once along the way. The private stone-strewn track leading directly to their holiday home was steeper and more uneven than expected. Kesey was glad Janet had opted for an SUV rather than a saloon or hatchback when making the arrangements. The four-wheel-drive feature was more than welcome. This final part of the journey was bumpy and a little demanding on both driver and passengers. But once they reached the villa, driving through the large metal gates, Kesey quickly concluded the effort of it all was very much worthwhile. The building itself was impressive, with a large, beautifully tended garden, planted with different cacti, and a welcoming swimming pool that raised Edward's mood to unbridled excitement as soon as he saw it. But the best thing of all was the view, which could only be described as spectacular. There was a far-reaching volcanic landscape dotted with white buildings as far as the eye could see. It was stunning, a genuinely awe-inspiring sight.

Kesey counted over twenty inactive volcanoes as she helped Janet with the luggage, emptying the vehicle's spacious boot. As the three reached the top of the steps leading to the front door, they looked out on the dramatic natural landscape, Arrecife, the distant island capital of about 30,000 residents, and the green-blue Atlantic Ocean beyond. Janet entered the four-digit number into the key safe, attended to the alarm system, a surprisingly simple process, and led them into the marble-floored villa, which was almost as pleasing as the location. Edward was in the pool within twenty minutes, splashing about as Kesey and Janet watched, drinking complimentary bottled water taken from the fridge and chatting. Kesey was so happy to be there. She could already feel the tension melting away as the bright sun warmed her body. Only now did she truly realise just how badly she needed the break. She pondered the dramatic contrast between her professional and family life, the horrors she often encountered at work, the worst of human behaviour. And she silently swore she'd make the most of the holiday, with no more thoughts of police work or the criminals and victims involved. Maybe then the headaches would become less regular, the irritable bowel less severe. There was more to life than crime. Lanzarote, she thought, had been a good choice. She was already in a holiday mood, and the daily grind now seemed so far away. It was the longest break she'd ever indulged. It was going to be three whole weeks of family fun. As she turned to kiss Janet gently on her right cheek, she'd never felt more determined about anything in her life.

9

Cerys was a worrier. She always had been, and she suspected she always would be. Nothing was going to change anytime soon. Her thought patterns were well established. She thought the same things most, if not every day. And she did again now as her head began to ache, an all-too-common affliction that nothing seemed to alleviate to any satisfactory extent. She'd given it a lot of thought over the years, reading one self-help book and well-meaning online article after another before finally concluding that it all started when she was just six years old. She and her four-year-old sister Lucy were spending the weekend in the care of Doreen, their much-loved maternal grandmother, in the lovely Pembrokeshire seaside town of Tenby, with its bucket-and-spade beaches, picturesque fishing harbour and impressive medieval defensive town walls. It was something the sisters did from time to time when their parents were otherwise committed or simply fancied some couple time. But that all changed one windy Welsh November day as a brisk autumn breeze swept sheets of cold rain off the Irish Sea, soaking everything in its path.

Cerys recalled her surprise discovering that her nana wasn't up and about on that causative morning when she rose from bed at around seven. She could still picture the events now, almost as if in real-time. And the emotions felt real, too. She was back there in Tenby.

Doreen usually prepared a delicious breakfast of scrambled eggs, pancakes, maple syrup and freshly squeezed orange juice before waking the girls with a jolly call. There would be music playing in the background, the radio, or a favourite CD the sisters particularly liked – something cheery, tunes to make them dance. Their nana would be smiling, happy, exuding positivity as she almost always did where the girls were concerned. But not that day. Cerys had found her much-loved grandmother lying prone on the multi-coloured floral carpet of the comfortable lounge, next to the gas fire. She'd thought the middle-aged woman was simply asleep. She sat at her nana's side and shook her, then again, using all her limited strength the second time, but she still couldn't rouse her. She'd begged her to wake up; she'd pleaded time and again, but to no avail. It was an emotional scar, Cerys pondered, that had never healed. And so she relived those events time and again as if hoping for a different outcome, but with the same inevitable awful result she still couldn't fully accept.

Cerys rocked gently in her comfortable garden office seat as she continued her all too familiar thought process. Even at the tender age of six, she'd had the wherewithal to pick up her nana's landline in the hall, dial 999 and summon help. That was to her credit, worthy of congratulation, a pat on the back. And she looked after her younger sister too, hugging her tightly, holding her close, wiping away her tears until an ambulance finally arrived about twenty minutes later. It had seemed such a long time that twenty minutes.

Cerys was suddenly still, knees apart, her eyes tight shut as she smiled thinly. She took some satisfaction in the fact she'd acted as she did at such a young age. She'd been brave, looked after Lucy and hadn't put herself first. But from that moment, life became a less predictable reality where the fear of loss was ever-present. And no amount of yoga, meditation, self-hypnosis, alcohol, prescribed anti-anxiety medication or any other therapeutic endeavours, however well-intentioned, would change that. She still pictured those events at the most unlikely and inconvenient times. As was the case now, as she sat at her desk, staring at her computer screen, urging herself to write the next chapter of her latest contemporary romance novel, the tenth in a little over seven years.

Cerys silently cursed her overactive mind as she pictured the past events. And it wasn't just the past. Once the anxiety kicked in, it seemed to spread, grow, reach out its tentacles to pollute everything and drag her down. She felt like screaming. She so wished she could still her troubled mind, focus and let the words flow, allow them to appear on the page as if by magic, as if dictated by someone else entirely. But for now, that was a lost cause. She knew it only too well as she stood, pacing the room, first one way and then the other, even more agitated than before. She worried about the present too and, of course, the future, that greatest uncertainty of it all. She worried about her writing career, her health, her headteacher husband, her five-year-old son, whether he loved her as much as she loved him. She worried about her mother's cancer diagnosis, the treatment, if she'd make a full recovery. Whether or not she'd die. And for some reason, of late, she was worrying more and more about her sister.

Cerys thought about that now as she stood at the floor-to-ceiling window, looking out on the garden as two black-and-white magpies pecked the damp ground, searching for worms after a light fall of early-summer rain. Yes, Lucy's career was going well, she was a talented artist, a skilled painter and sculptor, but her relationship was a disaster. And yesterday's meeting with the strangely named man at the café. How weird was that? Cerys couldn't help but feel that something wasn't right. She tried to push her nagging concerns from her mind, but they kept coming back. There was something about Moloch, for all his smiles, that put her teeth on edge. It was an instinctive thing, a gut feeling, something she couldn't ignore, however much she'd appreciate an easier life.

Cerys sat back at her computer now, folding one leg over the other, drumming the wooden desktop with the fingers of one hand, staring at the screen and willing herself to concentrate on the task at hand. She so wanted to write at least one chapter that day before picking up her son from school. But once again, her intrusive thoughts got in the way. She shook her head, closed her laptop and picked up her mobile. She looked up at the clock located on the wall to her right, next to one of Lucy's paintings, a brightly coloured, blue, purple and green acrylic abstract inspired by the sea. It was almost lunchtime; Lucy would soon take a break from her lecturing duties, and maybe she'd be available to talk. She suspected that conveying her concerns wouldn't be overly welcome, but she felt obliged to do it, anyway. Whatever Lucy's likely negative response, Cerys decided she would tell her exactly what she thought of Moloch and the offer of work mentioned by her mother. Some things needed saying.

Cerys locked her office, hurried across the patio towards the house and into the kitchen, where she opened a can of organic vegetable soup, bought from a nearby, independent health food store. She needed to eat if she was going to have the confidence to make this call. She heated the contents in a copper saucepan rather than the microwave, cut two slices of locally produced sourdough bread, and sat down at the breakfast bar with her mobile placed next to her dark-red pottery mug. She blew her soup repeatedly to cool it, dunked in a small chunk of bread, and thoroughly enjoyed it, waiting until just after one before making her call. Lucy answered on the third insistent ring of the shrill tone.

'Crufts Dog Show – woof, woof, woof.'

Cerys smiled but didn't laugh. Lucy was nothing if not predictable. She made the same childish joke almost every time she answered the phone.

'Very funny, Lucy, I can hardly stop laughing. Have you got time to talk?'

'Of course. What's up?'

Cerys felt her jaw tighten. She'd hoped to keep the conversation casual, as low key as possible, to express her concerns in a subtle way rather than jump right in. But it already seemed her tone had betrayed her concern.

'Why do you assume something's wrong?'

'Well, there usually is when you ring. Is it Mum again? I called at the house to see her; she's doing okay. She's having the right treatment, she's thinking positive, and you worrying yourself silly isn't going to change anything for the better. You're going to make yourself ill again if you're not careful. You have to try to relax.'

Cerys adjusted her position, trying to get comfortable as her lower back stiffened and complained.

'It's, er, it's not Mum, not this time.'

'Then what is it? Come on, I know something is bothering you. Just tell me and get it over with – you know I'll help if I can.'

Was that a hint of impatience in Lucy's voice? Or maybe it was frustration. It was sometimes hard to tell. Either way, it was time to get to the point.

'Mum told me about the problems you've been having with Andy.'

'Ah, yeah, okay. I wondered if that was where this was going. I've told him he's got to move out. It wasn't an easy conversation. I've been putting it off for months, but now it's done. Soon he'll be gone. It's a huge relief, to be honest. I wish I'd done it a lot sooner. The relationship has run its course.'

'Was he difficult? When you told him, I mean? I know he can be. Did he give you a hard time?'

'Same old, same old – a mixture of anger and tears, much as I expected. It's done, that's the main thing. I'm getting my life back.'

'You've done the right thing.'

'Yeah, I know, thanks. I'm glad you understand.'

Cerys smiled. 'You and me against the world. We'll always stick together.'

'Exactly, that's what sisters are for.'

It was now or never.

'There is one other thing,' Cerys said.

'Oh, here we go. What is it now? I just knew there was something else.'

Cerys crossed and uncrossed her legs and then stood before responding, taking her unfinished soup with her.

'That man you met at the café. Will you be seeing him again?'

'I hope to. He made me a great offer. The most generous I've ever had. It would be a shame to miss out on so much cash. I think he must think I'm a lot more famous than I am.'

'Don't do it, Lucy. There was something strange about him, something I didn't like.'

'Have you been talking to Mum about that too?'

'Well, yes, I have. I rang her yesterday evening, but it's not that. Didn't you notice something wasn't quite right about his appearance?'

Cerys heard her sister let out a long breath before responding.

'I thought he looked rather smart. A little old-fashioned, perhaps, but nice. I've got a quirky dress sense myself. A lot of artistic people have. You could say the same thing about me.'

Cerys made a face.

'No, you don't understand; that's not what I'm talking about. I was only sitting a short distance from the man. I studied him closely while the two of you were talking. It's an author thing – it's something I do; observe, searching for storylines. He had grey hair and a grey beard, but his skin and face didn't look old enough for that. There were no wrinkles. None that I could see at all. It was almost as if he'd dyed his hair that colour. As if he was trying to look older than he actually was. I think he was a man in his thirties trying to look fifty.'

Lucy laughed. 'Oh, come off it, Cerys, that's crazy talk. I was sitting directly opposite the man at the same table. You were at the other end of the room. I didn't notice anything of the kind. You're getting yourself in a tizzy again. You really are worried about nothing.'

'But you weren't wearing your glasses. And I know how much you hate your contact lenses. I bet you couldn't see him that clearly at all.'

Cerys heard her sister sigh. She could picture Lucy's disapproving expression and body language when she next spoke moments later.

'Look, I appreciate your concern – really, I do. But this is getting ridiculous. I'd have to be blind as a bat not to have seen what you're claiming. Some men go grey early in life, and he's one of them. He had uneven teeth too. Are you going to criticise them as well? You seem totally committed to character assassination. I'm sure there must be something else you can think of.'

Cerys rolled her eyes with frustration.

'I wish you'd take me seriously for once.'

'First, Mum persuades you to come to spy on me for no good reason at all, and now this. The man offered me work, and he offered to pay me well – much more than I've ever received for a commission before. Given I couldn't do it when he wanted, I probably won't even hear from him again. But if I do, and he's willing for me to do the work at the end of term, I'll grab the opportunity with both hands. Why on earth wouldn't I? You worry about everything, Cerys. This is my life. Let me get on with it. I'm grateful to Moloch for his offer. And don't even start going on about his name like Mum did. It's unusual, but so what? It's not a crime. I still hope his offer comes to something. I'll be disappointed if it doesn't.'

Cerys briefly considered a further attempt to influence her sister, but quickly decided she'd done her bit. Anything she said, however reasonable, would fall on deaf ears. It was almost always the same.

'Well, I've said my piece. It's up to you what you do with the information. I can't make you see sense. I just hope you don't end up regretting not listening to me.'

Lucy laughed, something Cerys found utterly infuriating. It was so like her sister, so very typical.

'Now you're starting to sound like Mum.'

Cerys shook her head, trying not to cry with frustration. It seemed the apple rarely fell far from the tree.

'I care about you, that's all. If I didn't tell you of my concerns and something awful happened, I'd never forgive myself.'

'Oh, Cerys. Nothing bad will happen. I'm an artist, not in some high-risk profession. Get a grip, for goodness' sake.'

'Okay, maybe I'm worrying about nothing.'

'You are, you definitely are.'

Cerys decided to change tack. She wasn't getting anywhere, which was no surprise. Time for a different subject.

'Do you fancy meeting for coffee one lunchtime next week?'

'That would be lovely. Just text me a time and place. Any day other than Thursday works for me.'

'I'll look forward to it.'

Lucy's tone was more upbeat when she next spoke.

'There is one thing I should probably mention.'

'What's that?'

There was a silent pause before Lucy responded.

'I'm pregnant.'

Cerys's mouth fell open.

'Did I hear you right?'

'You most certainly did. You're going to be an aunty.'

'Wow, that is not what I was expecting. Does Mum know?'

'I told her first, and now I'm telling you. I swore her to secrecy. I wanted to tell you myself.'

'Is it Andy's?'

'Yes, it's Andy's! Why does everyone keep asking me that?'

'How did he react to the news?'

'He doesn't know. I haven't told him yet. I will, but only when I think the time is right, maybe in a week or two when he's settled into wherever he ends up. I don't want him thinking there's any chance of us getting back together. That's the last thing I'd want.'

Cerys raised her free hand and rubbed the back of her neck. 'I don't know whether to congratulate you or sympathise.'

'After a good deal of soul searching, I've finally decided it's good news. I'm going to be a mother. You and Mum seem to manage it well enough. I like to think I can do the same.'

'In that case, congratulations! Life really can be unpredictable. You're going to be a brilliant parent. Just you wait and see.'

'How's the book going?'

'Oh, it's, er, it's going, that's about the best I can say. One of the main characters is pregnant too, twins. Although she's in a happy relationship with a famous rock star. I'll tell you more about it when we meet up. My last book wasn't as popular as I'd hoped. There's so much more competition these days. I need this one to be a bestseller. It's a little sexier than the others. I've let my imagination flow.'

'Oh, that sounds good, just my sort of thing. I look forward to reading it.'

'Have you thought about baby names?'

'Not as yet, but I think I'll opt for something Welsh like you did.'

Cerys took a final slurp of soup, emptying her mug, swallowing before speaking.

'Oooh, exciting, I'll give it some thought. I've got a book of Welsh names somewhere. I bought it before Dewi was born. I'll bring it with me when we meet.'

'That would be great.'

Cerys smiled.

'Right, I'd better love you and leave you. I know you've got arty things to be getting on with, and my book's not going to write itself, more's the pity. For some reason, I'm struggling with this one. I need all the help I can get.'

'Send me that text.'

'I will, and you think about what I said about that Moloch man. He made my skin crawl. I don't like him. I can't pretend I do.'

'Oh, my God, not that again – you and Mum are obsessed.'

'Just think about it, that's all I'm asking.'

'I'll see you soon, Cerys. I need to grab a sandwich and a quick cup of tea before my afternoon lecture.'

'Promise me you'll think about it.'

'Okay, okay. If it makes you happy, I'll think about it. But you're worrying about nothing as usual.'

As Cerys ended her call and returned to her garden office, she felt sure Lucy wouldn't act on her expressed concerns. As the older sister, it seemed she did the worrying for both of them. Lucy hadn't listened to her advice before, so why should she start now?

10

Gove had felt a burning rage that threatened to explode into a frenzy of uncontrolled violence as he left the café following Lucy's rejection. Her unwelcome and shocking response felt deeply personal. She wasn't just rebuffing his fictional offer of paid work; she was rejecting *him*. And that hurt, it stung, it festered as nothing had before. It ate away at his peace of mind like a wild creature tearing at flesh. He could easily have ruined her in righteous revenge, torn her to pieces, fed her to the birds. But as the hours passed, he began to view it differently.

Now, a day after their lunch, Gove lay on the stained wooden floor of his killing room with classical music playing quietly on a recently acquired laptop and pondered the unwelcome developments in his life. Strangely enough, despite all of Lucy's hateful and unreasonable behaviour, he still thought of her as a likely future soulmate; that was the truth of it. He found it hard to comprehend, but his warm feelings for her were still there. He didn't know if it was love because he didn't know how that felt, but he felt something. After thinking about it for an hour or so, he finally concluded that his current situation was a challenge sent to test him, rather than the end of things. It was the only explanation that made any sense. Gove sat cross-legged now, close to a sash window, looking out on his garden cemetery. He felt a sudden surge of satisfaction, pleased with the reasoned conclusions he'd reached. Yes, despite everything, lovely Lucy was still the one. Of course, she was. How could he have doubted it even for a single second?

He'd sat opposite her, he'd looked into her beautiful eyes, touched her warm hand as the blood flowed in her veins and arteries, pumped by a heart that would soon be his. And there was no doubt about it; she was the only female he'd ever encountered who didn't look like his bitch mother in one way or another, not even slightly. There was nothing about her, nothing at all that brought back dark memories of the painful past. How remarkable was that? A flame-haired woman with whom he could enjoy a fruitful relationship for however long it lasted. So many wondrous things had happened in such a short time. He'd won the lottery, moved to wonderful Wales – a country he'd never even previously visited – he'd found the perfect killing house, and now he'd found her too. The woman who was destined to be his. But, for all of that, there was only so long he could forgive her rejection. She needed to change her behaviour, and quickly too. There were limits to even his patience. If he had to kill her, then so be it.

As Gove sat in his spacious, well-equipped country kitchen, sipping camomile tea half an hour or so later, he decided he needed to kill again before welcoming Lucy to his Georgian home. An itch needed scratching. The pressure was building as it always did. It had to be satisfied, and there was only one way of finding relief.

Gove drove towards a familiar scrapyard later that same day. It was somewhere he'd been before, located in the same faded industrial town where he'd caught the train to the café meeting the day before. The owner was a friend and distant cousin of a patient he'd encountered at the secure hospital – one of several useful contacts he'd developed due to his professional psychiatric nursing role. He'd borrowed a suitable van from him in the past, a van with false plates and plenty of room for an unconscious victim in the back. Now he needed the vehicle again.

He planned to travel to Bristol that night, somewhere he hadn't been before, but which he'd chosen with care and attention while perusing an online map of the UK. The city wasn't too close, but it wasn't too far away. Far more convenient than the cities of the Midlands and North he'd used before. And Bristol had a red-light district, sex workers, vulnerable girls plying their trade in the dead of night. That was important too. It offered an ideal hunting ground, opportunities and easy pickings for an accomplished predator like him. Maybe he should have thought of the place before.

Gove carefully manoeuvred his expensive German SUV through the large, grey-painted gates that led into the shambolic scrapyard. There were mangled vehicles of every kind and description piled high on either side of the enclosure, and a rusty corrugated metal building which served as an office and workshop at the far end, where scrap metal was weighed and cash changed hands. Gove was pleased and relieved to see the white van in question parked directly outside the half-open door to the structure. Everything was working out as he'd hoped. Soon, the van would be his; he'd wait for darkness and be on his merry way.

Carl Fisher, the scrapyard owner, suddenly appeared from behind a tower of crushed cars, approaching Gove's SUV as he parked and got out. Fisher had a rolled-up cigarette hanging from one corner of his mouth.

'Carl, nice to see you again, my friend. I have another favour to ask.'

Fisher frowned hard, spat the fag from his mouth and ground it into the dirt with a light-brown cowboy boot heel. He spoke with a strong West Wales accent with rolled Rs and well-rounded melodic vowels.

'If you want the fucking van again, I'm not sure. You left it in one hell of a state last time. There was blood everywhere. I don't want any shit from the police.'

Gove's hackles rose, but he outwardly retained a calm composure because it suited his purpose.

'I told you, I ran a stray dog over. I put it in the back to take to the vet. How many times do I need to tell you the same thing? Why would the police be interested in that?'

Fisher looked as if he didn't believe a word of it.

'Well, you could have washed the fucking thing. Someone had to do it. And that someone was me.'

Gove looked at Fisher with an intense glare. He'd never loathed a man more. It would have felt so good to punch him in the throat, to crush his windpipe. To watch him fall to the ground and choke. But when it came to men, violence wasn't the answer. He wasn't big enough or strong enough for that. Gove took a wad of fifty-pound notes from an inside pocket of his summer jacket, shaking the money in the air with a grin.

'There's a thousand quid there, Carl, all in used notes. I think that should be enough to silence your concerns. I need the van for a few days, no more than that. Take the money, spend it well, and keep my SUV well hidden. I'll get the van back to you once I'm done with it. And I'll make sure it's clean this time. You've got my contact number. You know my address. You can always get hold of me if you need to. That sounds like a good deal to me.'

Fisher focused on the money greedily and then snatched it with an oil-stained hand. He stuffed the cash into a pocket of his dirty overalls as Gove smiled and nodded. Gove hurried after him as he walked back towards his office.

'I need the number plates changed before I go. And not just any old plates. Something matching the make and colour of the van but registered in a completely different part of the country.'

'For fuck's sake, do you think I'm an idiot? You say the same thing every fucking time.'

'I don't want any mistakes. I'm paying you good money, way over the odds. I want to make my expectations crystal clear.'

Fisher mumbled to himself as he took a bunch of keys with a worn green leather fob from a small metal hook just inside the office door. He threw them to Gove, who caught them easily in one hand. Fisher pointed at Gove and then at the van.

'A week maximum, and it's back here and clean, yeah? I don't know what the fuck you're up to, and I don't want to know. Keep that shit to yourself. It's got half a tank of diesel. Give me ten minutes to sort the plates, and you're good to go.'

11

Laura Kesey was starting to relax. The sky was a clear azure-blue, there was a pleasant sea breeze coming off the Atlantic Ocean and the average daily temperature was just perfect. Kesey wasn't one for extreme heat. She struggled with the blazing summer temperatures of the Mediterranean. But the Canaries, she observed, were spot on: not too hot but plenty warm enough for swimming both in the pool and the sea. The rigours of West Wales policing were already fading somewhere into the distance. She still thought of particular cases from time to time, individual victims, particularly women and children, who for one reason or another came to mind, but such thoughts were fleeting. It was amazing how quickly the stress seemed to melt away when she focused on the now. She was very much hoping it would stay that way and was looking forward to the rest of her holiday.

The morning hadn't exactly gone as planned. Much to Edward's disappointment and dismay, an intended visit to a nearby beach popular with surfers had to be cancelled when Janet realised she'd forgotten a necessary medication, a twice-daily treatment for heart arrhythmia she couldn't do without for very long. A visit to a public medical clinic in the nearby town of Teguise, hoping for a suitable prescription was unsuccessful due to complications to do with Britain leaving the European Union. And so,

Kesey drove the approximate twenty-minute journey to find a recommended private clinic in Costa Teguise, with Janet making repeated apologies and Kesey telling her it wasn't a problem. Not a big deal at all.

Kesey parked in a conveniently located car park in the same street as the clinic, a few minutes' walk from a surprisingly large Spar supermarket they also planned to visit before leaving the area that day. Kesey took Edward for ice cream in a busy seaside café while Janet waited to see a Spanish doctor.

Janet was at the reception counter paying the bill in cash when Kesey and Ed returned to meet her an hour later. Janet stood with a sheepish look on her pretty face. Another unnecessary apology followed, and to everyone's relief, Janet obtained the required medication in a small, well-stocked chemist shop almost directly opposite the clinic at a very reasonable cost.

Kesey and Janet soon decided that Costa Teguise, as popular as it was, wasn't the place for them. It was a bustling resort, busy with people of all ages. But they preferred a quieter life. It was interesting to see the place, and they were both glad they'd been there – albeit the circumstances could have been better – but felt glad they were staying where they were. It was a case of each to their own. The villa was exactly where they wanted it. The three spent about half an hour or so stocking up on provisions as planned and then made their way inland, back to Teguise, where they ate an early lunch in a vegetarian restaurant that catered for Janet's gluten and dairy sensitivities perfectly well. The welcome was warm, the food delicious, and both women knew they'd be back.

It was decided to put off the beach visit until the next day. So they returned to the villa, where Janet sat on a comfortable recliner in a shady spot reading a popular celebrity's autobiography. Kesey and Ed swam and played in the private pool. It wasn't heated, but it wasn't so cold as to be uncomfortable.

Kesey shuddered, shaking off unexpected feelings of fear and anxiety as she towelled her son dry and applied his sunscreen a short time later. She looked around her at the happy scene, asking herself what on earth was wrong? It was almost as if the holiday was too perfect. Life, she pondered, had the habit of biting her in the arse when it seemed to be going well. She told herself not to be stupid, but the feeling wouldn't go away. Kesey put it down to the realities of her job. As the afternoon passed, she finally pushed her anxious thoughts from her mind, interpreting them as proof of just how badly she needed the break. It was time for the family, time for innocent fun. Police work and everything that went with it could wait.

12

Gove crouched low in his rust-pocked van, watching intently as a young, scantily clad sex worker emerged from a dark doorway. He stared at her with unblinking eyes, motionless, transfixed, as she approached the open driver's window of a saloon car parked on the opposite side of the dimly lit street. Gove smiled hungrily, leering as the young woman bent at the waist, leaning towards her potential punter, undoubtedly negotiating a cash price, revealing thin legs accentuated by five-inch heels and a skinny arse, barely covered by her tight shiny black satin skirt. He saw a potential victim, a guest who would have to meet his needs as best she could until lovely Lucy's eventual arrival.

Gove was delighted when the metallic-blue saloon car he'd been watching suddenly sped off with a loud screech of its tyres, leaving the young woman standing stranded alone in the road, balancing awkwardly on her heels, giving the retreating car the finger and swearing in what sounded like a West Country accent. Something about the young prostitute reminded him of his bitch mother as she stood forlorn below a flickering streetlamp, close to tears. She had an undefinable quality he couldn't quite pin down. But he was sure there was a similarity. There always was when he first targeted a potential victim, whatever their age, ethnicity, hair colour, height or build. Yes, there was always something. And tonight was no different, as his anger gradually intensified, his blood pressure rising to a new and savage high.

The young woman's face slowly morphed into that of his mother, as if he was back there, before he was taken into local-authority care at the age of eleven. Before he met his abusive foster carers. From the frying pan into the fire.

Gove lent forwards, gripping the steering wheel with both hands, resisting the impulse to scream. He shouted out his anger, talking to no one but himself. 'The prossie is a total and utter fucking bitch!' He said it and believed it, spitting out his words as his anger intensified still further. His verbal assault was replaced by dark thoughts as he continued to watch her, taking everything in, every slight movement of her body. The bitch was mocking him, sneering, derisive! Look at her standing there, so full of herself, so lacking in shame or remorse for her many terrible sins. She would suffer for her lack of respect. Yes, the bitch would pay. He'd obliterate her features, tear her limb from contemptuous limb. How dare she look so much like the vile cow who'd so ruined his early life? Yes, the bitch was mocking him, laughing. She was doing it on purpose. It was the only explanation that made any sense at all. It was time to make his move, time to make her pay.

Gove finally started the van's diesel engine on the fourth turn of the key. He punched the dashboard in frustration, put on the headlights and manoeuvred out into the quiet road, never taking his eyes off her, scanning her body from head to foot, up-down, up-down, not looking away. He imagined sinking his teeth deep into her soft flesh as he drove on about twenty yards. And then he pulled up alongside her, a few inches from the kerb, using his right hand to wind down the window with a great big welcoming smile. He could hardly contain himself. He so wanted to get his hands on her. But he had to play the long game. However complex, he had to time it right. The last thing he wanted was to sound any alarm bells in the bitch's head. She may run, try to escape. He had to stay in control.

'Hello, my little darling. Are you available for some fun?'

He thought she looked eighteen, or maybe nineteen, possibly younger but certainly no older as she approached the van. Her age didn't matter to him. There was a cut to her upper lip and a slight bruising to one heavily made-up eye. He could see she'd been crying.

'It's cash upfront; that's the deal, take it or leave it.'

He put on his best smile as he imagined cutting her scrawny throat from ear to ear. The smile he always used at this stage of the grooming process. It had worked in the past, and it would again.

'That is no problem at all, my beautiful lady. Just tell me how much. I'm sure you're worth every penny.'

She leaned forwards, showing off her small tits, allowing the van to support her weight. There were multiple needle marks on both her arms that Gove couldn't help but see. Just like his mother. His filthy, stinking, junkie mother. Just like her.

'It's twenty quid for a hand job, thirty for a blowy, fifty for a fuck, and extra for anything else. And you've got to wear a rubber. Nothing is happening without one. Unless you pay an extra twenty.'

Gove took a wad of new notes from the glovebox, five hundred pounds in total and held the cash up in plain sight, watching her eyes light up, no doubt at the thought of her next chemical hit.

'There's a mattress in the back of the van. Get in, lie down, take your knickers off, keep your mouth shut, and you can have all of it. You can be out of here and as high as a kite in half an hour.'

She frowned hard, her entire body stiffening.

'I told you, it's cash upfront.'

Gove was wearing workman's overalls, a black baseball cap pulled down low and tinted glasses that hid his eyes as he exited the vehicle, handing over the cash with another manipulative smile she seemed to find reassuring.

'There you go, my little darling. That's a lot more than you asked for. Let's get you in the back. The quicker you let me fuck you, the quicker you're out of here with a needle in your vein.'

She screwed up her face. 'I don't do anal, and I don't do bondage. I don't like being tied up. Anything else is fine for five hundred quid, but you ask first. I don't like being forced.'

Gove made a mental note of her dislikes for future advantage. Such information was gold dust. He fully intended to use it against her the second they were back at his home.

'That's all good, my lovely, not a problem with me. I'm one of life's good guys – you're in control. I'm into the girlfriend experience, nothing kinky.'

He looked to left and right, checking the street for potential witnesses, led her to the rear of the van with a hand on her arm, opened both doors and encouraged her to enter first. He grinned as she climbed in like a lamb to the slaughter, unaware of her pending fate. He chuckled at the thought. Such a stupid girl, so willing to die.

'I'll be with you in a second, my lovely – I've just got to get the condoms from the cab. Make yourself comfortable. We're going to do this your way. I'll be gentle with you.'

Gove smirked as he opened the driver's door, reaching into the vehicle with a growing sense of confidence. It was amazing what you could get on the dark web if you had the ready cash to pay in whatever form the seller required. He'd learned that at the hospital; an apprenticeship for his true purpose. Everything was as it should be.

Gove had a fascination with altered states of consciousness. He always slept clean, free of any drugs, even alcohol, considering his body a temple, a divine creation not to be sullied by chemicals. But Harrison had shared with him his extensive knowledge of sedatives. Gove had asked pertinent questions, listening fascinated by the killer's advice and making detailed, alphabetically ordered notes, storing the information for later use in a file named 'Methods'. Gove noted the benefits and disadvantages of the various drugs, the time they took to take full effect, and the ideal dose required depending on the approximate weight of the particular victim. Gove had studied and learned the information by heart. And he used that learning to his advantage now as he took a black pouch from the glovebox with feelings of satisfaction and heady anticipation. Everything was going so very well. The universe was on his side.

Gove took a plastic syringe from the pouch, removed the packaging covering a needle and secured it carefully in place. While holding the syringe in one hand, he took a small glass vial containing a fast-acting sedative drug in the other. He broke off its top with a satisfying snap and placed the needle precisely through the mouth of the vial, slowly drawing the clear liquid into the syringe chamber. Finally, with practised skill and speed, he gently pressed the plunger with his thumb, pushing out the air until a tiny drop of the clear liquid squirted reassuringly from the top of the needle. He was ready. The bitch was waiting. Time to get it done.

Gove rechecked the quiet backstreet road for potential witnesses, and he was pleased but not surprised to see that all was well. The ordinary people of Bristol were asleep and lost in their dreams. It seemed he could act without fear of discovery. And so he smiled again as he opened one of the van's two rear doors, which creaked alarmingly as it swung on its hinges. He flinched as a light shone brightly in the first-floor window of a building opposite. A curtain opened and then quickly closed. That shook him momentarily, but his anxiety soon passed as the light went off. There was just him and the girl. The ugly, hateful bitch with his mother's face. It was as if they were the only two people in the world. What did a bit of noise matter? If someone had seen, they were gone.

He smiled again as the girl looked up at him, and then he climbed into the van alongside her, keeping the syringe hidden for the moment, closing the door behind him with a metallic click. He switched on his phone's torch, providing ample light.

'Lie back and relax, my darling. Why so worried? Turn that frown into a smile. You never know, you might even enjoy yourself. I'm not like anyone you've met before. It's your lucky night.'

She pulled her short skirt up around her waist. She wasn't wearing any underwear. An off-white lacy thong was next to her on the van's filthy metal floor among the blood and oil stains. There were multiple finger bruises to the top of both her legs; blue, purple, brown and black. She lay back with her haunted eyes fixed on him, not saying a word. He thought that strange, her sudden silence. She'd had so much to say for herself, and now nothing. All her bravado was gone. It was as if someone had cut out her tongue. Not such a bad idea – maybe he should do that. But not yet, tomorrow, now was not the time.

Gove focused on the task at hand, pushing his imaginings from his mind as his penis began to swell. He took the syringe from behind his back and held it out in front of him, just a few inches from the girl's tired eyes. He could have rained down blow after mighty blow, rendering her unconscious and bleeding. He considered it briefly. It would at least provide some entertainment. But the mind games were amusing him for the moment, so he decided to continue because he could. And the light in the window. What about that light? It may not be a good idea to hang around too long.

'Do you want some of this, my beautiful? It's fantastic stuff, the best I've ever had. It will blow your fucking mind.'

Her eyes widened as she sat up, holding out an arm, undoubtedly keen to welcome the latest chemical cosh. Anything to take the edge off. He inserted the needle, with care, using his nursing skills to ensure it entered deep into the girl's brachial artery, the major blood vessel just inside her elbow. He pressed in the plunger with a squeal of unfettered delight, administering at least twice the required dose to render her insensible in under a minute. He sat back, watching as she slowly drifted away. He didn't want to kill her there, not then, not yet. As pleasurable as that would be, it was better to wait. Preferable to drive back down the M4, over the Severn Bridge, across the Welsh border and on to his remote rural home, to his killing room where he could indulge his interests to his heart's content without fear of discovery.

Gove tore out the girl's stud earrings, ensuring she was asleep, then exited the rear of the van. He checked the street with quick darting eyes, jumped up into the driver's cabin and started the engine, which fired on the first hurried attempt. He took brief satisfaction from his triumph but cursed loudly on considering the length of the journey facing him. He'd be driving for around two hours before reaching his home. Two fucking hours! The waiting would be a challenge. It always was when a victim was waiting. It would eat away at him, testing his patience and resolve. He was so looking forward to seeing the fear in the terrified girl's eyes as she woke, naked, shackled to the wall, helpless and at his mercy. He keenly anticipated hearing her scream in terror and pain as her intermingling body fluids stained the floor around her feet.

Gove felt his penis swell again now as he pictured the scene. And then he ejaculated without even the need to touch himself. He was that excited, that aroused by the thought of it all. It would be so good, so terrific. Perhaps this time, the cellar was an appropriate place of execution. And maybe this time, he'd film the bitch suffering as no one had ever suffered before. Yes, he'd film the entire process, from the start to the glorious end as she breathed her last breath. He'd installed the necessary equipment. It was all there, ready and waiting. So, why not use it? He had to start sometime. And the film would be something to show lovely Lucy. A means of introducing her to his work. Yes, yes, that all made absolute sense. It was genius, total genius. Why hadn't he thought of it before? He'd create a work of art for his new love to celebrate and enjoy. And then, when she'd watched it and worshipped at his feet, they'd create a bloody new masterpiece together. A triumph to top all that had gone before. Something worthy of the highest awards.

* * *

The journey back to West Wales passed slowly, with Gove making good use of his smartphone satnav app until he hit the motorway when it was no longer needed. By then, he was back on familiar ground, an area with which he'd become thoroughly familiar as he'd made one hunting trip after another, seeking suitable prey. From Newport onwards, he listened and sang along to a favourite country music compilation but even that didn't help the time pass more quickly as the adrenaline gradually left his system and tiredness set in. It was past four in the morning when he finally drove down the stone-strewn track leading to his luxury home. He was so relieved to get there, so glad the night was finally ending. But there was still work to do – things which couldn't wait.

Gove parked the van on a large area of even gravel bordered by the lawn at the back of the house, keen to hide the vehicle from any potentially prying eyes – delivery people, the postman and the like. The earlier clouds had cleared by that time, and a bright moon lit the entire area in a pale-yellow light as an owl hooted in the far-off distance. But Gove didn't see the beauty. He was oblivious to the glorious sight before him. He was focused on only one thing. He opened the van's rear doors and dragged the unconscious girl from the vehicle by her bare feet, allowing her head to hit the hard ground first before closing the doors. A wound to her scalp left a thin trail of dark blood as he dragged her into the house and towards the kitchen. He'd decided not to utilise his killing room this time, but to imprison her in the cellar, as he'd considered earlier. He switched on the kitchen light, left the girl lying on the cold tiles, entered the utility room, opened a white-painted four-panel door to the right of the washing machine and looked down the twelve concrete steps that led to an extensive cellar, which had once been a coal house, among other things. He was tired then, yawning repeatedly as his eyes threatened to shut. But as always, when preparing a new guest for the slaughter, he somehow found sufficient strength to get things done to his satisfaction. He lifted her into a seated position, her thin legs dangling over the first four steps, and then he shoved her with all his strength so that she went tumbling down to the bottom. She landed with a final thud that amused him immensely.

Gove descended the steps after her, unlocked a second door, dragged her into the dark cellar by her hair and then returned to the kitchen. He made a cup of calming camomile tea, drinking it from an antique floral china cup with a matching saucer, enjoying it along with a chocolate digestive biscuit, building his strength up for the final task of the night. He'd decided to shackle the girl to the cellar wall before finally heading to bed for a few hours' much-needed rest. It was, he told himself, essential to ensure she was adequately restrained. There was no room for sloppiness, however exhausted he felt after all the driving. Better safe than sorry. And then he'd wake her from her chemically induced slumber when he rose in the morning. A bit of breakfast first, and he'd be ready. He began giggling as he imagined the look of horror on the girl's face when she first opened her eyes, hanging there from thin, twisted arms, the unforgiving metal cutting into the soft skin of her wrists.

He'd shout out, 'Wakey, wakey, welcome to your new home.' Ha! The sentence invariably amused him, however many times he used it. Why change what worked well? There was no point in reinventing the wheel. A bucket or two of icy cold water usually did the job well. Splash! He'd hurl it right in her bitch face. See how she liked that, the total and utter skank. There was so much to look forward to, so much fun to capture on film for posterity.

Gove had a skip in his step, a rekindled energy, as he approached the cellar door for a second time, one thought after another tumbling in his mind. Maybe it wasn't such a bad thing that lovely Lucy's arrival had been temporarily delayed. Maybe it was meant to be. Perhaps the universe had conspired to make it happen. Yes, that was it. His new guest was so like his mother. It was uncanny. Lucy would understand that; she'd see it too when he welcomed her to his country home. How could she not?

As he slowly descended the steps one at a time, he decided he had to make it happen. If he was to entertain Lucy, he had to be proactive. His first ploy had failed, and now it was time for another. He'd keep the van, maybe get the number plates changed, and then watch Lucy. He'd search for the opportune time to snatch her. She'd soon be his.

13

Myra Williams grimaced as a sudden stab of burning pain exploded in her chest, her upper abdomen aching. She put it down to indigestion, but a small part of her still feared the worst. Life had knocked her confidence. When her phone rang in the lounge, she was chewing two antacid tablets, washing them down with a slurp of still bottled mineral water. She briefly considered not answering but thought better of it. Maybe it was her husband or one of the girls. She was already feeling a little better. The pain was easing, thank God. The medication was working its magic. It was best to put on a brave face, something she'd been doing an awful lot of in recent months.

'Oh, hi, Cerys, what can I do for you? I was just about to make some lunch.'

'I just thought I'd ring and say hello. I can ring back later. If you like?'

Myra slumped into the nearest armchair, slightly out of breath but now feeling significantly better as the antacids neutralised her stomach acid. She felt ridiculous for thinking it may have been her heart.

'No, it's nice to hear from you. How's the family?'

'We're all fine. Dewi's in school, Mike's in work and I've been doing a bit of writing. How about you?'

Myra sucked in the air.

'I'm doing all right, all considered. A little tired as usual, but good other than that.'

'I'm glad to hear it.'

Myra paused, wondering how much to say. 'Has Lucy told you her news?'

Cerys's voice rose in pitch and tone. 'Yes, yes, she has. I can't believe she's going to be a mum!'

'I'm so very glad she's told Andy to go, and not before time. It's going to be tough on her, being a single mother. I don't think she fully appreciates that yet. But it would have been a lot harder with that twat still in her life.'

'She's going to be fine. I've still got a lot of Dewi's old baby stuff – his cot, a buggy and a load of clothes. I meant to get rid of it all but never did. Most of the clothes would suit a boy or a girl. We'll give her all the help she needs between the two of us.'

Myra frowned, ready to change the subject. As the months passed, there would be plenty of time for baby talk, assuming the cancer didn't get worse.

'Has Lucy made any further mention of that Moloch man?'

'Um, yeah, I did have a word with her about all that. I told her my concerns, but she's still hoping he contacts her again. You know what she's like, always seeing the best in everyone. I don't even think it's just the cash. She seems to find the whole idea of the work fascinating.'

'What sort of person writes a letter like that? I'm hoping she never hears from him ever again.'

'I feel exactly the same, Mum – let's hope we're wrong to be worried.'

'Has Lucy mentioned the talk she's giving at the gallery tomorrow morning? I think she said it's from eleven until one.'

'No, I don't think so, not that I can recall.'

'It's to a women's group. Domestic violence, I think – something arranged by social services. I'd go if I were feeling any stronger. Just to represent your dad and offer my support.'

'As soon as you are better, we'll have a nice day out together, all three of us. A spa day, perhaps, the theatre, or a meal in a nice restaurant?'

Myra closed her eyes for a beat.

'I'll look forward to it. I've always loved a girls' day out.'

'I'd better make a move. I can hear in your voice that you're tired.'

Myra yawned, thinking Cerys had never said a more accurate word. So much had changed. Even conversations could now be exhausting.

'Oh dear, is it really that obvious?'

'I love you, Mum.'

'I love you too. Give my best to Mike and Dewi. And bring my grandson to see me. I've been missing him.'

'It's only been a few days. How about Saturday? I don't think we've got anything else on.'

'Any time over the weekend would be perfect. And let's invite Lucy too. She said she'd be popping around sometime, anyway. I'll leave it to you to make the arrangements. Dad will be back late on Friday night. He's getting a train from Paddington. It will be wonderful to have us all back together again.'

14

Lucy saw the old white van parked on double yellow lines outside the Lammas Street Gallery as she hurried along the pavement with quick-moving feet, a few minutes late for her presentation on Thursday 4 June. The seemingly ordinary vehicle came to mind just once as she gave her talk, enjoying the company of the women, who were both friendly and enthusiastic as they discussed modern art and its significance in our world. It was the kind of thing Lucy thoroughly enjoyed doing, talking about a subject she loved to people who were interested and appreciated her contribution. All in all, the morning's events felt very worthwhile. For a time, as she stood at the centre of the white-painted room with the vari-ously aged women seated in a semi-circle around her, Lucy forgot about her worries – Andy, her pregnancy, her mother's cancer, the early-summer hay fever that wouldn't let up. She simply focused on the task at hand. It carried her away and relaxed her. For Lucy, work was a therapy of sorts. Something she could fall back on in times of adversity.

It had started raining by the time Lucy left the gallery a couple of hours later. She was feeling good, increasingly optimistic about the future. She was, she told herself, a strong woman who could deal with whatever life threw at her.

Lucy briefly considered sheltering until the dark clouds passed, but as she looked up to the sky, she quickly concluded the change in the weather was likely set in for hours, if not the entire day. She had about an hour before needing to be back at the college. So why not enjoy a bit of lunch in that pleasant Merlin's Lane café where she met Moloch while she had the opportunity? The meeting hadn't gone to plan, but their food had been good. It was important to look after herself, get the proper nourishment and not overdo things, perhaps more important than ever before.

Lucy took a small navy-blue umbrella from her handbag, raised it and was about to stride off in the direction of the vegetarian café when a sharp two-second beep of a horn caught her attention. She looked across to where the sound had come from to see Moloch looking back at her from the open driver's side window of a white van she'd noticed earlier, with that same friendly broad smile she'd seen before. He looked much the same as he did on the day of their first meeting: grey hair, grey beard and blue-tinted glasses with round metal frames. She studied his face closely, now wearing her contact lenses despite her hay fever, and thought that maybe her sister was correct, at least in part. Maybe he did look younger than his hair colour suggested. But to say he was deliberately trying to look older than his years? The very idea was laughable, a ridiculous hypothesis. Cerys worried about the funniest things. She always had, and probably always would. The girl should get a grip.

As Moloch raised a hand, beckoning Lucy to approach, she smiled back, thinking it was an opportunity to discuss his work proposition further. Maybe the chance was still there. Hopefully, he'd had second thoughts about the dates. Why else attract her attention and smile so very warmly? It seemed her earlier optimism had been entirely justified. Their unexpected meeting was fortuitous. Things really were looking up.

However, as Lucy crossed the road, she asked herself why a man who claimed to live in such luxury, a man who could offer her twenty-five-thousand pounds to complete a commission, would be sitting in such a dilapidated-looking vehicle. An old van that looked almost more rust red than white. But she assured herself there must be a reasonable explanation. Maybe she'd ask him.

Moloch met Lucy's itchy, pinkish eyes as she stood blinking with her umbrella held above her head as the rain got a little heavier.

'I thought it was you as soon as I spotted you leaving the gallery.' He spoke with an unmistakable, eager enthusiasm that raised Lucy's hopes still further. Everything about him was positive, his body language, expressions and words. Perhaps he had reconsidered. 'I've been giving our meeting at the café a great deal of thought. It was unreasonable of me to expect you to drop everything to focus on my request. I let my eagerness for the project get the better of me. Please accept my sincere apologies. I'd be both delighted and honoured if we could discuss the matter again. I'd still very much like you to do the work.'

Lucy made a face. Everything he'd said was welcome, but the inside of the van looked so very dirty, even more neglected than the outside. On the other hand, Moloch was as immaculate as he had been at their previous meeting. And that skin, it was so smooth – lucky man. He really did look younger than she'd previously thought. She pushed her observations from her mind.

'No need to apologise. I completely understand. I'd love to discuss the commission.'

His face lit up. 'That's good, I'm delighted.'

'I hope you don't mind me asking, but what are you doing in the van?'

Moloch laughed, but it seemed forced. There was a hint of tension too. A flash of something in his eyes for just a fraction of a second. Lucy picked up on it, but she put it down to his likely embarrassment. She immediately regretted asking at all.

'Ah, I thought you may be wondering. It's borrowed from a mechanic friend of mine. I was lucky enough to win a Georgian oak sideboard in an auction. It is a beautiful piece of furniture with fluted tapered legs and a delicate design, dated about 1750. It will fit perfectly in one of my reception rooms. I like to keep some aspects of the place in the period. I'm in town to pick it up.'

'I'd love to see it.'

'Really?'

'Yes, absolutely – it's a period of history I find fascinating.' Lucy smiled.

'Okay, great, that's wonderful to hear. We have so much in common. Have you got time now?'

'I need to get some lunch before heading back to college, but another time, certainly. We should arrange a date.'

His quickly vanishing frown was replaced by another smile; not so warm this time, a little uncertain, but still enough to put her at her ease as the rain suddenly got heavier, large drops bouncing off the tarmac.

'Well, at least come in and sit next to me before you get drenched. I'd love to talk again about what I've got in mind for my home.'

Lucy checked her watch before walking around to the van's passenger side, lowering her umbrella, opening the door and hurriedly getting in.

Moloch swivelled in his seat, turning his slim body to face her.

'There, that's it. Sorry about the state of this old thing – I had a bit of a shock too when I picked it up. But there was no time for cleaning. Try to make yourself comfortable as best you can.'

Lucy noticed a gold-coloured metal stud earring on the floor at her feet. She briefly considered picking it up before deciding to ignore it. It seemed a potential distraction from far more important matters. She decided to take control, and get to the crux of the issue.

'Just so we're both on the same page. Are you saying you'd still like me to do the work?'

'Yes, absolutely, if you're in agreement and still available. Why don't I run you back to the college? If delaying the work until the end of term is unavoidable, so be it. We can talk about it on the way.'

Lucy shook her head. 'My car's parked here in town, and I plan to get a bite to eat before heading back.'

Moloch reached down the far side of his seat, next to the door. Lucy thought he might have something in his hand, but she didn't know what and gave it little thought. There seemed more important things to focus on. He suddenly pointed across her towards the gallery to their left as she awaited his response.

'Isn't that your sister?'

As Lucy turned to look, she felt a sharp stabbing pain in the upper thigh of her right leg. She looked down to see a syringe in his hand, the sharp needle deep in her flesh. She was already feeling drowsy, the world becoming an impressionist blur of light colours as she attempted to push his hand away without success. All her strength was gone. She was as weak as a small child. Her words were slurred, barely comprehensible as she tried to process events that made no sense at all.

'What, the, what the h-hell, do you, d-do you think...?'

Moloch reached out with his free hand, grabbing her yellow cotton blouse, pulling her towards him, their foreheads touching.

'Shut the fuck up! Just sit there and shut your fucking mouth. Struggle or try to shout out and I will kill you! I'll cut your fucking throat. Have I made myself clear? Now go to sleep, give in to it, not another word.'

Lucy made one final hopeless attempt to pull away, to reach for the door handle. But it was no good. She could hardly move. Her thinking was confused and dreamlike, her nightmare all too real. Her head fell forward, her chin resting on her upper chest as he released his grip only moments later. She had a vague awareness of her new reality for a few seconds, but no more than that. She continued drifting away, further and further, deeper and deeper. And then everything went black.

15

Gove watched and he listened later that same day. He saw everything and heard everything. Even Lucy's shallow breathing as she lay senseless on the cold concrete floor of her new cellar home. Technology can do that. And it did it now as he stared at the 98-inch wall-mounted TV screen installed in the spacious ground-floor cinema room he'd prepared for the purpose, complete with popcorn dispenser and a glass-fronted mini-fridge stocked almost to capacity with various canned and bottled soft drinks. He didn't drink alcohol, never touched a drop. It was something he saw as an admirable example of his approach to self-care. His mother had been a drinker, that filthy skank of a woman from the darkest corner of hell. Alcohol could lead to carelessness, something he couldn't risk.

Gove surveyed Lucy's cellar prison on screen with gushing pride. It was all so clear, such a beautiful picture, and the sound was perfect, filling the cinema room as he turned up the volume, taking full advantage of the Scandinavian surround-sound speaker system. The cellar provided ideal guest facilities. The night-vision cameras were state of the art, the multiple embedded supersensitive microphones the very best money could buy. He'd researched his options online, chosen the equipment with the ulti-mate care and spared no expense with the installation because nothing mattered more. Everything had been in its rightful place to await lovely

Lucy's arrival. It was tried, tested, and now here she was as she was meant to be. The future held such incredible promise.

Gove relaxed back in his cinema seat, staring at the large screen. He touched himself through his trousers as he focused on Lucy, slowly licking his lips, first the top and then the bottom, taking in every inch of her shapely body, naked and helpless. It was good, so very good. Just how he liked them. And he'd demonstrated such admirable self-control too, not to tear her to pieces, not to kill her as soon as she arrived. This time was different. *She* was different. But she'd need to prove that. If she were to live, she'd need to meet his expectations. That was entirely reasonable.

He undid the zip of his lightweight green chino trousers, rewound the recording, then played it back in slow motion, fully appreciating the ultra-high-definition feature for only the second wonderful time. He could hardly contain his excitement as he wallowed in his success. He really had excelled himself. His guest had no privacy, none whatsoever. He wouldn't miss a thing, however dark the room, and from any angle. And that made him feel like a god, an all-powerful entity with the power of life and death. There was nowhere for his latest captive to hide. Not for a single second, at any time of the day or night.

Gove watched as Lucy turned over in her chemical sleep, pulling her knees up to her chest, hugging them close, shivering slightly for the lack of a warming quilt as the cellar's ambient cold began to bite. She'd be awake soon, still in darkness, confused, scared, oblivious to time or place. Day or night would mean nothing to her. And then he'd speak to her if it took his fancy. He'd welcome her to her new abode if he thought it would enhance his day. Maybe he'd utter kind words, words of comfort. Or a threat? Something that made her shudder, alone and vulnerable, a prisoner with no chance of escape; the first test of many. Her reaction would tell him so much of her character.

Gove became increasingly aroused as he indulged in his fantasy, picturing the fear in Lucy's eyes as she began to understand her new reality for the first awful time. There was so much to look forward to; his most remarkable and darkest imaginings were becoming a glorious reality before his very eyes. Lovely Lucy was his. He'd made it happen. He'd done his bit. Now it was up to her to live up to his expectations.

16

Lucy opened one bleary eye and then the other. Her head pounding, the searing pain hard to bear as she attempted to blink it away with little hope of success. She instinctively tried to pull her summer quilt over her naked body to combat the unseasonal chill, but there was no quilt to pull. She reached out in every direction, trying to find it on the bed, still not fully awake. She raised her aching head, eyes flickering, looking around her, and seeing nothing but darkness. Not the familiar half-darkness of her night-time bedroom, but total, impenetrable blackness, without even a hint of reassuring light. She couldn't even see her trembling hand as she held it inches from her face. It was as if she'd gone blind. As if some unseen force had plucked out her eyes while she slept.

Lucy froze, her heart beating faster, her muscles tense. Oh, shit! What the fuck? Was she dead? Was that it? Had she died? Or was it a dream? Maybe it was a dream. It could be, couldn't it? Please let it be a dream. She hoped that her strange awakening was some frightening and unpleasant creation of her subconscious mind. But the aches and pains seemingly emanating from almost every part of her body told a very different story as a sudden uncontrollable, all-engulfing fear gripped her, making her shake and shiver. It wasn't simply fear she felt; it was terror. Realisation gradually dawned; she was awake, she was fucking well awake. It was real, oh God, it was all too real.

Lucy closed her eyes tight shut and prayed to a God whose existence she sometimes doubted. She prayed with all she had, every part of her being; she begged for help, she pleaded for strength. She tried to cling to hope as her tears freely flowed. She opened her eyes again moments later, desperately hoping that all would be well, that she'd be in her familiar bedroom. But once again, all was darkness. She told herself not to panic, that hysteria served no purpose and provided no gains. But some things were more easily thought than done.

Lucy felt around herself with quick frantic fingers, first one way and then another, trying to make sense of the unfathomable, searching for any clue that may help at all. Her thoughts were racing now, faster and faster, one unresolved question after another coming to mind, beating her down. What was happening? Where the hell was she? What was that stink? Drains, maybe, or rotting meat? And why no light at all?

As Lucy sat there shivering, rocking to and fro, clutching her knees to her chest, she began wailing. She gulped in the fetid air between repeated convulsive sobs as the horror of it all truly sank in, reluctant acceptance replacing anguished denial. She wasn't in bed. Oh, God, she wasn't in bed. That wasn't good; it wasn't good at all.

Lucy released her knees, feeling around herself again, learning what little she could with the touch of her fingers. She was on a hard, cold floor. Stone or concrete.

She asked herself if Andy could be behind the awful situation in which she found herself. His idea of revenge for her rejection? Yes, that could be it, couldn't it? Maybe he'd appear at any second, switch on the light and laugh in that infuriatingly childish way of his. Momentarily, for a few brief seconds, she clung to the idea like a determined limpet. She thought please let it be Andy. Please let it be him. But she dismissed the hypothesis almost immediately afterwards. He was an idiot but not a nasty man. Someone wanted to scare her shitless.

Lucy searched her mind, attempting to peer through her mental fog. The last thing she remembered was sitting in the van talking to Moloch, and then nothing, absolutely nothing. It was as if time had stopped, as if her life had ended at that moment, and then this, she'd woken in hell. And then it dawned on her. Maybe it was Moloch who'd brought her to this place. He had something in his hand. She'd felt a sharp pain in her leg, and then, God, yes, her mother and sister were right all along. She should have listened. Why the hell didn't she listen? Moloch! Yes, that made sense. Maybe it was the only thing that made any sense. Someone had put her in that terrible place. It could have been Moloch. What did she really know about the man beyond what he'd told her?

Lucy glanced in every direction, seeing nothing, hoping her eyes would soon adjust to the gloom. But it didn't happen. However hard she looked, however much she attempted to focus, there was nothing to see. She shouted out now, calling for help time and again, screaming out her fear as loud as feasibly possible until her voice was hoarse and her throat sore. But all she heard in response was the echo of her own words coming off the walls. Her wailing yells vibrated around the room, mocking her predicament, making it worse, if such a thing were possible.

Lucy was suddenly aware of her nakedness as she slowly stood, forcing herself to her feet, tears flowing. She wrapped her arms around herself to combat the cold, which seemed to be getting more intense with each minute that passed. Her spirits fell still further as she lost control of her bladder, the warm urine running down her legs, pooling around her feet where she stood. There was only so long she could hold onto it. Her bladder had felt like bursting.

She slowed her breathing, calming herself, desperately attempting to summon hope, talking to herself in her head. There had to be a way out of there, wherever she was. All she had to do was find it. And then her waking nightmare would be over. She'd be back in the light. Back in the world of the living and looking up at the big blue sky, appreciating the sun's warming rays like never before. It would happen. She had to make it happen. It was just a matter of time.

Lucy felt her heart pounding in her chest like never before as she stepped slowly forward in the darkness, her hands held out in front of her as she searched for anything that might offer a semblance of hope – a light switch, a door, or even a window if such a thing could exist in this dark and foreboding place. She took one short, tentative step, then another, urging herself on, sucking in the stinking cold air, blowing it out. *Come on, Lucy, girl, you can do it.* There had to be a way out of there if she looked hard enough and didn't give up.

Lucy found what felt like a wall with the tips of her fingers, tracing its cool surface, she moved to her left, one cautious sideways step at a time. She ran the palms of both her hands over the slightly uneven surface in every direction, but she found nothing that could conceivably help. Her heart sunk, the disappointment crushing, but she willed herself on, repeatedly talking to herself in her head, mantra-like. *Please don't give up, Lucy. Keep going, take another step, don't give up. You can do it, girl, one more step.*

The smell of excrement was worse now. It seemed to assault her nostrils, making her wretch. It wasn't her shit; she was sure of that. Someone else had been there, scared and trembling in the dark. She had to keep going. There was no other choice.

Her stomach heaved and Lucy spat a mouthful of acidic vomit from her mouth. Collecting herself, she continued to move slowly to her left. Her bare foot collided with something unseen, causing her to stumble and fall, hitting the concrete floor hard, grazing an elbow and cutting a knee. She rose to a seated position, reaching out tentatively and then recoiling when she touched what felt like a small, cold human hand with stiff fingers. She called out. 'Hello! Say something, please say something.' But all was silence. A strange, awful silence that seemed to fill the space, encircling her without mercy.

Lucy counted slowly to three and then reached out again, keen for human comfort, feeling what could only be a female breast. A cold shudder ran down her spine as she spoke. Even in the strange circumstances she felt the urge to apologise. 'Sorry, please say something, *please*. We can escape together. You're not alone any more.'

But once again, there was no reply, not even the slightest sound. Lucy told herself that her newfound companion must be asleep or unconscious. Just as she'd been, they were probably drugged and taken to this place too. But as she went to shake the girl awake, deep down, Lucy already knew the truth. She heard the girl slide to one side. Lucy reached down in the darkness, touching the girl's face. And then she screamed out, loud and piercing, on realising the girl's nose was missing. It wasn't there. There was just a wound where a nose should have been.

Lucy retreated quickly, scuttling back on all fours, adrenaline surging through her system, desperate for escape. She found a corner where two walls met and curled up on the cold concrete floor in the foetal position like an unborn baby, her back curved, her head bowed, and her limbs bent and drawn up to her torso.

* * *

Lucy uncurled her body sometime later. She had no idea how long she had laid there, whimpering like a young puppy in need of its mother. She feared she might never stop. That she'd lie there crying until she was old, wrung out and dry.

Her mind filled with a strange, potent combination of hope and dread at the sound of a door creaking on its metal hinges on a floor somewhere above. She listened intently, suddenly on full alert, her hearing picking up even the slightest sound. She considered calling out again. 'I'm down here! Help me, get me out.' Words along those lines. But her intended cry stuck in her throat, silenced by her cautionary thoughts. What if the dead girl was murdered? It seemed likely. What other plausible explanation could there be for her presence in such a place? And her injuries, what about her injuries? Surely, she must have been murdered. She didn't cut her own nose off. Some vicious bastard did that, some psycho without mercy. What if the killer was about to appear? What then? Oh, God, no, please, no.

Lucy cowered at the sound of a metal key in a lock. Closer this time, a different door. She flinched at the blinding light of a ceiling-mounted fluorescent bulb bursting into active life above, dazzling her as she urgently raised a hand to protect her eyes from the intense electric glare. Lucy could see everything around her now as her sight painfully and gradually adjusted to the brightness. It was a concrete space with dark walls and mouldy damp. Wall-mounted cameras, what might be microphones, a red plastic bucket, the stiffened body of a young woman with multiple awful injuries, and a man, very much alive, who strode to the approximate centre of the room. He stood facing her, no more than ten feet away. He was around six feet tall and slim, with an entirely bald head and a clean-shaven face. His eyes were piercing, looking only at her and never looking away. He had what looked like a bright-yellow police taser in one hand and a bone-handled knife with a long thin blade in the other. Lucy noted a sharp point at the blade's end. A point she imagined piercing her flesh, driving the life force from her body. She felt her gut twist as she raised her line of sight, looking from the knife to his face. At first she thought she'd never seen him before. But she knew his voice as soon as he spoke. His indefinable English accent left her in no doubt it was Moloch. He'd trapped her, brought her to that place. And now what? Would she be the next mutilated corpse propped up against the cellar wall? Was this the end?

'Welcome to your new home. I'm delighted you chose to accept my kind invite.' Moloch projected his words as if giving a Shakespearean performance on a theatre stage. It was almost as if he'd preprepared a speech. 'I was so very sad to see you crying. Your eyes look so sore, puffy and red, as red as your hair, almost the colour of blood. I couldn't help but notice as I watched you on the big screen upstairs. I see everything you do. And I do mean *everything*. Nothing escapes me, not a movement of your body nor the blink of an eye. Wipe away your tears. Why stain your pretty face? Look on the positive side. You're still very much alive. I can see your chest rising and falling as you suck in the air. That's more than the bitch who's been keeping you company can claim. She provided me with some entertainment before your welcome arrival. It's all recorded on film for our later delectation. We'll watch it together if and when you've earned my trust. It's up to you to gain my respect. You're mine now. Whatever I tell you to do, you do it without question. That's the only way to stay alive. I will kill you if you let me down. Women fail me, all of them, the bitches, but I'm hoping you're different. Show me the appropriate degree of reverence, and maybe you won't end up like her.' He pointed the knife at the young woman's corpse.

Lucy used her arms to hide her nakedness as best she could as she shuffled backwards. Her entire body was shaking so much it seemed the whole cellar was trembling; as if at any moment, the walls might come tumbling down. She briefly considered jumping to her feet and running for the open door no more than twenty feet away. But Moloch was standing in the way, blocking her potential escape. No doubt, that was deliberate. He might be looking for any excuse to stab her. Maybe he enjoyed the chase. What to say? Was it worth pleading? Was he even capable of rational thought?

'Why, Moloch, why? Please, I'm b-b-begging you. I won't s-say a w-word to anyone. I'll still, I'll still do the p-painting.' She stammered. 'I'll do everything you ask of me. And you needn't even pay me. You can keep the money. Spend it on s-something else. It will be my g-g-gift to you. I'm begging you. I'll kneel if you want me to. Just say the word. Please, please let me go.'

There was a serpent-like coldness in his eyes as he looked back at her with a smirk, chilling her to the core. It was cold, so very cold. She shuddered as he spoke again, more loudly now, not quite shouting, but close. The words seemed to assault her ears. There was so much hatred in them, so much venom.

'Be very careful, Lucy – I don't miss much. I could see you looking at the door. I can see inside your head. I can read your thoughts. If you even *think* about trying to escape, I'll punish you. Take a long, hard look at what happened to your young friend there. She screamed blue murder until her last painful breath. You can't even begin to imagine the horrors I can inflict if the mood takes me. You'll come to appreciate that given time.'

Lucy spoke between sobs, desperately trying to appease him, hoping he'd see her as a person, trying to be liked, anything to survive. 'I, I w-w-wasn't thinking about escaping, honestly it, it n-never, never crossed my mind. If you still want me to d-d-do the painting, I'm ready to, to start whenever you w-w-want me to.'

He took a step towards her and grinned, his head tilted to one side.

'Get on your knees.'

She dry-gagged, once, then again. 'What?'

'Get on your fucking knees.' This time he did shout, loudly, at the top of his voice, like a military drill instructor barking out orders.

'Do not annoy me, Lucy. It's a simple enough instruction. It would not be a good idea to piss me off any more than you already have. Show me even the slightest resistance, and I'm likely to lose control. Maybe I'll decide that you're like my mother after all. Maybe I'll conclude you're a bitch too.'

Lucy had no fundamental understanding of the significance of his words as she avoided his eyes. But she understood enough to believe that following his orders was the only viable option left open to her. She had to escape but not yet. She had to choose her time. She lowered herself to the hard concrete, ignoring the pain from her cut knee, which was bleeding, staining the floor.

She watched as he looked down at the blood, licking his lips with a darting tongue. His voice was quieter now, lower in tone. If anything, she found the sound of it even more frightening than the shouting. There was an evil lunacy to his persona. He was mad as well as bad. She was already sure of it as her mind raced. The man was insane, totally fucking insane.

'Praise me, worship me, Lucy, demonstrate your adoration as if your life depends on it. Because it does, believe me, it does. Lower your eyes. Shout out your praise. Worship me – I am your god!'

Lucy somehow resisted the impulse to scream. She feared that if she started, she might never stop. Not until she breathed her last breath. The last thing she wanted was to anger him. She knew where that would end. Maybe if she said more, he'd change. Perhaps there was a spark of humanity still in him somewhere. If only she could find it with her words.

'Please, Moloch, please, I'm begging you. I'm pregnant, I'm going to have a b-b-baby. Please, please let me go.' She regretted sharing as soon as she said it, silently admonishing herself for not keeping it to herself.

He took two strides towards her, smiling as he performed a lively, gleeful jig, leaping from one foot to the other, dancing on the spot.

'Well, congratulations, that is *wonderful* news. Unexpected but immensely pleasing. I can't begin to tell you how delighted I am. It's a sign, you see. You *are* the one. I was correct all along. It's meant to be. None of this is happening by accident. I adopted the name Moloch for a good reason. He was an ancient god of child sacrifice. The spirits inspired me to choose his name. His followers are said to have boiled children alive in a huge bronze statue with the body of a man and the head of a bull.'

Lucy was almost lost for words but she had to say something. As long as she was talking, he wasn't hurting her. She had to normalise the insanity of it all, get him to see her as a friend. But what to say? What the hell to say? *Come on, Lucy, you've got to say something.*

'I thought, I thought, Moloch was a Welsh n-name?' For fuck's sake, was that really the best she could do?

He laughed until tears ran down his face.

'I appreciate your interest. It's to your credit. Very well done, lovely Lucy – eight out of ten, you've passed the first test. But Welsh? Why would you think that? Moloch is of ancient Hebrew origin. You can use that history as an inspiration for decorating this place. Can you imagine the cauldron, the burning fire and the terrified young victim waiting to die? I've bought the paint, I'll provide the brushes and you can do the work. I was fascinated when I first read Moloch's story, and now I have the pleasure of sharing it with you. It's synchronicity. Everything is clicking into place. Can you imagine the fun we can have together when your brat is born?'

She rose to her knees. The words poured out of her. She could no longer hold them back.

'You need help! You're mad, you're fucking mad!'

He bared his teeth, lips drawn back.

'Oh dear, Lucy, and just when you were doing so very well. You're not the first female to tell me that. A moronic psychologist at the hospital where I worked said much the same. I do understand society's mundane banalities have brainwashed you. Fortunately for you, I have the capacity for forgiveness. But there's only so much I'll tolerate before tearing you apart. I'll give you one final chance to mend your ways and live. Now, worship me, bitch. Worship me! Your life hangs by a thread.'

Lucy shook her head slowly, weeping, wailing, again weighing up the possibility of trying to run past him, to sprint for the door. But as her mind raced, he raised the taser and fired. Lucy heard him cackle like a demented hyena as she collapsed to the floor, having lost all muscle control as the sharp metal barb hit her bare chest, cutting into her tender flesh, hooking her like a fish.

Shooting, excruciating pain shook her brain like a pea in a jar. She lay there on the unforgiving concrete, twitching with Moloch looming over her, gradually recovering from the electric assault. He punched her twice to the side of her head, secured her slender ankles in shiny metal shackles connected with a ten-inch chain, tore the barb from her flesh, looked down at her and smiled, taking obvious pleasure in her suffering. There was a noticeable bulge in his trousers. The sick fuck had a stiffy. Although it disgusted her, it told her so much of his drives and motivations. Even in her vulnerable state, she told herself that she might be able to use that against him one day. All she needed was a chance.

'Worship me, Lucy. Get back on your knees, scuttle towards me, lower your face to the floor, kiss my feet and tell me I'm your god. Tell me you recognise my greatness. I'd be cautious, if I were you. I'm starting to enjoy myself. This is your last chance to get it right. If you think the taser hurt, the knife would be infinitely worse. Your young friend could tell you that were she still alive and able to speak. Praise me now. Tell me how much you love me, or I'll cut your fucking throat.'

Lucy did precisely what she was told, drawing on her past amateur dramatic skills, making her performance as convincing as possible. She still clung to hope. She told herself that she would escape as soon as the opportunity arose. But now was not that time. It was all about survival. For now, she had to play his game.

Ten minutes or so after Lucy began calling out her praise, feeling as if it may go on forever, he finally raised a hand to silence her, seemingly satisfied with her feigned reverence. Lucy decided to risk one request while he seemed in a better mood. Something to make the intolerable burden just a little bit easier to bear.

'I'd find it easier to work without the smell of the corpse, sir. I wouldn't; I wouldn't w-w-want to be distracted while creating our masterpiece. Will, will you please take her body away?'

Moloch glared at her. Lucy first thought she'd made a terrible error of judgement, but then his expression softened.

'It's good that you're focusing on your new purpose, Lucy. You've passed your second test. That, again, is to your credit. You're doing rather well up to this point. Although, of course, there are far more challenging examinations to come. I'll dismember your fellow guest soon enough while you begin your work. I'll need some help to carry her bits and pieces to the garden, but we can talk about that nearer the time.'

Lucy wanted to scream and cry and shout, but instead, she maintained as calm a persona as possible, trying to reach out to him emotionally, to make a connection, seeking to influence his behaviour and decision making. She knew it was a gamble. There was so much to lose, but she felt she had no option but to try. The talk of the garden gave her hope. It was either persevere or accept her fate.

'Could we, could we get rid of the body n-n-now, please, sir?'

He began slowly circling her, closer now, about six feet away. 'I said soon, not now. My word is the law. Do *not* ask again.'

She wasn't ready to give up quite yet.

'I'm c-cold, Moloch. Can I please have, have my clothes?'

He raised the taser again and fired, the second barb cutting into her left breast this time, causing temporary paralysis as she fell, twitching to the concrete. She lay there, gradually recovering, saying nothing at all as he tore the barb from her bloody flesh and walked towards the exit.

Moloch left the light on when he left, locking the door behind him. Lucy heard a second metallic click less than a minute later, and then the same creak of hinges she'd heard earlier. As she looked around her, focusing on anything other than the young woman's mutilated body, a part of her wished he'd returned the room to darkness. She had the opportunity to surreptitiously glance around the entire cellar, confirming there were no windows, and just one door, which looked like metal. If she was going to escape, it had to be through there.

Lucy crawled to the furthest point possible from the corpse, the plastic bucket held tightly in her teeth by the handle. She struggled into a seated position, allowed the wall to support her weight, and rested there, whimpering quietly to herself until exhausted sleep finally provided a welcome release.

* * *

Lucy was awoken, back on full alert sometime later. Her entire body stiffened as she sat shivering, witnessing the scene, as if seeing the cellar and its contents for the first awful time. Moloch was back and striding towards her. The taser was attached to a nylon belt around his slim waist in a black holster. There was an orange plastic bowl in each of his hands, of the type one would use to feed a large dog. One bowl was piled high with baked beans, and the other filled with water, a small amount of which splashed from the bowl onto the floor with the movement of his body. He placed the bowls on the concrete one to either side of where Lucy sat cowering. She went to speak but silenced herself immediately when he moved a hand to touch the taser's handle. Sometimes silence was best. She was a fast learner. Any words she uttered, however reasonable in the world outside the cellar, may result in punishment. She had to choose her battles with care.

'Very wise, lovely Lucy, you've passed the next test. You've learned when to keep your pretty little mouth shut. I want you to eat, and I want you to drink. The bucket serving as your en suite facilities is now full of cold water. Wash, clean yourself, make yourself attractive. I'll be watching upstairs. If you please me, tomorrow's water will be warm. If not, icy cold. Now would be a good time to thank me. I've never shown a guest such kindness before. I fear that sometimes I can be too generous of spirit for my own good.'

She avoided his eyes as she did as she was told. She'd never experienced such intense hatred towards another human being. 'Thank you, sir.'

'You'll undoubtedly be pleased to hear that you're going to start working tomorrow. If you're going to make this place a masterpiece, you need to get on with it. I'll bring down the paints and everything else you're going to need. I hope you've given some thought to the designs.'

She nodded.

'Yes, sir.'

'I'm glad to hear it.'

She looked up at him, trying desperately to hold her nerve, to appear as compliant as feasibly possible, and chose her words with the utmost care.

'Can I, can I, p-p-please ask you one thing, sir?'

He was silent for about thirty seconds before answering. To Lucy, it seemed like an age. She urgently looked away as he undid his zip, took out his erect penis and began masturbating while talking, as if doing nothing out of the ordinary.

'Ask away. I'm not an unreasonable man.'

Lucy had thought she could no longer be shocked. She'd been wrong. It seemed there was no normal, no rationale, reason or logic. Anything was possible in this world within the walls. Maybe that was something she should seek to manipulate as well as fear. If there was even the slightest chance of facilitating contact with the outside world, she had to do it whatever the risks.

It was now or never. But how would he react? Was she doing the right thing by saying anything at all? She rushed her words.

'My mother has cancer. She's going to be worrying. Will you p-please let her know that I'm alive? I told h-her I'd be doing the artwork. I'd love her to know that's what I'm doing. It would mean such a lot to m-m-me.'

His quickly vanishing frown became another lascivious grin as he looked first at Lucy and then the dead girl behind her.

'Who knows? Maybe we can have some fun with that. Let me give it some thought.'

'Thank y-you so very much, sir.'

She could hear his hand moving faster and faster.

'Occasional acts of kindness are a character flaw of mine. I've often thought about it, and now here it is in action. But don't go thinking you can use it to your advantage. There are limits even to my generosity.'

Suddenly, he ejaculated with a guttural groan, sticky white semen spraying Lucy's leg.

'You'll find that out if you push too hard. You've met Mr Nice. Displease me, and I'll introduce you to Mr Nasty. They both live in my head. It's up to you which one you meet.'

17

The Right Honourable Graham Williams MP stood in the recently refurbished reception area of West Wales Police Headquarters at 9.35 in the morning on Friday 5 June, and repeatedly tapped on the toughened-glass security screen with the first two knuckles of his right hand.

'I'm here to see the chief constable.'

The young PC looked up from his paperwork with a bored expression on his oval face. He couldn't have seemed less interested if he'd tried.

'Have you got an appointment?' He spoke with a strong, nasal North Wales accent, very unlike the locals, a natural consequence of a childhood spent close to Merseyside.

Williams stiffened, his frustration evident as he made an unnecessary adjustment to his silk tie, an instinctive response to stress. He noted the number on the young officer's epaulettes before responding.

'No, I haven't got an appointment, PC 134, but I know she's in – I saw her Range Rover in the car park. My name's Williams, Graham Williams – I'm the local member of parliament. And this is urgent. I suggest you pick up that phone and speak to her right now if you want to keep your job for very much longer. You are seriously straining my patience. I haven't got time to mess about.'

The officer swallowed hard before doing precisely what he was told.

'I've spoken to the chief constable's secretary, Mr Williams. She says to take you straight up.'

Williams's relief was palpable as the young officer pressed a button, opening the steel-and-glass security door leading from the reception to the inner rooms of the police station. The officer led the way, first to the lift, up three floors, and then down a long, well-lit top-floor corridor to where the chief's excessively large office was located at the far end.

'It's the second door on the right, sir. Just knock and go straight in.'

Williams was met by the chief's middle-aged, long-serving female secretary, who offered him tea or coffee, both of which he declined. A buzzer sounded. The secretary approached a second door emblazoned with the chief constable's rank and name in gold letters, opened it and invited him to enter. Chief Constable Jenny Harris was already standing and waiting, resplendent in dark-blue dress uniform with silver-coloured buttons, when Williams walked into the room. The office was an ample space with a sweeping view of the town and the green hills beyond. Chief Constable Harris reached out to shake Williams's hand a little more firmly than he'd expected.

'It's good to see you again, Graham. It's been too long. When was the last time we met? Now, let me think. It must have been the Welsh Government conference in Llandrindod Wells. If I recall correctly, we were talking about multi-disciplinary child protection services.'

He began speaking the second she stopped, rushing his words. As if he feared keeping them inside may result in him stalling. A single tear ran down his cheek, finding a home on his shirt collar.

'I can't quite believe I'm saying this. But I haven't got time for small talk – my daughter is missing.'

The chief constable's expression darkened as she handed him a tissue taken from a box on her desk before sitting.

'Take a seat, Graham. I'm here to help. Tell me all about it.'

Williams nodded his grateful acknowledgement. Sometimes contacts were useful. If he could wield influence, he was happy to do it, Anything for his girl.

'Lucy is an artist, a lecturer at the local college. She was giving a talk to a women's group at the small gallery in Lammas Street from eleven o'clock yesterday morning until one. It's something she does on a fairly regular basis. That's the type of person she is – selfless, public-spirited, a chip off the old block. She likes to give back to the community. She's been missing since.'

'We don't always get involved as soon as this where an adult is concerned.' Williams thought he identified a hint of impatience in Harris's response. Maybe he'd said too much, let his mouth run away with him, not focused on what really mattered. She continued. 'But I understand your worries. I'm a parent myself. And I'm sure we can make an exception given our professional relationship. You said your daughter is missing. The background is useful. It creates a picture, but let's focus on the pertinent facts for now.'

He bounced a knee, tapping a foot against the floor.

'Yes, sorry, I'll, er, I'll try to concentrate – this is just so hard to accept. It's the sort of thing one expects to read about in the papers. It's not something you ever expect to happen to you.'

'Take your time and give me the facts as you know them. She was at the gallery. Now, what happened next?'

He closed his eyes for a beat, opening them again before continuing.

'I spoke to the woman who manages the gallery, Helen Evans, before coming here. She was at the talk. Lucy left shortly after one and was due to be back at the art college at two. But she never turned up. It's not like her – she's reliable, a stickler for timekeeping. Her colleagues were concerned. She wasn't answering her phone. She still isn't. It goes straight to messages. Her line manager rang Andy – he's Lucy's partner, Andrew Baker – at around three, and then he finally contacted me at shortly after nine yesterday evening when she didn't come home. I'm worried, Jenny. She's never done anything like this before. There's something very wrong. I know there is. There's no other reasonable explanation. I should have contacted you sooner rather than wait. But I felt sure she'd turn up. I'm regretting that now.'

The chief constable took a notepad from a desk drawer, positioning the nib of a silver pen above the first blank page. She spoke slowly and calmly, clearly enunciating each word.

'Have you contacted friends, relatives, everywhere you think she could be?'

'My wife and oldest daughter made some urgent calls, but nothing. I've even rung the various hospitals in the area, but again nothing. There's no trace of her. It's as if she's disappeared off the face of the Earth.'

Harris tapped the tip of her pen against her desktop three times.

'Okay, let's start with the basics. What's your daughter's full name?'

'It's Lucy, Lucy Williams.'

'No middle names?'

He shook his head.

'We wanted to keep it simple.'

'Her date of birth?'

'The 22 October '97, she's twenty-five.'

She quickly scribbled a note in black ink.

'And you said she works at the art college.'

'Yes, yes, she does. She's been there since shortly after graduating with a master's in fine art. They were keen to take her on. I'm a very proud father. She's something of a protégé.'

Harris gave a quickly vanishing smile.

'You said she lives with a boyfriend.'

'Yes, at flat one Picton House, the new red-brick block opposite the main entrance to the park here in town. They've been there for about eighteen months or so. The mortgage is in her name. I helped her with the deposit.'

He could feel her eyes on him as she studied his face, expressions and body language as if trying to read his thoughts. Perhaps his comment regarding the mortgage arrangement had given her some clue that all was not well.

'How's their relationship?'

Williams dropped his chin to his chest, considering his response. He'd thought long and hard as to whether to share what he was about to say. He'd pondered the potential negative media attention given his public role. Now he felt as if he had no choice. To hell with politics; his daughter had to come first.

'It's not something, I, er, I know a great deal about myself. But, um, Lucy, Lucy has talked to her mother about some problems she and Andy have been having. Nothing major, you understand, but there have been issues.'

The chief constable met his wet brown eyes, holding his gaze as he fidgeted with a cuff of his bespoke grey suit jacket.

'This isn't a time to hold anything back, Graham. If you've got something to say, you need to say it. We need as much detail as possible if we're going to help you.'

He made a face.

'I'm, er, I'm not sure it's relevant.'

'Tell me everything and let me decide. Sometimes the most seemingly innocuous details can be key to cracking a case. A lot of adults go missing. Most are found, but not all of them. We need to do all we can to ensure your daughter's not one of those unfortunate people.'

He hadn't thought of his daughter's situation as a case before, and the term stung. It ate away at him. Surely she'd turn up, wouldn't she? Oh, God, what if she didn't?

'They're in the process of separating on Lucy's instigation. He's still at the flat but won't be for much longer. They met in college, and Andy seemed nice enough. Not the go-getter I hoped she'd settle down with, but decent, from a decent family.' He paused and then continued, speaking more quietly now, avoiding Harris's eyes, looking past her, at the walls, the windows, anything but her, fearing what he was about to say might somehow reflect poorly on him. 'Now, what I'm about to recount next is what my wife has told me, and I want to stress that I've only heard it from her.'

Harris glanced at the clock on the wall behind.

'Give me a second. I don't want us to be disturbed.'

She picked up her phone and dialled, only waiting for a second or two before speaking.

'Tell Chief Superintendent Halliday that I'm moving our meeting on an hour, please, Alison. I'm running a little late.' She returned her attention to Williams, who pondered what best to say and how to say it. 'Sorry about that, Graham. You were about to tell me about some problems your daughter was experiencing with her partner.'

It was now or never.

'Everything seemed fine until Andy lost his job at a local call centre. He was selling insurance, that sort of thing. He'd wanted to be an artist, but it didn't happen for him – he hasn't got Lucy's talent, that's the truth of it. Or her work ethic, to be honest. He started drinking a little too often and getting jealous, green-eyed, and not just of her success. It seems he resents her having any form of male attention. I put it down to insecurity, low self-esteem. She's more accomplished than him, and he can't handle that. I think it really is that simple.'

'Okay, I hear what you're saying. How bad has it got? I need you to tell it as it is.'

Williams shifted in his seat. What to say, what the hell to say? Oh, God, there was no avoiding it. He had to bite the bullet.

'There was one time about six months ago when Lucy turned up at our home with bruising to her face. It was only faint, but it was there. I was in London, at the Commons, so I didn't see it myself, but my wife was adamant the marks were in the shape of fingers. As if our daughter had been slapped. Slapped by an adult hand.'

'Were the police called?'

He was beginning to wish they had been.

'No, no, Lucy denied everything, claiming it was an accident, and my wife only told me about it weeks later when it was far too late to do anything. She was sworn to secrecy, apparently.'

'Have you ever talked to your daughter about what happened?'

He crossed and uncrossed his legs, thinking maybe he should have.

'No, no, I haven't. My wife, er, my wife's better at that sort of thing. Lucy never really talks to me about anything personal, not women's stuff – I leave that to the girls. I'm not even supposed to know about it at all, as far as Lucy is concerned.'

The chief constable made some hurried notes.

'We're going to need to speak to your wife – I'm sure you can understand the importance. It won't be me who interviews her – it's not my role – but as a mark of respect, I'll keep an eye on things. One of my best officers will contact her later today. The quicker we get on with this, the better for everyone. I'm sure I don't need to explain.'

'I'll give you her number and tell her to expect the call.'

'Okay, let's move on. I have to ask this, and it's crucial you give me an honest answer. Please think carefully before you reply.'

He tilted his head at a slight angle, eyes narrowed.

'Has your daughter ever suffered depression or any other mental illness? Do you think there's any possibility at all she may have harmed herself?'

'No, absolutely not. There's not even the slightest chance, none at all. Lucy's always been an extremely cheerful girl – she embraces life and always sees the best in everyone. She's very much like her mother in that respect. If we were talking about Lucy's sister, that might be different, but Lucy, no.'

Harris didn't look entirely convinced despite the strength of his statement. But for whatever reason, she didn't pursue the matter further.

'Have you got a recent photo of Lucy, something that clearly shows her face?'

He lifted his mobile out of the inside pocket of his jacket. 'Yes, I have – I've got several on my phone.'

'Speak to my secretary on your way out. Send them to me before you leave. I'll take it from there. I'm going to ask Detective Sergeant Raymond Lewis to take on your daughter's case. I've known him a long time. He's a good detective with a great deal of experience. A little rough around the edges, but I trust his judgement. If anyone can find Lucy quickly, Ray can.'

Williams rose to his feet, pushing back his chair. 'I was hoping DI Laura Kesey might be involved. I've heard good things. She comes recommended.'

Chief Constable Harris walked towards her office door, holding it open.

'Laura's away on holiday with her family, Graham, a much-needed extended break after a difficult few months, twenty-one days, and I'm sure you'll find DS Lewis more than up to the job. I'll brief him as soon as you're on your way. Give Alison yours and your wife's contact details. And don't forget those photos. He'll be in touch very soon.'

Williams looked back as he left the chief constable's office. 'I hope you're right about Lewis. I've been a reliable supporter of the police for some time now. It's time for that investment to pay dividends. Find my daughter. I don't think that's too much to ask.'

18

Detective Sergeant Raymond Lewis had made an effort with his appearance. He sometimes did when he thought the situation demanded, although it was the exception rather than the rule since his wife's leaving years before. Interviewing the wife of the serving local member of parliament, he'd decided, probably warranted the best of him. The chief constable had said as much in that oh-so-insistent way of hers. He didn't appreciate the feedback one little bit as he stood in her overlarge office taking orders, but he acted on it, anyway. Policing was a top-down profession. There was no point in an argument he couldn't win. Within reason, he'd do what he was told, anything for an easy life.

Lewis had shaved with a wet razor and soap in the police station's men's toilets, something he usually reserved for court appearances. He'd put on a clean shirt he kept hanging in his locker, albeit creased, and he'd added an old red polyester rugby-club tie to the mix, pulled loose at the collar. There was a fat stain on the tie halfway down, the remnants of a fried breakfast in the police canteen, but he ignored it. It was hardly noticeable unless you looked closely, which was good enough for him. He'd even considered polishing his well-worn brown leather shoes, something he hadn't done for months, but in the end, he'd decided against it, cleaning them with a moist toilet wipe instead. There were limits to what was necessary, even when working with the toffs.

The DS knocked on the Williams's front door with gradually increasing force until he saw the silhouette of a woman he correctly assumed to be Myra Williams rushing down the hall. There was a stiffness to her movements, as if she was struggling with the effort. Lewis was already holding his warrant card up in plain sight when she opened the door. The sound of classical music floated out from somewhere inside the house. He thought it might be Beethoven, but he wasn't sure, and he didn't ask. Eighties rock was more his style. He returned his identification to the inside pocket of his well-worn tweed jacket when she didn't choose to look at it. Very few people ever did.

'Good afternoon, my name's Detective Sergeant Raymond Lewis, West Wales Police.'

She spoke with urgency, rushing her words.

'Please come on in, Sergeant – I've been expecting you. My husband mentioned you'd be contacting me at some point today. Thank you for coming. I'm just making a hot drink – would you like one?'

He followed her back down the hall towards a large modern family kitchen located at the rear of the house. There were two double-glazed windows to either side of matching patio doors with a leafy garden view.

'Call me Ray. There's no need for formalities.' It was something he often said to witnesses, never to suspects. 'And yes, thank you. A hot drink would be lovely.'

Myra switched on a stainless steel kettle on a light oak worktop next to the cooker before turning to face him. Her voice was faltering as she asked her question.

'Is, is there any news?'

Lewis shook his head regretfully. He was a proud father himself and felt genuine sympathy for the middle-aged mother standing in front of him. Her deep anxiety and dread couldn't have been more evident. Everything about her communicated sorrow.

'Every officer in the force has been given Lucy's details, and I've got detectives looking at all the relevant CCTV as we speak. But there's nothing to report as yet, sorry, Mrs Williams. When I find something significant, you'll be the first to know. You have my word.'

She sighed loudly, one of the saddest sounds Lewis had ever heard.

'What about Lucy's car?'

'Yeah, I've made some enquiries, but I'm afraid it doesn't help us. The car is exactly where Lucy left it in the car park a short walk from the gallery where she gave her talk, the one next to the library. I've explained the circumstances to the council. It will be left where it is for the time being. You don't need to concern yourself about that.'

'What about her bank cards?'

He was quick to reply.

'She hasn't used them. Not since two days before she went missing. She may have had cash on her, of course. But there's no record of her withdrawing any large amounts for quite some time.'

Myra turned away again, taking two matching green pottery mugs from a white, wall-mounted cupboard to the left of the ceramic sink. Her entire body was shaking despite the room's early-summer warmth. Lewis surmised she was operating on autopilot; polite, friendly, going through the motions, doing familiar things, a coping mechanism of sorts. In reality, she would be close to falling apart.

'Tea or coffee?'

Lewis sat his not inconsiderable bulk on a tall, three-legged wooden stool at the breakfast bar. It wasn't the most comfortable seat he'd ever sat on, but it would have to do. There were bigger things to worry about.

'Coffee, please. Black with four sugars.'

A single tear ran down Myra's face as she handed Lewis his mug, filled almost to the brim. She sat opposite him, meeting his eyes and holding his gaze. Apart from the deep sorrow that her body betrayed, he thought he saw a stoic determination in Mrs Williams too. A spark of hope. She spoke calmly and slowly, controlling her emotion as best she could. Lewis respected her for that. There was a dignity to the woman that he admired.

'Right, I want you to listen to me very carefully, Sergeant. My daughter has been missing since yesterday afternoon. It's totally out of character. Something has happened to her. I know it. I wish I didn't, but I do. If you haven't got any news for me, what exactly are you doing here? Tell me what I can do to help.'

Lewis took his police-issue pocketbook from a jacket pocket, turning to a page folded down at one corner. A part of him couldn't help thinking that he wouldn't have been there at all were it not for the fact that Lucy's father was an MP. Far more likely, a more junior officer would be investigating at this stage. It was the first time in a very long career that a chief constable had given him a direct order. It pointed to favouritism, which didn't sit comfortably. But he had a job to do, which mattered, so he'd get on with it. He'd do the job right as he always did.

'I need to ask you some questions.'

She took a tablet from a brown plastic medicine bottle on the counter, popped it into her open mouth, blew her coffee to cool it, then sipped and swallowed.

'Okay, ask away.'

'Can you think of anywhere where Lucy may be? Do you think there's even the slightest possibility that your daughter has gone off the radar of her own free will? We all need a bit of space from time to time. It wouldn't reflect badly on her if she has taken some time for herself.'

Myra pushed her mug aside. There was a new determination in her demeanour. She sat more upright, shoulders back, her neck craned towards him.

'Sergeant, I'm not well. I've been undergoing cancer treatment for some time now, and Lucy has either rung me or called at the house to ask how I am every single day since I first told her of my diagnosis. There is *zero* chance that she'd suddenly disappear of her own volition without contacting me. I believe my husband told the chief constable that something is very wrong. It breaks my heart to say this but, I have to agree with him.'

'Where is your husband now?'

'As far as I'm aware, he's driving around town, hoping to get a sight of our daughter before heading back to London. I suppose anything's better than sitting here praying for the phone to ring.'

Lewis solemnly nodded. He'd very likely be doing the exact same thing in the father's place. Although he wasn't sure he'd be so keen to head back to London with his daughter still missing.

'Okay, I've heard what you've said – let's move on. Do you think there's *any* possibility your daughter has harmed herself? I'm sorry, but I've got to ask.'

She took a deep breath, obviously irritated, losing patience, which didn't surprise Lewis at all.

'Lucy had some eating issues in her teens, but nothing since. Your boss asked my husband the exact same thing. The answer was no then, and it still is.'

And now, the question that really mattered to Lewis. If someone had done something to the girl, which he had to accept was a possibility, it was likely someone who knew her. Attacks by strangers were rare, particularly in that part of the world. He stuck to a familiar investigative method because it worked. Ask the question, wait for the answer, look for inconsistencies, clues or corroboration. Often open questions were best.

'Tell me about Lucy's relationship with her partner.'

When Myra's face tensed, Lewis knew he was on to something. Experience had taught him to notice the little things, body language, tone, gestures and telltale signs that told their own story.

'What do you need to know?'

'When did Andy and Lucy get together?'

'They met at art college. They were both doing fine art degrees. She was in the second year and he in the third. From what she tells me, they hit it off straight away. From what I could see, he was a pleasant enough boy at that time, but he didn't have her talent. She went on to a successful career in art, and he sadly didn't. She completed her master's a year after her BA.'

'A bright girl.'

Her expression softened. 'Yes, Sergeant, she is.'

'You said Andy was pleasant enough *back then*. So, what's happened since?'

Myra pressed her lips together, the tension back on her face. 'He's changed so very much. There's no other way of putting it. He's, um, he's not the same person any more. He lost his job and became obsessed with body image about a year or so ago. He spends a lot of time in the gym lifting weights. Either that or he's in the flat playing video games. He's put on about three stones of muscle but never believes he's big enough. Lucy thinks it's a confidence thing. He doesn't think he's good enough for her. He seems to think she'll go off with somebody else the first chance she gets.'

Lewis turned to the next page of his pocketbook.

'Do you think she may have?'

'I think you already know my answer to that is no.'

He nodded. 'I had to ask.'

'I don't want to make too much of this, but lately, Andrew's behaviour has become increasingly concerning. I can't bring myself to think he'd harm Lucy in any significant way, but I can't rule out the possibility altogether. I feel I have to consider the unthinkable where my daughter's safety is concerned.'

'Can you expand on that for me?'

'He's become rather jealous and controlling.'

'Steroids?'

'I, er, I don't know. Lucy has never said anything. But that doesn't necessarily mean he isn't a user. My daughter keeps some things to herself.'

'Any threats of violence or actual violence? Your husband mentioned there may have been.'

'Well, there was some slight bruising to Lucy's face some months back. I did ask, but she was adamant it had happened by accident. She insisted that he's never physically assaulted her, but I'm not nearly so sure. Particularly given what's happened now. If he's hurt my daughter in any way, I will never forgive him.'

'I'll have a word with him, see what he's got to say for himself.'

Her expression softened. 'Thank you, Ray, it's appreciated.'

'Is there anything else, anything unusual, anything out of the ordinary that could have any potential relevance to your daughter's disappearance?'

Myra was silent for a second or two. For a brief moment, Lewis thought she might be holding something back. He was about to give her a verbal nudge when she started talking.

'Well, there was one thing. I'm, er, I'm sure it's probably of no significance, but I did think it strange at the time. I was in two minds about sharing it. The last thing I'd want is to misdirect the investigation. I don't want to send you off on some wild goose chase that achieves nothing at all.'

'Let me be the judge. Tell me about it. Whatever it is, I need to know.'

'Lucy was sent a handwritten letter. I'm not sure when exactly, and to be honest I didn't ask, but she'd definitely received it before the end of May. The writer wanted her to paint a picture of his home and garden. He offered to put Lucy up for the duration of the commission.'

Lewis made a face. 'Did anything come of it?'

'Lucy did meet him for lunch to talk the proposal through, but the timings posed a problem. He wanted the work done straight away, but Lucy's college commitments meant that wasn't possible. She was disappointed. He was offering a great deal of money. She was very much hoping he'd have a change of heart about the dates and get back in touch.'

'Do you know who this man is?'

'He simply referred to himself as Moloch, that was it, nothing more. It's a Welsh name apparently. Although not one I've heard of.'

Lewis thought it a potential lead that had to be followed.

'And the letter you mentioned, any idea where that is?'

She shook her head.

'Again, I'm sorry, I haven't seen it.'

'It's probably nothing, but I'll take a look if I find it.'

'It might be worth checking the flat and Lucy's office. She said the letter was a work of art in itself. She may have kept it.'

Lewis nodded; he'd already decided to do precisely that.

'When did Lucy meet this man, and where?'

'That would have been at the Good Health vegetarian café in Merlin's Lane at one o' clock lunchtime last Monday, 1 June. My older daughter Cerys was also there at my request. I asked her to keep an eye on events, much to Lucy's dismay. She accused me of interfering, which I suppose I was. Cerys will be able to give you the man's description if you think that's useful. She took an instant dislike to him – there was something about him that unnerved her.'

He drained his mug in one generous gulp, tilting his head back, pouring the warm, sweet liquid down his throat. 'It may be worth exploring. Is there anything else at all you can think of that may be relevant?'

'Lucy recently found out she's pregnant – it's Andy's. I don't know why I didn't think to tell you before.'

Lewis sighed, nodding his acknowledgement. 'Okay, noted, if you can give me Cerys's contact details, I'd like to interview her. I'll speak to her later today.'

Mrs Williams provided the number as requested and they both stood, Lewis preparing to leave. He silently cursed his aching knees as they stiffened and complained. She reached out to touch his arm just above the elbow.

'Please do everything you can to find my Lucy, Ray. She means so very much to me. I couldn't bear to lose her. The cancer has been hard, but this is infinitely worse.'

Lewis always chose his words carefully in such circumstances. He'd learned not to make promises he couldn't keep. False hope was no hope. All he could do was his best.

'I can't guarantee I'll find her, but I can guarantee I'll leave no stone unturned. I'm going to do *everything* in my power to find your daughter. You have my word.'

She reached out to shake his hand.

'And you'll keep me up to date with every development?'

He handed her a business card, black print on white. 'I will, and please don't hesitate to contact me day or night if you think of anything else.'

'Thank you, Sergeant, your help is appreciated. I'm counting on you. Please don't forget that. You're the best hope I've got.'

19

Lewis took a different approach to all his suspect interviews, depending on the person. He already knew exactly how he was going to deal with this one.

'Where is she?' he bellowed directly into Andrew Baker's ashen face the second he answered the door.

The musclebound young man took a defensive stance, a prominent vein bulging on his neck, pulsating. There was fear in his face, which Lewis couldn't help but see; he could recognise weakness in the blink of an eye.

'Who the fuck are you?'

Lewis put a knee in the door as Andy tried to slam it shut. The detective was a big man, more than eighteen stone, overweight but still powerful, with big arms, wide shoulders. And he knew how to use his bulk to his best advantage. He forced the door back open with relative ease.

'DS Lewis, West Wales Police. I'm looking for Lucy.'

'Have you got a warrant?'

Lewis shoved Andy with an open hand, pushing him backwards, causing him to stumble and fall to the floor, banging his coccyx on the tiles. The sergeant moved in on him quickly for a man of his weight and fleshy build, closing the door behind him with a mule-style kick of his foot. He noticed a wet stain forming around the crotch of Andy's overly tight shorts. Nothing surprised Lewis very much any more, not even Andy's crazy reaction. His suspect had a criminal history, he was anti police, that seemed obvious. And now his bravado had melted away like an ice cube in the hot summer sun.

'Don't be so fucking ridiculous. You've been watching too many detective shows. I'm here to find your girlfriend. You invited me in. You're cooperating with my enquiries. Why would I need a warrant? Unless you've got something to hide, of course. Is that it? Is that what you're trying to say?'

'I don't know where she is. I haven't got a clue. I've been shitting myself that something bad's happened to her. I love the girl. She means everything to me. It was me who told her father she's missing. Why would I do that if it was anything to do with me?'

Lewis reached down, pulling Andy to his feet by the front of his vest and then shoving him through the open door to the lounge, where he closed the sky-blue venetian blinds before speaking again.

'Sit the fuck down.'

Andy did as he was told.

'Do you like hitting women, muscle boy? Does it make you feel like a big man? Does it make your prick hard? Is that what turns you on? If you touched my daughter, I'd beat the fucking shit out of you. It would be the last thing you ever did.'

Andy looked stunned. He was like a rabbit caught in the headlights, eyes darting from one part of the room to another.

'I've never touched Lucy, not even once. I'd never hit a woman. That's not the sort of bloke I am.'

Lewis stared back at him with a dismissive smirk. 'Do you really expect me to believe that crap? Have I got *stupid* stamped on my forehead or something? I've been talking to Myra Williams. She saw bruises on her daughter's face. Bruising you put there with those big hands of yours. If I ask around, I'm sure I can find other witnesses who saw the same injury: her father, sister, students and people she works with at the art college. Now would be a good time for the truth. I don't appreciate tossers like you wasting my time. I've got better things to do.'

Lewis could clearly see Andy was close to tears. He was a boy in a man's body. Lewis watched as his suspect psychologically disintegrated before him, just as he'd hoped he would. Occasionally, it was that easy, not always, but sometimes.

'I slapped Lucy once when I was seriously pissed. Just the once, and never again, I swear on my life. It was out of character. She forgave me. It was months ago. I've never regretted anything more. I've got no idea where she's gone. I wish I did. I've lost her, I know that. She's made it clear our relationship's over. But like I said, the girl still means everything to me.'

Lewis moved to the rear of Andy's chair, placing a hand on each shoulder and digging in his thumbs. He spoke directly into the younger man's ear at touching distance as he made him wince.

'I've been checking up on you, Andy, my boy. Naughty, naughty, you've got a history of violence. I'd be willing to bet you never told Lucy and her posh parents about your conviction. I bet you kept that one quiet. Am I right? Come on, spit it out; it's confession time. I haven't got all day.'

'I was *sixteen*, just *sixteen*. I was in the wrong place at the wrong time. What happened has got fuck all to do with Lucy being missing now.'

'Is that meant to be funny? You were convicted of assault. Violence is violence. You punched some bloke to the ground and then hit your girl-friend. That's a pattern; past behaviour is the best indicator of future performance. Didn't anyone ever tell you that? Where is she? I'd be willing to bet you've done it again.'

Andy tried to rise from his chair, but Lewis pulled him back.

'I was at a football match. The guy butted me. I hit back, and he fell, banging his head. I had a shit lawyer. I was stitched up. I should have gotten off with self-defence. Why do you think I don't trust you lot? I should never have been banged up in youth detention at all.'

'Yeah, yeah, that's what they all say. I know the case. I've talked to the officer who dealt with it. You fractured the kid's skull. You were convicted beyond all reasonable doubt – GBH – that's good enough for me.'

'I do *not* know where Lucy is. I don't know what more I can say. This is getting fucking ridiculous. I want a solicitor before I say any more.'

Lewis laughed, a harsh laugh that had nothing to do with humour.

'First, you want a warrant, and now you want a lawyer – what a come-dian! You're not under arrest. We're having a nice, friendly chat, just you and me. You're cooperating by answering my questions. We can do it here or at the station, that's up to you.'

'I've got fuck all else to say.'

'Lucy was kicking you out. How did that make you feel? Did it make you angry? Did you hit out? You seem like the type to me.'

Andy wiped the tears from his face as Lewis changed his position, now standing facing his suspect, feet spread wide.

'I told her if she wanted me out, I was willing to go.'

'Is that a fact?'

'Yes, it fucking well is.'

'Seems unlikely.'

'That's what happened. It's the truth, nothing but the truth.'

'But you're still here. Lucy going missing was rather convenient, wasn't it? You've still got a roof over your head. From what I've heard, you can't afford to rent a place yourself.'

'She gave me two weeks to move. I've still got time. I'm going to sleep on a mate's settee for a few days and then head off to stay at my mum's house in Swansea until I can get my own place.'

Lewis knew he didn't have enough evidence to make an arrest, not yet. His visit was a fishing exercise more than anything else. Pile on the stress, see where it got him.

'I'm going to need both addresses.'

'That's not a problem; I've nothing to hide.'

Lewis scribbled the details Andy gave in his police-issue pocketbook and then decided to double-down on the pressure. Maybe his suspect would blurt out something he'd later regret. He played what he considered his trump card.

'How do you feel about becoming a father?'

Andy stared back at Lewis, his eyebrows curved and high, horizontal wrinkles across the forehead.

'What the fuck are you talking about?'

'Oh, come on, give me a break. You're not going to claim you didn't know, are you?'

Andy began weeping now, tears running down his face.

'She d-didn't say a word. Not a fucking word.'

'If you know where she is, now would be a good time to tell me. That's your baby we're talking about.'

'I haven't got a fucking clue where Lucy's gone. I swear it on the baby's life.'

'So, I'm assuming you won't object to me having a good look around this place?'

'Look wherever the fuck you want to. Why would I care? She's not here. You'd be wasting your fucking time.'

'If I find any sign of a struggle, any sign of a disturbance, you'll be in cuffs and down the station. The scenes-of-crime team will be all over this place like a rash.'

Andy wiped his nose with the back of a hand, dragging snot across one stubbled cheek.

'There's nothing to find.'

'Up you get. We'll start in here and go on from there, one room at a time.'

Lewis found nothing until he put on the bathroom light. He looked down, focusing on a small dark-red spot next to the sink on the wood veneer floor.

'What's that?'

Andy screwed up his face.

'I sometimes get nosebleeds after a heavy session on the weights. I thought I'd cleaned it up. I must have missed a bit.'

'Turn round.'

'What?'

'Turn round, put your hands flat on the wall, spread your legs wide. You're coming with me.'

'Over one drop of blood, what the fuck's wrong with you?'

'You've got a history of violence, you're alleged to have assaulted an ex-girlfriend who's dumped you, she's missing fuck knows where, and there's blood on your bathroom floor. That's good enough for me.' Lewis hand-cuffed his suspect, first the right wrist and then the left. Andy made no effort to resist physically, and Lewis was grateful for that.

'I'm arresting you on suspicion of murder. You're not obliged to say anything, but anything you do say could be used in evidence. Have I made myself clear?'

'Murder? No fucking way! It's *my* blood, I've told you, it's *my* fucking blood. It's got nothing to do with Lucy. She left the house yesterday morning and didn't come back. That's what happened, no more than that. Lucy's disappearance has got nothing to do with me.'

As Lewis led his suspect to the unmarked CID car, shoving him repeatedly when he stalled, he was already starting to think of him as an unlikely answer to the case despite the blood spot. The sergeant hadn't ruled out Andy, not wholly, but instinct told him he was very probably looking in the wrong place. It was a gut feeling more than anything else. Something Lewis often relied on.

The short journey back to the police station passed quickly, with Andy making repeated denials regarding his involvement. Lewis left him locked in a cell for about an hour until a nervous young duty solicitor in an ill-fitting business suit finally turned up. Andy was formally interviewed under caution and said much the same as at the flat. Lewis changed his tactics at one stage, becoming less aggressive, less assertive, more understanding, good cop and bad cop all rolled into one. He again asked Andy if he had any idea where Lucy may be, when he'd last seen her and if he'd heard anything from her since. He listened to the answers, looking for any sign of inconsistency. But Andy told Lewis precisely the same as he'd told Graham Williams. Lucy went out on the morning of her disappearance and he'd not seen her since. The more Lewis thought about it, the more he concluded it was very probably the truth. Andy was released on police bail pending further enquiries. Nothing he'd told Lewis had helped, not one little bit.

20

Lewis arranged to interview Cerys Williams at West Wales Police Headquarters at seven o'clock that same evening, 5 June. He was ploughing through piles of unwelcome paperwork, a part of the job he hated, when the phone rang in his shared CID office at five to the hour. He picked it up on the second ring, glad to break the red-tape monotony, and he wasn't in the least bit surprised to hear the duty constable on reception telling him his witness had arrived.

'Thanks, Mike, I've been expecting her. Put her in whatever interview room's free and offer to make her a cup of tea if she fancies one. I've got one quick call to make, and I'll be down in five minutes.'

'Okay, Sarge, will do. Are you going to the darts at the club tonight? I'll see you there if you are. I actually made the team.'

'No, not tonight, mate – I'm knackered, and anyway, I've got too much on.'

'Maybe next week.'

'Yeah, maybe – I'll see how things go. The team must be fucking desperate to be picking you. You couldn't hit a barn door from ten feet away. Have a pint for me.'

The young constable laughed, amused as intended, before putting down the phone. Lewis was well aware he was something of a legend in the station, both well-liked and well respected. A bit of a dinosaur, perhaps, grumpy at times, old-school certainly, and he didn't suffer fools, but he was no less a good copper for all that. He got results, that's what mattered.

Lewis took the lift rather than the stairs, but he was still slightly out of breath when he entered Interview Room One on the ground floor of the large modernist building. He could feel his chest tightening as he pushed open the door. He needed to lose a bit of weight and he knew it only too well. And Kesey never stopped telling him in that Midlands drone of hers. But beer and stodge were two of the few pleasures he had left. He'd occasionally cut down from four sugars to three in his tea and coffee when feeling motivated, but that was about it. Good intentions didn't solve anything in themselves.

Cerys had a look of fearful apprehension on her face, unsurprising in the circumstances, as the detective sergeant reached out to shake her pale white hand. He noticed her fingers were cold and trembling despite the room's relative warmth. That didn't surprise him a great deal, either. Police interviews could be stressful, whatever the circumstances. Witnesses reacted in different ways. Her sister was missing and was God only knew where. Why wouldn't the poor woman be filled with trepidation? The work mattered to Lewis and cases such as this more than most. He silently committed to making the interview process as painless as possible.

'Take a seat, love. I'm DS Lewis, but then I guess you already know that. Call me Ray – there's no need for formalities. And please don't be nervous. I'm on your side. I'm going to do all I can to help. Did the constable on reception offer you a cuppa?'

They sat on either side of the small interview-room table, Cerys with her arms crossed in front of her as if hugging herself tightly. He could see the tension in her face as she spoke in a voice resonating with raw emotion.

'He did, thank you, but I declined. My husband's cooking a meal for when I get home. I don't know how I'm going to eat it, though. I've got no appetite since my sister went missing, none at all. I pray to God she turns up. It's like a waking nightmare. I can't quite believe what's happening. I see such terrible things on the news. There are some awful people out there. Why can't people be kind? I'm terrified I may never see her again.'

Lewis took a statement form from a drawer below the tabletop.

'I know none of this is easy, love. But try to stay hopeful. It's far too soon to be thinking the worst. I'm heading up the investigation, and you can help. The more relevant information I can gather, the better the chance of finding your sister. It's like a jigsaw. I need to put together the pieces until a picture emerges. Hopefully, then, I'll be able to find out what happened. I'm going to ask you a series of questions, and I want you to be totally honest with me when you answer them. If there's something you're not sure about, just say so, don't guess at it. And please don't keep anything back. I'm interested in hearing your opinions as well as the facts as you know them. The more information you can give me, the better. Are you ready to make a start?'

Cerys nodded once. 'As ready as I'll ever be.'

'Are you sure you don't want that cuppa? It's not a problem if you do. The kitchen's only a couple of doors down. I wouldn't mind one myself.'

'Not for me, thanks, I'm sure. Kind of you to ask. I'd rather get on with it, if that's okay with you.'

Lewis took a clear plastic biro from an inside jacket pocket. The pen's top had been well chewed. 'I've already spoken to your mum and Andrew earlier today, and I've read the information your dad gave the chief constable, so I'll already know some of what you're going to tell me. But I still want you to say it anyway. I want *your* perspective on things. Do you understand?'

She rubbed the back of her neck, every muscle tense, and then folded her arms again.

'I'll do everything I can to help.'

'That's good. Let's make a start. Has Lucy ever talked about going off somewhere on her own for however long?'

'No, she wouldn't ever do that. We're a close family – she always keeps in touch. We always have. We speak regularly and text daily.'

'Your mum said much the same.'

She lowered her arms, gripping the table's edge with both hands, holding on. 'That's because it's true.'

'Okay, next question, let's move on. Has anything been worrying your sister, anything at all?'

'Well, there's, er, there's the pregnancy. She only found out she was expecting shortly before she went missing. It wasn't something that was planned. I don't think she'd ever thought about being a mother before that positive test. And then there's Andy, of course. Things haven't been great between the two of them. It hasn't been for months.'

'When you say "things haven't been great", what exactly do you mean? How bad had it got?'

Cerys was quick to reply. There was a new determination to her, a harder edge to her voice as she got her point across. 'I don't think Andy's done anything to Lucy, if that's what you're thinking. I'm sure he's gutted she finished with him. He gets angry from time to time, and he's prone to jealousy – she's told me that. He finds it hard to trust. But I really think he loves her deep down, despite all his faults. I'd be *amazed* if he had anything to do with her disappearance. If someone has hurt my sister, God forbid, I'm confident it wasn't him.'

Lewis was thinking much along the same lines. He'd been wrong before. It wouldn't be the first time. But experience still told him Andy was an unlikely suspect. He needed to look elsewhere.

'Is there anything unusual, anything out of the ordinary, that's happened in Lucy's life in the period leading up to her disappearance? I'm not talking about what you've already told me. I need to know if there's anything else.'

'There was that meeting with Moloch.'

Lewis made a face as Cerys continued.

'It's a Welsh name – something to do with praise. Or at least that's what Lucy told me. It's not a name I've ever heard before. She received a letter from him offering her an artistic commission.'

'Your mum mentioned it.'

'Did she tell you he gave no address or contact details? Just a request to meet him at the café in Merlin's Lane last Monday at lunchtime, if she was interested. Lucy told Mum about it; Mum didn't like the sound of it, so she asked me to be at the café too, to keep an eye on Lucy. It did all seem a bit weird, so I agreed to go.'

'Just to clarify, he only gave that one name, yeah?'

'Yes, that's correct, Moloch.'

'Strange.'

'That's what I thought.'

'And he didn't give an address?'

'He told Lucy he lived in a big house somewhere out of town, and that was it.'

'You've got no idea in what direction?'

'No, and he could have been lying even if he had.'

Lewis leaned forward in his seat; his eyes narrowed and brow furrowed. He nodded his agreement before asking his next question.

'Any idea where this letter is now? I'd like to take a look.'

'Maybe at the college. She's got a small office there. She said the letter was beautifully written, so she may not have thrown it away. She likes pretty things, anything arty. She can be a bit of a hoarder.'

'Okay, that's something I can look into. Did you see this man?'

Cerys nodded enthusiastically, no doubt pleased to reply in the affirmative.

'I was already in the café when Lucy arrived, and then Moloch arrived a few minutes later. He and Lucy sat at one table close to the door, and I sat on a sofa at the other end of the room, by the serving counter. But I could see both of them well enough. It's not a big place. And he was facing me. I had a clear view of him, but I couldn't hear much of what was said. There were too many other customers there.'

'Right, I want you to think very carefully. And I want you to take your time. This really matters. Imagine you're back there at the café that day and describe him for me. Picture him in your mind's eye. Let's start with his hair. What were the colour and the style?'

'Short light-grey hair and a neatly trimmed matching beard.' She paused for a beat and then continued. 'But this is where it gets odd. The more I looked at him, the more I thought the hair didn't match his face.'

Lewis raised an eyebrow. All of a sudden, he was a lot more interested. 'Sorry, I'm not clear what you're trying to say. Are you saying it was dyed or something?'

Cerys shrugged, slightly raising her shoulders. 'I don't know. I've given it a lot of thought. It could have been dyed. Or he could have been wearing a wig and a false beard. Or maybe, his hair apart, he just looks younger than he is. I can't be sure. But I can't help thinking there was something about his look that wasn't right.'

Lewis cleared his throat. 'Right, okay, let's take this one step at a time. How old would you say he was? We needn't put your answer in your statement. It's for my ears only at this stage, nobody else's. What would you say if you had to give it your best guess?'

She blew the air from her mouth. 'From a distance, I'd say in his fifties or early sixties. But closer up, and this is what I'm getting at, in his thirties at most. He had the skin of a young man. I told Lucy what I thought, but she wouldn't listen. She thought I was being ridiculous, but I hope to God I'm not being. The last thing I'd want to do is mislead you. I'd never forgive myself.'

'How certain are you that he was younger than his initial appearance suggested? Put a figure on it for me.'

'I'd say 70, maybe 80 per cent.'

Lewis hid his disappointment as best he could. He'd been hoping for 100 per cent. If the evidence was significant enough to ever get to court, he knew any decent barrister would tear it to pieces. Cerys seemed far from certain. There was an obvious element of doubt. But it wasn't like he had anything else to go on.

'Okay, that's helpful. What about his eyes? What colour were they?'

'He was wearing blue-tinted glasses. But as for actual eye-colour, I'd be guessing. The truth is, I haven't got a clue.'

Another disappointment, but there were more questions to ask.

'Describe the glasses for me.'

Cerys described them as she remembered them: gold metal with round lenses.

'How tall was he?'

'He was tall and thin. Somewhere between five ten and six foot.'

'How thin?'

'I'd say about ten, maybe eleven stone at most. Wiry but fit-looking. There was nothing frail about him. He didn't have the body of an older man.'

Lewis made some hurried written notes.

'Okay, that's helpful. Keep picturing him for me. Imagine him sitting there at the table. What was he wearing?'

Cerys described Gove's outfit from head to foot.

'And any distinguishing marks?'

She shook her head. 'Not that I saw.'

'What about his accent?'

'English, but I can't tell you what part.'

'You're sure, not Welsh?'

'Yes, that I am certain of.'

Lewis had expected a very different answer given the name Moloch. He considered asking again but decided against it. If witnesses felt pressured, they sometimes volunteered inaccurate information in an effort to please. False information was worse than none at all.

'I'll need you to get together with our photofit guy as soon as possible. He's only in Monday to Friday nine to five. When are you available? I'll arrange it for nine Monday morning if that works for you. I'm thinking the sooner the better.'

'I'll be there.'

'Good, that's great – I'll have a word with him to set it up. He's good at what he does. Describe Moloch to him *exactly* as you have to me, and he'll come up with an image we can share if necessary. Ask for Paul Davies when you arrive at reception. He'll be expecting you.'

'Thank you, I will.'

Lewis smiled thinly. 'Okay, let's get back to that afternoon at the café. Did Lucy and Moloch leave together?'

'Not as far as I know. But I can't be certain. I left before them. Lucy asked me to go when he noticed I was staring at them.'

'That must have been a bit awkward.'

'A bit, but it hardly matters now.'

'No, I guess not. Did Lucy agree to do the work? Did she accept the commission?'

'No she had to turn it down due to other commitments despite a very generous offer.'

'Did they speak again after that day?'

'Lucy hoped they would. She still hoped the commission would come to something. But, no, I don't think they spoke again. Or not that she told me about. She knew I didn't like the man. So maybe she wouldn't have told me, anyway. I wouldn't be shocked if she kept it to herself.'

'Okay, thank you, Cerys, that's all been very helpful. Unless there's something else you want to say or ask me, let's get your statement down on paper.'

'Is there CCTV covering Merlin's Lane?'

Lewis shook his head. 'No, sadly not, nor in the two streets leading to the lane from either end. I'll get my officers to check the cameras covering the main streets. But if he is our man, he likely avoided them. The areas of town covered by cameras have been well reported by the local press, so the odds are against us, I'm afraid.'

Cerys looked very close to tears. She was holding them back but only just. Before speaking, she took a paper tissue from a plastic packet in her jeans pocket.

'Do you really think this Moloch man could have something to do with my sister's disappearance?'

Lewis poised the point of his pen above the statement form as he had many times before. 'Let's just say he's a person of interest. Maybe he can help me with my enquiries or maybe not. Either way, I need to talk to him. He may even provide the answers we're looking for. It's a possibility we can't afford to ignore.'

21

Kesey, Janet and Edward woke to a warm but cloudy morning on Sunday 7 June. The sky was a greyish white with only small sporadic areas of blue on the far distant horizon, which raised hopes of sunnier times later in the day. Kesey read for half an hour or so, seated on the villa's spacious patio, something she rarely did at home in Wales, while Edward watched a cartoon on a tablet and Janet prepared a tasty breakfast in the well-equipped kitchen. BBC Radio 2 played in the background on Janet's mobile, the mixture of modern music and friendly DJ chatter giving the place a familiar and cheerful vibe that reminded them of home.

Kesey smiled warmly when called to the table in the dining room adjoining the lounge, looking forward to sustenance to start the day well. There was a smoked-glass bowl of fresh fruit salad, slices of gluten-free brown toast with a non-dairy olive oil spread, sweet apricot jam and clear honey, all bought from the well-stocked Costa Teguise supermarket. The three ate together and happily chatted, washing down the tasty fare with glasses of chilled bottled water. Janet had read in a guidebook that due to scarcity of rainwater, much of the tap water was desalinated seawater, and therefore not to many people's taste. Kesey and Janet tried it once, quickly deciding it wasn't for them. It was bottled water from then on, bought in large plastic containers in multiples of six. It was surprising how much they went through. Fortunately, there was a small shop that sold it just a five-minute drive away in Nazaret.

Kesey washed up while Janet collected together all they'd need for a trip out. They'd decided on a morning visit to Arrecife. It had the cafés and shops both women would enjoy, a long, wide promenade on which to stroll, and Playa Reducto, a pale-yellow sand beach on which Ed could play safely while they relaxed on rented sunbeds. They set off from the villa at just before ten, arriving at their destination half an hour or so later. Traffic was busier than in other areas of the island they'd visited, but not to such an extent that it caused any significant delays. Kesey struggled to park, driving around for a few minutes before finally finding a suitable spot in a quiet side street a short distance from the seafront. Ed was impatient to get to the beach despite the clouds, but both women agreed on a walk along the promenade and a café visit before any thoughts of sandcastles. Within a short time, they were sitting at a table, drinking coffee – or lemonade in Ed's case – and eating fruit sorbet from small metal bowls. Kesey picked up a day-old red-top UK tabloid newspaper left by a previous customer, turning the pages and glancing at the various articles with only passing interest, until page six, when she saw the face of a young woman she recognised looking back at her. She read the brief report with interest and concern; eyes narrowed, a frown on her face.

Janet sipped her hot coffee, placed her china cup back on its saucer and looked her partner in the eye. 'What is it, Laura? Your face is very serious all of a sudden. I can see there's something.'

Kesey lowered the paper, folding it in half, placing it to one side. 'It's Lucy Williams – she's missing. There's a short article in the paper. Ray's quoted – he's heading up the case.'

Janet adopted a puzzled expression, shaking her head.

'Lucy Williams?'

'Yes, *Lucy*, you must remember her. She's the artist. We met her at that yoga class we went to downstairs at the library. You commented on her outfit, the bright colours. She had yellow ribbons in her hair.'

'No, I still can't place her. Did I talk to her?'

'Yes, yes, you did, more than once.'

Kesey picked up the paper and opened it to the relevant page, showing her partner the small black-and-white photo of the smiling young woman with shoulder-length hair and a low fringe.

A look of recognition suddenly dawned on Janet's face, followed by a frown.

'A lot of people go missing. You've told me that yourself. Why has it made a national paper? The locals I get, but a national?'

'She's the daughter of the local MP.'

'Ah, okay, that makes sense.'

Kesey placed the paper aside for a second time. 'She was always friendly; I liked her. Let's hope she's okay.'

Janet gave Kesey a look that said a thousand words, none of them good.

'Don't even think about it, Laura. It's not happening.'

'What?'

'You know.'

'I've got no idea what you're talking about.'

Janet reached across the white plastic table, griping Kesey's hand, holding it tight and not letting go.

'We're on holiday, the first one for ages. And we're enjoying ourselves. I wish you'd never picked up that newspaper. I know what you're like – we're staying here and you can forget about work. You said Ray's on the case. You've told me he's a good detective. Focus on us for once in your life. I'm sorry Lucy's missing – truly, I am – but leave the case to him.'

'I hadn't even considered getting involved.'

Janet fixed her with a steely glare. 'And you're not going to. We're here now and we're staying. You're not the only police officer in West Wales. It's a job, just a job. And someone else will be doing it just as well as you do long after you're gone.'

'How about a bit of shopping? You said you need a new bikini. There must be a place to get one around here somewhere.'

Janet stood, taking Ed's hand in hers.

'I know you're changing the subject. I don't want you even to ring Ray, not until we're home. You need the break – we all do. I want you to promise that's the end of it.'

Kesey held her hands wide.

'Okay, okay, I promise. Happy now? Are we done? I can't believe you actually think I'd cut the holiday short because of a case.'

Janet took a twenty-euro note from her green leather purse, preparing to pay.

'Nothing would surprise me with you, Laura. But if you did do that, it would be a deal-breaker, the last straw. Sometimes you've got to put your family first.'

'I've promised, and I meant it. Please, Jan, you've said enough. There's no point in upsetting Edward. Let's leave it at that.'

22

Lewis hadn't visited the art college before – he'd never had a cause – but he'd driven past the campus many times over the years, so he was entirely familiar with the route. He silently acknowledged it was day five of Lucy's disappearance as he negotiated the surprisingly quiet road. He'd already searched her flat for a second time over the weekend with Andy looking on, the college closed. But there was no letter to find. It seemed Andy wasn't even aware of the letter's existence. The detective was hoping he'd have better luck now. That's how policing was, sometimes. It wasn't all about clever detective work, analysing clues. Sometimes you just needed a break.

Lewis stretched and yawned on exiting the unmarked police car, glad to be out in the fresh air. He'd slept poorly on the Sunday night, as he often did, his lower back aching and his bladder sensitive, resulting in one night-time bathroom visit after another. But he pushed his chronic health issues from his mind as he locked the car, heading in the direction of the college entrance, no more than a two-minute walk across the car park, even at a stroll. He wasn't in the best of spirits as his left knee began to ache, the unfortunate result of an old rugby-union injury, but he refocused back on work. Lucy deserved that.

Lewis spoke to the first person he met, a beautiful young woman of Asian origin with long, shining black hair and almond-brown eyes, who made the detective sergeant feel old and worn out simply by being so young and full of life. She exuded an energy that Lewis recalled he'd once had himself. She pointed him in the direction of the principal's office at the far end of a ground-floor corridor, the walls of which were covered from floor to ceiling in brightly coloured student art. Lewis was surprised to find himself liking the place, the last thing he'd expected. It was so very different from his working world, but there was nothing intrinsically wrong with that. As a child, he'd enjoyed art. He had a flair for colour, or at least that's what his teacher claimed. Perhaps, if he hadn't joined the police force, he could have lived a very different life. But he'd made his choice and was happy with that.

Lewis shrugged, bringing his rumination to an end as he knocked on the principal's office door, pushing it open and entering without waiting to be invited. He smiled on approaching the middle-aged, brown-haired woman dressed in a loose-fitting multi-coloured kaftan, seated behind a desk, the top of which was only just visible under piles of papers. He felt unusually self-conscious as he introduced himself and explained his reasons for being there. Within two minutes, Lewis was surprised to find himself sitting opposite the principal in a comfy armchair, drinking peppermint tea from a glazed pottery mug, a new experience so very different to his usual overly sweet milky coffee or tea in the police canteen. Dr Charlotte Johnson spoke with a broad Texan accent that reminded Lewis of the cowboy films of his youth; Southern with a twist. She was friendly and welcoming, unnerving him slightly with her confident, relaxed behaviour and bearing. He considered asking her what had brought her to Wales, but decided against it. It was all about the investigation. It was easier that way. He just didn't have the confidence to chat. Not to such an appealing woman to whom he felt unusually attracted.

'Tell me, Sergeant, are you any closer to finding poor Lucy? It upset me terribly to find out that she was missing. It's not something one expects to happen, not in a quiet part of the world like ours. Will you have good news for me soon?'

Lewis crossed his legs one over the other. For some reason, he couldn't understand, he felt awkward, not knowing what to do with his feet. He looked down, wishing he'd polished his shoes. He felt his face redden. What was it about this woman that so affected him?

'We're, er, we're following several lines of enquiry. That's the most I can say.'

Lewis noticed her red-painted fingernails as she sipped her tea, wetting her lips. He imagined their touch on his skin, and blinked the image away.

'You look overheated, Sergeant. Shall I open a window? A little cool morning air may help.'

Lewis knew he was blushing crimson. He felt like an old fool, reacting as he was. He was there for work. And even if the woman was single, she was so far out of his league – a ten compared to his three or four. He'd never been a looker, and he hadn't dared ask anyone out for years, let alone someone as beautiful as her.

'No, I'm, er, I'm okay, ta. I must be coming down with something. There's a bug doing the rounds. Now tell me, did Lucy ever mention receiving a letter from a man named Moloch? It's likely to have been relatively recently, and definitely before the end of May. She was asked to paint an artwork at his home.'

'No, no, she didn't say anything, not that I can recall. I'm sure I'd remember if she had. Do you think this letter played some part in her disappearance?'

He uncrossed his legs, holding the almost full mug in one hand, resting the other on his knee. The peppermint tea was proving a challenge to a man with such a sweet tooth.

'It may be helpful. I'm hoping it might be somewhere in Lucy's office. Her sister suggested I might find it there.'

He was surprised by how tall the principal was when she rose from her seat, walking out from behind her desk. She had to be close to six foot, even in her flat leather gladiator sandals. Her toenails were painted the same bright colour red as her fingernails. There was a silver ring around one sun-bronzed toe, which Lewis found strangely attractive. He found everything about her fascinating, which unnerved him even more.

'Well, then, let's take a look, Sergeant. Her office is on the first floor. I'll show you, and then, I'm afraid, I'll have to leave you to it.'

Dr Johnson led the way with Lewis following, focused on her shapely backside much of the time as she walked a few feet in front of him. He found himself thinking about sex for the first time in what felt like an age. His wife had lost interest long before she left. There had only been one unsuccessful date since, a drunken Indian meal with a woman then living at a domestic-violence refuge, which led to nothing. He'd made such a fool of himself.

'Right, this is it, Sergeant. I'll leave you to it. Take as long as you need. I'll be in my office if required. You know where it is. Although, I'll be leaving for a meeting at ten.'

Lewis could barely look her in the eye. All his confidence was gone. He'd never felt so silly or insecure.

'I should be fine now, ta. Thanks for your help. And the tea, thanks for the tea.'

Her American drawl was music to his ears.

'You're very welcome.'

Lewis glanced in Dr Johnson's direction for one final time as she walked away with the effortless elegance of a catwalk model. He shook his head, frustrated with his lack of concentration. He wasn't usually so easily distracted. It was time to focus on the simple task at hand. He was back in work mode, back in his investigative comfort zone, when he opened Lucy's office door.

The room was small, with a desk and chair located close to a window with a view of the college car park and the rolling green countryside beyond. There were posters of famous impressionist paintings, most of which Lewis recognised, on each of the four walls, and a pine bookcase full of art textbooks stood to the right side of the desk. A blue vase containing several wilted daffodils sat on the desk, along with what looked like an appointments diary and a book of Picasso's work with an abstract representation of a woman on the cover. Lewis looked around the small room with interest, now entirely focused on what he was hoping to achieve. He started with the desk drawer, finding nothing of interest. There was nothing significant in the diary either, despite his having looked through it for almost ten minutes. In fact, Lucy hadn't seemed to use it very much at all. He'd almost given up on finding the letter when his eye was strangely drawn back to the book of Picasso's paintings sitting on the desktop. It was the only book not in the bookcase. And that, Lewis pondered, may or may not be significant. He picked up the book, which opened easily at the centre pages, and there it was: a letter written on ivory-coloured paper in flowing red script. Lewis put on a pair of thin latex gloves taken from a sealed clear plastic packet before picking up the letter by one corner, minimising contact. He read it with interest, confirming the lack of a full name, address or any means of communication. *Moloch*. There it was, that name at the bottom. What the hell was that about? He accessed the internet via his smartphone, running a Welsh to English translation, something he told himself he should probably have done before. *Please praise*. A certain red flag; it had to be some nutter with delusions of grandeur. And that writing, that blood-red ink... It couldn't be real blood, could it? He couldn't rule it out. Something he'd need the lab to check out as a matter of priority.

For Lewis, as he scanned every inch of the letter's surface, it sounded alarm bells, not just the content but its style. Everything about it screamed danger. But he could completely understand why a young woman like Lucy, with her artistic bent and very different life experience, may not have seen it that way. The letter did look stylish and creative if you didn't look deeper with a critical eye born of painful experience. Some might even say it was romantic, if they'd lived a very different life to him.

Lewis folded the letter carefully, placed it in the plastic packet for safe-keeping, peeled off his gloves, opened the office door, and made his way back down the corridor towards the staircase leading to the ground floor. He felt a degree of hope as he crossed the car park towards his car, not exactly optimistic, but more positive than when he'd arrived. There may be fingerprints. And if there were, those fingerprints could be of someone with a criminal history. He could have a name, and quickly too. A real name, not some bullshit pseudonym that was frustrating the hell out of him every time he considered it.

Lewis climbed stiffly into his car, started the engine on the second turn of the key, reversed out of his tight parking space and drove off, still deep in thought. Fingerprints, a name, an arrest, rescue the girl, celebrate with a few pints at the rugby club? Could it really be that simple? It sometimes was, but not often.

He shrugged and then changed gears, second to third. Oh, well, there was only one way to find out. Get the letter looked at, get the results expedited and move on from there.

23

Gove decided to shave lovely Lucy's head on Tuesday 9 June, the sixth day of her captivity. Not simply because the idea amused him, which it did, but because he'd dreamt that her body would be almost entirely free of hair, much like his own, when she first killed alongside him, a plan he fully intended to implement in the coming days. His night-time vision was a prophecy. It was a clear message foretelling future events, sent by some wondrous, unforeseen dark supernatural force, directing the dance of life. He saw himself as the centre of everything, the sun around which the Earth revolved.

Gove had a recently purchased navy-blue plastic sports bag clutched tightly in one hand as he unlocked the hardwood security door in the utility room next to the kitchen. He hummed happily to himself as he flicked the light switch, hurried down the newly illuminated concrete staircase with an excited skip in his step and opened the steel security door at the bottom with a turn of the same key. A second light switch just outside this second door lit the cellar. There had been a switch inside the room too, but he'd had it removed, thinking it a bad idea to give an involuntary guest any semblance of control. The last thing he wanted was to offer his victim's any hope of self-determination. Lucy apart, they'd been there to die. Her future? Well, that was still to be decided. Maybe she'd die too?

Lucy had a pained look on her face as he approached her, propped up in one corner of the cellar, her delicate ankles still secured in steel shackles that had cut into her raw, red skin. She had a haunted look to her eyes, dark shadows portraying her angst, which pleased him. He saw beauty in her slow decline. She was losing weight and hope too, and that, he told himself, was a good thing. She'd be more compliant that way, less likely to attempt escape before the realisation of her true calling as his future soulmate dawned in her societally brainwashed mind.

Gove pulled Lucy away from the wall by her feet without speaking, dragging her backwards with all his wiry strength. He flipped her onto her front as she called out in distress and then sat astride her, pinning her to the floor with his body weight. This time she didn't struggle. It seemed her fight was gone. He began singing a jolly sixties pop song made popular by a recent washing powder television advertising campaign. He took an electrically charged hair trimmer from the sports bag and began roughly shaving off Lucy's shoulder-length red hair as close to her scalp as possible, grazing the skin more than once. He planned to return to the cellar later in the day with a bowl of hot water, shaving foam and a sharp razor to finish the job correctly. Attention to detail, he told himself, was crucial to getting everything precisely right. She had to look *exactly* as she'd appeared in his dream. Nothing could be left to chance. He was creating the future, making prophecy reality.

Gove gathered the newly cut hair together while still sitting astride his captive, placing it in a large padded brown envelope taken from the bag for later use. He spoke to Lucy for the first time that day as she lay under him, her face pressed against the concrete floor.

'I've been thinking about your request, and you'll undoubtedly be glad to hear I've decided to grant you your wish. I'm going to reach out to your sick mother, but I suspect not quite in the way you had in mind.'

Lucy groaned under his weight, but she didn't speak, turning her head from one side to the other, struggling to breathe between repeated sobs.

'I'm certain you must have guessed my intentions by now. But I'll tell you anyway, just to be sure. I plan to send your mother your newly cut hair. Can you imagine the look on her face when she first opens the envelope? Won't that be a lovely surprise on a bright summer morning? I briefly considered tearing out your fingernails and sending them, or perhaps cutting off your pinky fingers one at a time with a lopper I keep in my garden shed. But after a good deal of thought, I finally decided such things would interfere with your work. And so your hair will have to do for now. I can always reconsider at a later date if I think it's justified. Let's see how the painting goes before we decide. Please me, and you'll keep your pretty fingers. Disappoint me one more time, and, well, they'll have to go. I'm sure you'll agree that's fair. I'm nothing if not a reasonable man.'

He stood, turned Lucy over onto her back, took four paintbrushes of different sizes from the bag and placed them alongside her on the floor.

'Come on, girl, don't just lay there. Sit up, pay attention – we have a project to discuss! Stop your pathetic snivelling. Look at the state of you, snot everywhere. What the hell is wrong with you, girl? You can be so self-indulgent at times, so self-focused. Pull yourself together. I haven't got all day.'

Lucy followed his instructions without comment. She did open her mouth at one point as if about to say something, but no words came. He interpreted this as a sign she was losing the will to resist, gradually coming around to his way of thinking, evolving as he had in the time leading to his first killing. Harrison had been his mentor, and now he was hers. In his eyes, it was a triumph, the beginning of better things to come.

'Pay attention, Lucy, look me in the eye before I'm tempted to poke yours out. You need to give this 100 per cent. Nothing less is acceptable. I'm sure you'll recall what I told you about the cult of Moloch. I'm sure you find it as fascinating as I do. I'll provide the paint today, the best quality, all the colours you'll need to make your new home a place of infinite beauty. You can use the story as your inspiration, as I mentioned before. I'm sure you'll have given it all some thought. You can come up with something truly creative, something that pleases me, a work of art worthy of my destructive genius. And remember the children, I don't want you to forget the children. I want to see the terror in their eyes.'

Gove had no actual interest in children, but the negative psychological impact of the project on Lucy as an expectant mother genuinely interested him. He had initially planned to assess the effect on her simply as a female, but now the news of her pregnancy offered a surprising and welcome bonus he hadn't expected. It added spice to the recipe, and if she was *the one*, as he increasingly thought she was, she'd deal with it, she'd overcome.

'I'll fetch the paint and my various butcher's tools, and you can stay right there. I'll be locking both doors on my way out. I do realise you haven't yet fully embraced your new life yet. That will take some time. I'm going to need to leave the security doors open as we discard the bitch's remains – it's just too impractical not to – but don't forget those shackles. You can walk, but you can't run. I've got my taser, my knife and I'm fast. There is *zero* chance of you getting away. I would strongly advise you not to try.'

Within the hour, all the paint cans were in the cellar, along with an aluminium step ladder and Gove's cleaver and bone saw. He began dismembering the young sex worker's corpse while Lucy started her work, creating an outline in black paint on one wall, starting with the mythical creature with the body of a man and the head of a bull. She cried as she worked, but Gove was pleased with her efforts. He encouraged her to sing along with him as he sawed through the victim's neck, joyfully rolling her head to one side with a shout of triumph.

'Stop crying! How can you sing with all that ridiculous sobbing? You wanted the body out of here, and I'm doing as you asked. Is there no pleasing you? Are you never satisfied? Sing, girl, sing, before I cut out your tongue.'

Lucy sang as she painted, out of tune, forcing out the words despite her tears, which he found satisfying. Maybe congratulations were in order. Perhaps he should occasionally encourage her along the way. Or was his tendency to kindness clouding his thinking?

Gove removed the last of the young woman's limbs with another celebratory yell of delight. He was panting hard, covered in various body fluids as he stood, throwing his bone saw to one side, the sound of it clattering on the concrete reverberating around the underground room.

'Right, that's done. Look at me, Lucy, look at the body parts, stop looking away. I know what you're up to. Come down from the ladder, come here, take a close look. It's essential that you start to truly appreciate what we're doing here.'

'I was, I was just c-c-concentrating on the, on the painting.'

'Ah, she speaks! Now get off that fucking ladder as I told you to.'

She descended slowly to the floor, repeatedly gagging as she approached him.

'Pick up the head.'

'What?'

'Pick up the fucking head.' He began shouting now, his face contorting with rage as Lucy stalled. He could quite easily have killed her at that moment. The thought was there, the intention, but he somehow retained control. 'It's a simple enough instruction. What the hell is wrong with you? Do what you're fucking told.'

He drew his arm back, slapping her face with all the force he could muster when she didn't respond. He lurched forward, punching her twice to the upper body and face as she stumbled. He kicked her leg as she lay on the floor.

'Now, get the fuck up, pick up the head and follow me towards the garden. This is what you asked for – you're a part of it. Do what you're told and do it with enthusiasm, or it will be your body I'm cremating. No more chances. Get the fuck up.'

Lucy dragged herself to her feet. She vomited as she bent at the waist, picking up the girl's head by her blood-matted hair. She continued being sick until there was nothing left but green acidic bile.

Gove clapped his hands with glee. 'Okay, that's good – we're making progress at last. You can clean that mess up later. Follow me, and I'll introduce you to my garden cemetery. It's a place of beauty. A memorial garden where all my guests end up one way or another. I've been looking forward to showing you since your arrival. It's going to be a momentous day.'

Within half an hour or so, all the young sex worker's body parts, except for one hand, were doused in petrol and awaiting cremation. Gove insisted that Lucy light the match that ignited the death pyre into life. And then he insisted she dance as he sang various high-tempo songs at the top of his voice. Lucy often stumbled on the uneven ground as the shackles limited her movement, which made him laugh. He recalled he'd always been a fan of slapstick, and this, he thought, was priceless. He insisted she dance for another twenty minutes after that until she finally collapsed a few feet from the oil drum. He left her there panting until he decided she was sufficiently rested to stand, ordering her to her feet. Once again he asked himself if he was sometimes too kind for his good as he shoved her back towards the house.

'You've done rather well today, my lovely Lucy, all considered. I do appreciate our endeavours are all a little new to you. It's not the sort of activity you've enjoyed before. Although, this is the creative art I love, as you love yours. We have that in common. It's only a matter of time until you love it too. Later in the week, if you keep up the good work, as a reward for your efforts, I've got some entertainment in mind.'

He shoved Lucy again when she slowed her pace, talking the entire time, never shutting up. Within minutes she was back in the cellar, this time in darkness. He gave her no thought as he locked the second of the two security doors and headed for his kitchen. It was time for a meal, something simple, something delicious, to keep up his strength before heading to the post office. There were big things ahead, exciting times. Today had only been the start. He'd need to be at his best.

24

Myra Williams collapsed to the floor when she opened the large padded envelope delivered by her smiling postman at around nine that morning, 10 June. It seemed like an ordinary event when she opened her front door to accept her post, dressed as she was in a comfortable primrose-yellow dressing gown and dark-blue slippers. The two exchanged pleasantries as they sometimes did, and then the postman, whose name she didn't know, went on his way. There was nothing very remarkable about the letter, not on the outside, and no clue as to its contents. It was just a small package like many others, except for the flowing pen-and-ink copperplate script that provided the address. That did impress her. Beautiful writing wasn't something one often saw in these days of printers, particularly not in dark-red ink. And it was addressed to her rather than her husband. That surprised her too. For some reason she gave no thought to the letter mentioned by Lucy, written in a similar style. She later put that down to the pain medication, which sometimes clouded her thinking. Opioids could do that; they affected the mind.

Myra found herself holding a handful of bright ginger hair when she first reached into the envelope. Her initial surprise was quickly replaced by shock as she looked down at it in her hand, raising it close to her eyes for the lack of her reading glasses. She recognised the colour of the hair immediately as she moved it slowly between the fingers and thumb of her right hand. The horrible reality hit her gut like a physical blow just a few seconds before her world went blank.

When Myra awoke on the cool hallway tiles, she checked her wristwatch, a small, much cherished fourteen-carat gold Swiss timepiece inherited from her mother the previous year, and saw that only brief minutes had passed since she'd accepted the parcel. She raised herself into a seated position using the wall to aid her movement, ignoring the acute pain from a badly bruised hip. And then she stared at both the brown envelope and red hair again, still not quite able to believe the evidence before her startled eyes. She was desperate to deny the truth, wishing it wasn't real but knowing in reality that it was. She told herself she had to face that reality, however distressing, however traumatic. That's how life was sometimes. She had no other choice.

Myra felt her gut twist as she reached for the envelope for a second time, fearful of discovering its remaining contents but feeling she had no other choice but to face whatever reality it held. She held the envelope up and shook it, emptying the entire contents onto the hall tiles. There was more hair, long strands in bunches, and what looked like a note or letter written on both sides of a single page. In some strange way, the communication gave Myra hope. Her immediate initial thought was that the letter was likely to be a demand for ransom money – money she'd be only too happy to pay whatever the cost to free her daughter from the hands of her captor. She knew her husband would feel the same. There wasn't even the slightest doubt in her mind. If they had to sacrifice their entire savings, fine. If they had to sell the house, then so be it. What did material possessions matter where a loved one's freedom was concerned? In that brief moment, Myra's spirits were raised. She thought the end of the living nightmare might be in sight. But as she held the letter close to her face with a trembling hand, reading the flowing red script, a very different picture emerged.

My dear Myra,

Please excuse my familiarity. I do realise we haven't been properly introduced. The last thing I'd want is to be impertinent. Manners maketh the man, after all, as my bitch mother often said when beating me to within an inch of my life. But I feel the use of your first name is entirely appropriate, given how well I've got to know your lovely daughter in recent days. You'll undoubtedly be delighted to hear that she's here with me, imprisoned at my mercy, naked, cold, shivering, bound in chains, a plaything whose only role in life is to please. She's doing some decora-tion for me, making the best use of her artistic talents. So you'll know she'll be breathing the breath of life for some time yet. After that? Well, we'll have to see. I don't want to make promises I may be unable to keep. It wouldn't be the first time my desires got the better of me. And then, well, young women tend to die.

I hope you appreciated my little gift. I thought it a nice reminder of what you've lost. Lovely Lucy looks very different now, as I'm sure you'll realise. She's not quite as conventionally lovely as she once was, but she's still alluring to me. I have unusual tastes. I'm not your typical man. I'm better, stronger, more powerful than you could ever imagine. I don't let conventions hold me back. There are no limits in my world. Of course, that's good for me, but not so much for her.

I think that's an adequate introduction. As time passes, I may send you additional gifts, a pinky finger perhaps, or a toe. Or maybe Lucy's pretty little nose. That would be amusing, if a little messy. Something for you to look forward to as you deal with your illness. That cancer that eats away at you. A gift to make you squirm.

Well, bye for now, I'll be back in touch very soon. Busy, busy, busy; places to go, people to see. I may even visit that other daughter of yours one fine day sometime soon. Cerys, isn't it? She's such a bitch. A lot like my mother. Maybe I'll capture her too.

With very best wishes,

Moloch xxx

Myra wept uncontrollably as she stumbled down the hall towards where her mobile was charging on the windowsill in the lounge. She disconnected it from the charging cable, clumsily dropped it to the carpet, bent down stiffly and picked it up again with a frustrated groan. Less haste, more speed; everything had become so much more difficult in recent months. Even the simplest of tasks could prove a challenge. She blew her nose before hurriedly dialling Lewis's direct number, which she'd learned by heart. *Come on, Sergeant, come on, pick the damned thing up.*

It was only a matter of seconds before she heard his voice.

'DS Lewis, West Wales Police.'

'Hello, Ray, it's Myra, Myra Williams. I need your urgent help.'

'What can I do for you, Mrs Williams?'

Myra outlined the morning's events in a voice faltering with emotion. She talked of her daughter's hair, the letter and its contents as Lewis listened in silence.

'Where's the hair, letter and envelope now?'

Myra rested her weight on an arm of the sofa, exhaustion setting in. 'I dropped them all to the hall floor before making the call. Do you want me to fetch them?'

'No, no, leave them *exactly* where they are until I get there. There's likely evidence we can use, forensics. Please don't touch them again. If there's anyone else in the house, tell them the same.'

'My husband's back in London for an important vote. He's not back until late tonight. There's just me.'

'Right, I'll be with you in fifteen minutes max. I'm on my way.'

'What about Cerys? The maniac threatened her.'

'I'll give her a ring now, put her in the picture and send one of my best officers to discuss security. We'll offer her what protection we can until the bastard's caught and locked up.'

'And you're coming to see me now, yes?'

'As soon as we end the call.'

'Thank you, Ray – I'll be waiting.'

Myra took two more strong painkiller tablets, washing them down with a tot of French brandy before pacing the room first one way and then the other, staring through the lounge window, repeatedly checking the time, waiting for Lewis to arrive. It was a huge relief when she saw his dark-blue saloon car pull up, half on and half off the pavement, directly outside the house. As she met him at the front door, she was desperately hoping Lucy would survive and that Cerys would stay safe too. She saw Lewis as their potential saviour. Him and his investigative team.

'Please come in, Ray. It's been a terrible morning. I'm so glad you're here.'

Lewis closed the door behind him.

'I know this must have been one hell of shock, Mrs Williams, seeing the hair, reading the letter. But maybe the bastard has made a big mistake. Let's hope he's got overconfident. That happens sometimes, and they give themselves away.'

She nodded her understanding, silently watching as Lewis took a pair of thin, blue latex rubber gloves from a sealed clear plastic package in his jacket pocket. He looked first at Myra and then the various items on the hall floor.

'Do you think it is Lucy's hair?'

Myra wiped a tear from her face. Talking about it made it feel all the more real.

'Yes, unfortunately, I do – I'm certain of it. It's her exact colour, and the length looks right too. She so loved her hair. What kind of lunatic does something like that? My poor girl, she's in the hands of a madman. What has she ever done to deserve that?'

'Right, you make us both a nice cup of tea and leave me to deal with this lot. I can already see the writing's familiar. It's our man, all right. I'll get the hair DNA tested and the results back as a matter of priority. Every new piece of evidence gets us closer to catching the bastard. He's too cocky by half. That's when they slip up. Sometimes these people get too sure of themselves for their own good.'

25

Detective Chief Superintendent Nigel Halliday kept Lewis waiting in the brightly lit corridor outside his office door for almost ten minutes before finally calling him in at quarter past ten in the morning on 12 June. Even then, after what had felt like an age, he left Lewis standing while he looked down at his paperwork, his grey metal-framed glasses perched on the tip of his nose. Lewis quietly seethed, having expected no different. It seemed the head of the force's Criminal Investigation Department felt the need to drive home his importance at every possible opportunity – as if his rank and status weren't enough to provide the validation he so obviously craved. Halliday kept everyone waiting. Or at least those who were junior to him.

Lewis swore silently under his breath as he shifted his weight from one foot to the other, oblivious to his involuntary dance. He glared at the senior man with a dislike he'd first felt on meeting him years before. First impressions weren't always correct, but they had been on that occasion. He and Halliday were chalk and cheese. Halliday was a pompous and condescending idiot with far too much to say for himself. And everything about the chief superintendent screamed insecurity: the framed academic certificates prominently displayed, the cream-coloured leather swivel chair that was more a throne than a seat, his name and rank emblazoned on his office door. Even the silver golf trophies on top of the bookcase polished to shining perfection were strategically positioned close to the window to catch the light. Halliday had moved to Wales from London's Metropolitan Police Force, having risen quickly through the ranks with only limited front-line experience. And that, Lewis concluded, was the crux of the problem. Halliday was a money man, concerned with reports, statistics and budgets, not a real copper. He wouldn't spot a criminal if one crept up behind him and bit him on the arse.

Lewis looked at his watch, a cheap quartz with a black rubber strap. He'd had enough.

'Are you going to be much longer?'

Halliday finally looked up from his papers. He took off his glasses, began cleaning them with a small white cotton cloth.

'Do I need to remind you who you're speaking to, Sergeant? I don't appreciate your tone.'

'Are you going to be much longer, *sir*?' Lewis's heavy emphasis on the *sir*, exuded contemptuous sarcasm from every pore.

Halliday looked back with a scowl. 'Take the weight off, Sergeant. There are matters we need to discuss.'

Lewis sat in the only available seat, a black leather armchair with a metal frame. He felt inclined to laugh as he made himself as comfortable as his aching joints would allow. His chair was smaller and lower than Halliday's. No surprises there. It was more of the same. It didn't take a detective to work out the significance. The prat really had thought of everything.

'I was told you want an update on the Williams case,' Lewis said.

Halliday gave a barely perceivable nod.

'Quite so, it's been nine days since the Williams girl went missing. We both know what that means. The risks increase with every day that passes. Surely you must have something positive to report by now. Or was I wrong to trust you with the investigation? I hope that wasn't a mistake on my part. I had hoped your years of experience would serve you well.'

'The chief constable gave me the case.'

Halliday snapped out his reply. 'I'm the head of this department.'

Lewis crossed one leg over the other, slowly, taking his time, not allowing Halliday to rush him. 'She spoke to me personally.'

'I'm very well aware of your mutual history, Sergeant. I know you and the chief were PCs together, but don't go thinking you can use it to your advantage. How long have you got until retirement?'

Lewis shrugged. 'Why do you ask?'

'Indulge me.'

'Three years.'

'Let me make myself clear. Show me the respect I'm due, or you'll spend those final years in a non-operational role. Perhaps the training department, or how would you feel about administering the cycling proficiency scheme? Not the best way to end such a long and dynamic career.'

Lewis chose to ignore the super's snide remarks. There was nothing to be gained from continuing an argument he couldn't win. Halliday was holding all the cards. Best say what the prat wanted to hear and get out of there as fast as his size nines could carry him.

'Do you want that update or not?'

'Get on with it. I haven't got all day.'

Lewis raised a hand to the side of his head in mock salute, one last act of rebellion before putting his resentments aside in the interests of both the case and an easy life. He then outlined a concise, clearly expressed summary of progress with the Williams case to date as Halliday listened in sullen silence. It appeared the chief superintendent was not a happy man. His expressions and body language said it all. He waited for Lewis to finish before asking his question.

'The hair in the envelope was Lucy Williams's, yes?'

'That's been confirmed by DNA. Whoever sent it has or had Lucy, that's beyond a reasonable doubt. It's the only explanation that makes any sense. I had the results rushed through. This case is the lab's number one priority.'

'All right, let's go through the available evidence. You've told me we've got the same suspect's fingerprints on the padded envelope, the note accompanying the hair and the letter sent to Lucy only days before her disappearance. And the writing matches – it's of the same style. You can confirm that with a suitable expert if you haven't already done so. That may well be of great benefit at a later date if and when an arrest is made, and the matter comes to court. But as of now, it doesn't help us a great deal.

Our man hasn't got a record. His fingerprints aren't on the database. But we have got a good idea of what he looks like, albeit you believe he may have been in disguise when he met Lucy in the café that day. I'm assuming you've circulated that description widely within the force?'

Lewis confirmed that he had. The words *granny* and *sucking eggs* came to mind as Halliday continued, now in full flow. It seemed there was no stopping him once he'd started. And Lewis had to admit to himself that the senior man was talking some sense, even if most of it was blatantly obvious to any copper with half a brain.

'It's regrettable that CCTV covers so few streets. It was very different in London. Do you think we're dealing with a kidnapping?'

The detective sergeant shook his head. It was always 'London this' or 'London that'. If the prat pissed off back there, Lewis would have been a very happy man.

'I really don't think we are. There's been no demand for a ransom. I'm confident there would have been by now if this was about money. The note sent to Myra Williams was the sick bastard's idea of a wind-up. The writer wants her to know her daughter is in terrible danger. It's sadistic. Whoever's got Lucy wants her mother to suffer. And both the note and letter are written in blood, very likely with an old-fashioned fountain pen. The expert thought the blood would be too thick for the modern version unless it was fresh and watered down. And it isn't Lucy's – I've had it tested. I was hoping it was red ink, but it's not. We're dealing with a psycho. The contents of the note suggest he may have offended before. I've got an officer checking the system for similar crimes in other parts of the country.'

Halliday pulled his head back. He'd suddenly recoiled as the impact of this new revelation fully sank in. The colour had drained from his face.

'Why the hell haven't you told me about the blood before now? Didn't you think it was important? You didn't think to mention it?'

'Would it have made a difference? I've not long found out myself.'

'Oh, come on, for goodness' sake, man, it's crucial information. The sort of thing it's essential I know, no surprises.'

Lewis gave a little shrug. 'The lab sent me the results earlier today. The report arrived less than an hour ago. They hurried them through after a bit of pressure. I've told you now, so what's the problem?'

Halliday didn't have his head in his hands, but he may as well have. He looked as if he had the weight of the world on his shoulders. It seemed all of a sudden his world was a darker place.

'Blood! That suggests a serious element of psychopathy. That's not good!'

Lewis found Halliday's reaction almost comic. In any other circumstance, he'd have laughed. 'Nobody's saying it's good.'

The chief super seemed back in control of his mood as he slowed his breathing. His tone was sardonic.

'Is there anything else you haven't told me, any other revelations you haven't deemed to share?'

Lewis imagined himself punching Halliday right in the mouth, knocking him from his oversized chair. The mental picture made him smile.

'That's it – you know as much as I do.'

'Right, I don't want the media finding out about the blood. We keep that detail in house. And don't share it with the parents either, not yet. They're likely to panic. Talk to your team. Make sure they're fully briefed as to my orders. Anyone who breaks confidence will have me to answer to.'

Lewis trusted his officers; he didn't see the need to say anything of the kind. But he kept his opinion to himself, keen to bring the interaction to a close.

'I'll get it sorted. Anything else?'

'Talk to a profiler. That professor at Cardiff University has done a good job for us in the past. I can't recall his name, but you'd easily find it. Get hold of him. Tell him it's urgent. Do it today. Speed up your enquiries. We need to find this Moloch, whoever the hell he is, and find him quickly. Find the man, and we find Lucy. Hopefully, we find her alive.'

'I've had officers going from business to business in the relevant areas of town in the hope a member of staff saw something significant either on the day of the café meeting or after Lucy left the gallery on the day of her talk. We're working our way through each shop, bank, office, et cetera. There are a lot of people to interview. Increase the size of my team, and we'll do it more quickly. Moloch left the café shortly before Lucy, I've already established that. He claimed to live outside town. We live in a rural area, so public transport is limited, Therefore, there's every chance he had a vehicle. And someone must have seen the direction Lucy took after leaving the gallery. She didn't return to college. She had to go somewhere. It was a market day. It's in a busy street with a fair amount of footfall. There's got to be a witness out there. We've just got to find them.'

Halliday moved forward in his seat.

'It's not all about resources, Sergeant. There are limits to the CID budget. I will assign additional officers, that will be done today, but it would help if you managed the investigation more efficiently. I can't say I'm overly impressed by your performance to date. I expected better of such an experienced detective. The chief constable has had the home secretary on the phone. Did you hear what I said? The home secretary! She's a personal friend of the father. The national press is already sniffing around. I want a report outlining how many additional officers you'll need on my desk within the hour, not a second longer. We'll bring them in from other divisions as necessary. And I'll be keeping a close watch. I'll give you two more days – I want you back in my office forty-eight hours from now with an update. If you haven't made significant progress, I'll replace you with a more senior officer. If you don't think you're up to the job, say so now – we haven't got time to waste.'

Lewis stood, cursing his arthritic joints, keen to get out of there before his notoriously sharp tongue got the better of him. He imagined himself shaking Halliday like a rag doll and felt a little better.

'It's not all about rank. I've been in this job a very long time. If anyone can find Lucy Williams alive, I can.'

'Let's hope so, Sergeant. Your job may well depend on it.'

'Are we done?'

'We're done when I tell you we're done and not before. The sister is clearly in danger too. What are you doing to mitigate the risks? One MP's daughter in the hands of a maniac is bad enough without a second joining her.'

Lewis had never wanted to punch a man more.

'She's been fully briefed, advised not to go out alone, and there's a panic button installed in her home with a direct link to the station. Hit it and uniformed officers will be there in minutes. Short of putting an officer with her twenty-four hours a day, that's the best I can do.'

'Is there not an alternative address she can stay at, with a relative perhaps, somewhere out of the area until the abductor's caught?'

'It has been suggested, but it's not something she wants. It's got to be her choice – I can't force her.'

'You've got two days. I want significant progress, or you're off the case. And don't go thinking the chief constable is going to protect you. I've already spoken to her. She's in full agreement. Now get on with it. There's not a second to lose.'

26

Lewis was sitting back with his feet resting on his overly cluttered desk, perusing the recently compiled list of potential suspects on the evening of that same day, when Detective Constable David Oakes burst into the room with a mischievous grin on his boyish face. Oakes looked eighteen but was ten years older and had been in the job for a little over five years. He still seemed to find being a detective as much of a novelty as he had on his first day. Just looking at him made Lewis feel old.

Lewis raised a hand in friendly acknowledgement, but he didn't otherwise move. He was tired. It had already been a long day. 'What the fuck are you doing here, Dai?' he called. 'It's gone eight. That new wife of yours is going to be well pleased. She'll be kicking you into touch if you're not careful.'

'Ah, she won't mind. She married a copper. She knew the score. It goes with the territory.'

'Fuck knows what she sees in you. You're punching well above your weight with that one.'

The DC laughed in response to his sergeant's familiar banter. Humour was a coping mechanism of sorts; if you were on the receiving end, you were part of the team. Both men understood that, instinctively.

Oakes was still smiling when he spoke again moments later. 'We've got something.'

Lewis lowered his legs, sitting upright. All of a sudden, he was paying attention. They needed a break, lucky or not. Maybe this was it.

'This had better be good.'

'Do you want the good news or the bad?'

Lewis shook his head with a frown. He could tell the younger man was playing to the gallery, enjoying his moment in the spotlight. On another day, he may have indulged him, but not now.

'For fuck's sake, Dai, stop pissing about and tell me what you've got.'

Oakes allowed a wall-mounted radiator to support his weight. 'I took a statement from a Rhian Harris a couple of hours ago. She works as a waitress in the small Italian restaurant opposite the gallery where Lucy gave her talk. It's only today she's back in work. She's been off sick for a few days, flu, otherwise I'd have seen her before. Rhian knows Lucy – they were in secondary school together. Not the same class but the same year. Rhian looked out of the window that day to see if it was still raining, which it was. She saw Lucy leave the gallery, walk towards a large white rusty van, lower her umbrella, talk to the driver briefly and then climb into the passenger seat alongside him. The driver drove off with Lucy still in the front seat a minute or two later. The driver matches the description of Moloch given by Cerys – grey hair, beard and glasses.'

'That is fucking brilliant – well done, Dai. You'll get some brownie points for this one. Have you got a full description of the van? Please tell me the answer's yes.'

'It's even better than that.'

Lewis beamed. All of a sudden, he wasn't feeling tired at all.

'Okay, come on, let's hear it.'

'The driver went straight through the centre of town. Can you believe that? He's either very confident or very stupid, or maybe a bit of both. We've got him on camera. We've got the number plate. We see him, and we see Lucy. The picture quality isn't great – it's all black and white and a bit grainy, what with the rain – but it's definitely them. Lucy's slumped in the passenger seat, either unconscious or asleep.'

Lewis had a third potential explanation in mind. Lucy might already have been dead. The hypothesis ate away at him, but he kept it to himself. The young detective had done well. There was no point in bursting his bubble. Morale mattered when the going got tough.

'How did we miss this, for fuck's sake? We've been going through CCTV all week. They had one fucking job...'

'To be fair, I might have missed it myself if I hadn't known what I was looking for, boss. Like I said, the pictures aren't that clear.'

Lewis let out a long breath. He still felt more than a little irritated but decided to let it go.

'But they're clear enough for us to nail the bastard – that's what matters.' Lewis punched the air. 'It looks like we've got him.'

'Not quite.'

'What the fuck are you talking about?'

'The number plate is registered to a Steve Smith in the Benwell area of Newcastle. The make and colour of the van are right. But the age is wrong. My dad runs a garage. I grew up helping the mechanics. Our van's got a different grill. I've checked. The model was only made between 1998 and 2008. But the index number is for a van seven years newer. I'm sorry, Sarge. Our van's got false plates.'

Lewis rubbed his knee, groaning. His newfound energy was already melting away. So close, but no cigar.

'You had better be fucking sure, Dai. This matters.'

'I'm sorry, I'm right, boss. I wish I weren't. I double-checked online. And I had a word with my dad. There is no way the number plate and our vehicle match.'

'Oh, for fuck's sake.'

Lewis rose to his feet, weighing up his options and quickly formulating an immediate action plan. He prided himself on being good in a crisis.

'Get on the blower, ring Northumbria Police, give them the heads up and tell them we need them to check out this Smith character pronto. We need to know where his van was at the relevant time and get it on record. We don't want some paper-pushing twat telling us we didn't cover all the angles if the case goes tits up.'

'Okay, will do.'

'Do it now, and give that missus of yours a ring once you're done. Tell her you're not going to be home for a good few hours. We're going to start putting together a list of all vehicles registered in our area matching our van. We'll start with a twenty-mile radius of town in every direction and then move out from there. Let's see who the registered keepers are and if any of them has a relevant history. There's a map on the wall in the training room. I'll grab that and a marker pen. It'll be easier than using a computer. I'll be back in five minutes. Make those calls.'

'Coffee?'

Lewis turned when he reached the office door, his hand on the handle. 'Strong, plenty of powdered milk and four heaped sugars. There's some biscuits in my drawer. Help yourself, but make sure there's plenty left for me.'

Oakes picked up the phone but didn't dial.

'I thought you were down to three sugars.'

'Fuck the diet. I'm going to need all the energy I can get. The canteen's shut. It's going to be a long night. And anyway, I'm lovely as I am.'

27

Lucy lay alone in the dark, her bruised and battered body aching, her virtually naked scalp sore, awaiting Moloch's next inevitable appearance with trepidation. Her mind raced, one invasive thought after another. She'd never experienced such pain, such despair. She quietly hummed a lullaby her mother often sang to her as a child, listening to the sounds echoing in her head, trying to shut out her new world. But the gentle song brought little comfort despite its familiarity. Her situation was so far out of her control, so seemingly insurmountable. What use were memories of the long-gone past? In that terrible place, they simply mocked her. That was one life, and this was another. Everything good had gone.

Lucy groaned as she continued her reluctant rumination. Her existence had become nothing but misery; a horror film come to life. She tensed at every sound, always on full alert. There was little, if any, point in hoping the devil in human form wouldn't come again, because he always did. The lights would shine bright, she'd flinch, screw up her eyes, and then there he'd be.

What the fuck was wrong with the man? There was no reasoning with him, no giving him the 'right' answer. She'd tried to agree with him, to do what he wanted. Hell, she'd even tried telling him no. Nothing satisfied him.

Lucy sat up on the hard, cold concrete floor, trying to ignore the pain in her buttocks and hips. There was always pain, everything hurt. She wept as she gently ran the palm of one hand over her naked belly, picturing the little life inside her. It had seemed such good news not so very long ago, a new chapter, a milestone she'd quickly come to accept and even welcome. But now what? The thought of a baby entering her new world of darkness, fear and suffering was unthinkable. The more she considered it, the more impossible it seemed and the more intense her weeping. Moloch must never, ever get his filthy, murdering hands on her child. She repeated it in her head, *Never, never, never!*

At that moment, as she sat there trembling, Lucy made a decision. She couldn't stop trying. She'd struggle on; she'd persevere for as long as feasibly possible, hoping for rescue, searching for any chance of escape, however slight. She'd cling on to what little hope she had, not for her sake but for that of her baby. It was escape or die.

28

Gove kept the young sex worker's severed hand in the coldest part of his fridge after its removal from her body. He'd nibbled the end of one slowly decomposing finger still attached to the hand before freezing it, quickly deciding that cannibalism wasn't for him despite his earlier ambitions. He was a little disappointed in himself, seeing his reluctant omission as the first limitation he'd encountered on his murderous journey to greatness. But he was glad he did at least have another positive use for the hand as he held it up in plain sight, sealed in a clear plastic bag, just a few inches from Lucy's increasingly haggard face. He shook the bag in front of her with a grimly mocking, dominant smile he thought entirely suitable for the circumstances. Nothing was left to chance. Everything was planned – even the expression on his freshly shaved face.

'What do you think, Lucy? Nice, eh? I did consider cooking it up for us both with a little garlic butter, but I've decided on another use. I hope you're not too disappointed. I'm certain you'll cheer up once I tell you more.'

Lucy tried to look away as she sat against the cellar wall. He gripped her face to either side of her chin, pulling her head sharply to face him.

'Look at me, bitch, look at the bag. Do not *dare* turn your head again.

Test my patience one more time, and it'll be the last time. Look at the bag. I'm interested to know your thoughts.'

She looked at the hand now, tears welling in her eyes. He noticed she was thinner than when she'd first arrived, losing at least a pound a day in his estimation. She looked older too. Her face appeared to sag. He could see her ribs under a thin layer of flesh. Even the strength of her voice had weakened.

'I don't know w-w-what you want m-m-me to say, sir.'

'Oh, come on, surely you must realise what I've got in mind. Do you think your mother would like it? You know her well enough. Would she appreciate the gesture? I'm thinking of putting it in the post.'

Lucy was trembling now, her entire body shaking from head to foot.

'Please, no, God, no, n-n-not that. Don't you think we'll need it?'

He took a backward step, glaring at her, thinking she'd said the most ludicrous thing he'd ever heard. He spat out his words, every muscle tensed, teeth bared, jaw clenched, lip curled.

'I wonder what the fuck's wrong with you sometimes. I've sent the ridiculous woman your hair. She'll have received that well before now. It's time for another gift, another nice surprise to make her wince. Surely you can see the logic in that? It's hardly complicated. It's not fucking rocket science. I thought you had a degree of intelligence. You need your hands and fingers for the painting, at least for now. So I thought, why not send this hand?'

His mood calmed slightly as he studied her reactions. She was cringing, dropping her shoulders, making herself smaller, trying to retreat, pressing herself to the wall. He interpreted all that as her acceptance of his dominance, and he took some satisfaction in that. He continued to watch her closely while touching his genitals through his trousers. Her tears were in full flow now, staining her face. She was swallowing hard. He could see the movement in her throat. Even her neck seemed to be getting thinner. She'd been slim to start with, so maybe one can of beans a day wasn't enough. And she wasn't even eating all of those. Perhaps he should ram them down her stupid throat.

'I'm still waiting, girl. Tell me your thoughts.'

He tilted his head to one side, listening with sardonic interest as she went to speak. What laughable nonsense would she come up with next? A small part of him was beginning to wonder if she was the one after all.

'I'd, I'd f-f-find it a lot easier to w-work if, if you didn't s-s-send the hand to my mother. Please, Moloch, I'm, I'm begging you. She's not like you and m-m-me. I could use the h-hand as inspiration for our m-masterpiece. Can we keep it, please?'

Her words confused him. Her reasoned argument was the last thing he'd expected. And maybe she had a valid point. He asked himself if Lucy was indeed coming around to his way of thinking despite his earlier doubts. Or was she simply trying to manipulate him in her mother's interests? Without further assessment, it was hard to tell, even for a genius like him. He handed her the bag, closely studying her reaction once more, her body language, her expressions, telling himself actions spoke louder than words.

'Think of this as your next test. Another examination you have to pass. Open the bag, take out the hand, study what's left of the cold flesh. Take your time to appreciate its dark beauty. Come on, reach in, out it comes, Why the hesitation? I'll need to get it back in the freezer soon, of course, before posting, but you've got time. Do it now – this is your final chance.'

She followed instructions, repeatedly gagging, bent in fear, her distress written on her face as he loomed over her, leering.

'There, that's it, that's better. Smell it, breathe deeply, touch it with your tongue, imprint it on your memory, never to be forgotten. Now, you're getting it. Sniff, sniff, lick, lick, sniff, that's all the inspiration you'll need.'

After a minute or two, Lucy lowered the hand slowly from her face, very obviously preparing to speak. All the crying had left her eyes so very red they were almost the colour of blood. There was vomit on her chin and chest.

'Please, p-p-please don't send it. Please c-c-can we keep it? It, it would m-m-mean so much t-to me.'

He reached for the taser.

'Am I your god?'

She placed the severed hand back in the bag and then on the floor next to her. She struggled into a kneeling position.

'Yes, sir, y-you are m-my god.'

'Then, praise me, lovely Lucy, sing out your praises as if your life depends on it. Because it does. I can promise you, it does.'

She began calling out her adoration between whimpering sobs. He stood there, shouting if she stalled, kicking her leg twice when her apparent enthusiasm slightly lagged. She continued for another ten minutes as he masturbated, ejaculated and then finally silenced her.

'That's good, lovely Lucy – you're making progress. You still have some way to go, but we'll count this morning as a pass. And that, I've decided, is worthy of reward. Say thank you, come on, say it. I'm tired of waiting.'

'Thank, thank y-you, sir.'

He refastened his trousers.

'You'll no doubt be delighted to hear that you're cordially invited to the world premiere of a short film I've produced and directed. You'll join me in my cinema room later this week. You recently sent the star up in smoke, but I also played a leading role. I'll be interested to find out what you think of my performance. Watch the film, and you'll truly understand my life's work. It's my greatest masterpiece to date, but you and me, my lovely, will go even further. There will be other films, other masterpieces. We'll choose the participants together. You can help me trap them, as Hindley did for Brady. That's true teamwork; they cast aside society's moral constraints in a frenzy of violence, and so will we. We may even invite your sister to be an active participant one fine day. She reminded me of my mother, her repulsive look, the grating sound of her voice. Cerys, isn't it? Isn't that the bitch's name?'

Gove kicked Lucy hard in the face when she looked towards the cellar door. Blood ran from her nose and mouth as she curled up in a ball.

'Oh dear, that is disappointing, Lucy, another black mark. And just when you were doing so very well. Was the mention of your sister's name too much for you at this early stage of your development? I can't help thinking participating in her murder would be your greatest test yet. Pass that, and anything is possible.'

Lucy protected her head with her hands as best she could as she lay there, whimpering.

'No, please, n-no, not my, my sister. Kill m-me if you have to, anything b-b-but that. Aren't I the special one? Shouldn't you be focusing on me?'

'On your feet, get to your fucking feet. Don't even think about questioning my devotion.'

She struggled into a standing position, dizzy, in danger of falling. 'Yes, s-sir.'

'I do not want to hear another fucking word.'

He landed a powerful hooking blow just below her elbow, turning his body, swinging an arm, cracking a rib, causing her to fold over with a gasp.

'Oh, for fuck's sake. Come on, girl, straighten up. You look like shit. It would help if you cleaned yourself up. There's water in your bucket. Come on, get over there. Don't make such a fuss about nothing. What are a few blows between friends?'

Lucy struggled towards the plastic bucket, the chain between her ankles limiting her movement.

He sat alongside her as she gently washed her face and body, a knife in one hand.

'That's it, lovely girl, wash away, wash away. It's good that you're doing what you're told. Let's see how well you progress in the coming days. Kill you, kill your sister, kill you both on film? We can decide about all that once your painting's done. The bottom line: you need to impress. You're starting to sound a bit like my mother, and that's never a good thing. I'd be careful if I were you. Things could get infinitely worse.'

29

Lewis felt a deep sense of foreboding, as Halliday glared at him with what seemed a strange combination of glee and resentment at their scheduled meeting on 14 June. He was surprised Halliday was even there on a Sunday and wishing he wasn't. It was all too familiar. Lewis had once told Halliday to fuck off back to London when drunk and celebrating a colleague's pending retirement. Halliday had pulled rank rather than responding in kind, initiating disciplinary proceedings that resulted in a written final warning being placed on Lewis's file. Several years had now passed, but it was obvious to Lewis that the burning resentment was still mutual. It had festered over time. And now, Lewis thought, the arrogant, supercilious twat was finally in the perfect position to make him pay. He was creaming his fucking underpants. Lewis decided to break the silence. What other option did he have?

'You said you wanted an update and I've given you one. Are we done? Can I get on with the job?'

Halliday waited a few more excruciating seconds before responding, all the time tapping his cleanly shaven chin with the first finger of his left hand. Lewis was hoping for the best but fearing the worst. He'd made progress with the case but was it enough?

'So, let me see if I've got this right, Sergeant? You know what this Moloch character looks like, you know when and where he abducted Lucy Williams, you have his handwriting and fingerprints, and you know what vehicle he was driving at the time of the abduction. One of your officers has even established that a similar vehicle is of interest in the disappearance of a young female sex worker in Bristol. You know all that – you've even got much of it on CCTV – and yet you're no nearer to arresting our suspect?

'Despite all the additional resources I've given you, you haven't got even the slightest idea who this Moloch is or where he took the Williams girl. You don't even know if she's alive or dead. It's not good enough. It's not nearly good enough. I've said as much to the chief constable. She's in full agreement. I'd be tempted to resign were I in your position. Have you considered early retirement? You're due a generous lump sum and a good pension. You've got the years in. I've got the figures here if you'd like to see them. The job has moved on, and you haven't. You're a dinosaur, man. There's no room for people like you in the force any more. What have you got to say for yourself?'

Lewis felt his entire body tense. He knew Halliday was hoping to provoke a reaction he could use against him. It was just his style.

'Oh, you'd love that, wouldn't you? I was arresting criminals when you were still in fucking nappies. I'll retire when I'm ready. And don't think you can shove me into some pointless role not equal to my rank and experience. I'll be speaking to my federation rep as soon as I'm out of here.'

'You have failed dismally, Lewis. You must realise that – it's staring you in the face. The Williams family deserve better. And frankly, I deserve better. You'll be replaced as soon as a suitable officer is available. In the interim, perhaps you can get on with the investigation and do a better job. You are truly testing my patience.'

Lewis rose to his feet, grinning. Once again, Halliday seemed full of crap, all bark and no bite. Bullshitting because that's all he could offer. Perhaps the chief constable wasn't in complete agreement after all.

Lewis had a skip in his step as he headed for Halliday's office door. For now, he was still on the case. For all of Halliday's heated bluster, nothing had changed. Lewis saw that as a victory of sorts. One day, he'd tell Halliday precisely what he thought of him. But for now, finding Lucy Williams was still his responsibility. He'd have to be satisfied with that.

Kesey and her family woke to a perfect blue sky morning on Monday 15 June. The air was already warm by eight as they ate breakfast together on the sunny patio in front of the white-painted villa. There wasn't even a single cloud in the sky, not in any direction as far as the eye could see. It really couldn't have been more perfect. According to the weather forecast, it would be a warm but slightly breezy day, just as Kesey liked it. An ideal day for a family trip to the beach.

Janet had suggested a visit to Papagayo the previous evening when perusing a list of Lanzarote's best beaches online. Kesey had agreed. It meant an approximate one-hour drive through Teguise, on to the popular tourist resort of Playa Blanca via the LZ-30, and then along a rough, stone-strewn track for a mile or two to reach a series of five beautiful crescent-shaped beaches with soft pale sand and crystal clear-blue water. Some areas were nudist, but that didn't bother either woman a great deal. And anyway, it was clear from the many scenic online photos and traveller comments that it was easy to find your own undisturbed area of beach if you wanted to. There was a small three-euro charge to enter the area, which seemed like excellent value, given the unspoilt beauty on offer. All three were looking forward to enjoying a wonderful day.

The happy family arrived at their destination a little after ten that morning after a bumpy journey along a windblown road riddled with multiple potholes. It really couldn't have been more different to the busy resort only a few short miles away. And that, Kesey decided, was a good thing. The walk from the car park to their beach of choice was a bit of an effort and Kesey struggled at times while carrying the picnic bag, which seemed to get heavier by the minute. But as they looked out on the magnificent vista – the rocks, the beach, the sea, the yachts and pleasure boats – it all felt very worthwhile. It was their little slice of paradise. Somewhere new they could relax and enjoy. They were settled on the beach in a quiet spot only a few yards from the sea within ten minutes.

The rest of the morning was spent playing beach games, making sandcastles, enjoying the sun and swimming. The sea was a little rougher than expected, the power of the rolling waves enough to knock you back with ease if you ventured too far from the shore. Ed was only allowed to enter the water in the close company of one or both of the women while wearing his buoyancy aid, a bright-yellow sleeveless jacket tied at the waist and zipped up the front. And even then, they stayed in relatively shallow water, going no deeper than his waist while standing.

They ate their picnic lunch together at around twelve, sitting under the shade of a large orange sun umbrella, carried to the beach by Janet. Everything was laid out on a large multi-coloured beach towel. There were crisps, garlic hummus, green olives, gluten-free brown bread, sweet Medjool dates and slightly sparkling mineral water, so perhaps more a snack than a substantial meal. They planned to call at that same favourite vegetarian restaurant in Teguise for a takeaway on their return journey. The salads were fabulous, and the dream cake was to die for.

Kesey lay back on the warm sand, enjoying a bit of quality me-time as Janet took Edward for a wee in the sea. She was just thinking how very peaceful the place was when her mobile rang in her beach bag next to her. She considered ignoring it for a fraction of a second, but she was never going to do that, not really. The ringtone demanded her attention. Kesey fumbled in the bag, finally found the phone, sat upright, held it to the side of her face and said hello.

She recognised Chief Superintendent Halliday's voice as soon as he spoke. 'Hello, Laura, I hope I haven't caught you at an inopportune time. Unavoidable, I'm afraid. There's something we need to discuss.'

Kesey disliked Halliday intensely. She considered him a misogynist; a worm of a man who seemingly wallowed in his self-importance. Some of her female colleagues called him handsy, which summed him up very nicely. Although she could think of a good few names worse.

'I'm on holiday.' Kesey snapped back her reply.

'I'm very well aware of that, thank you, Laura. But you're still a serving police officer. Duty calls. Work has to come first. You know that as well as I do. And I always thought three weeks was a bit excessive.'

Kesey looked across the beach to where Jan and Ed played at the sea's edge. She had a terrible feeling of foreboding. As if things were about to go horribly wrong. As if Halliday was about to smash her happy family idyll into a myriad jagged pieces. She didn't hold back.

'What the hell are you talking about? This is my first foreign holiday in years. I booked the leave well in advance. You knew I was going. We talked about it. The DCI approved it. I'm almost three thousand miles away. I need this break.'

She heard him sigh at the other end of the line. She waited for him to speak, as she knew he inevitably would.

'We have a missing young woman, the daughter of a local MP, and we have every reason to believe she's in grave danger if indeed she's alive at all. That's more important than your holiday, don't you think?'

'Yeah, Lucy Williams, I know the girl. I read an article in the paper. It said Ray's dealing with the case. He was quoted. He's more than capable. What the hell would you need me for?'

'I strongly suggest you calm yourself down, Inspector, before you say something you later regret. I'm not sure I agree with your assessment of Lewis's capabilities. But that aside, the case is fast becoming newsworthy. The home secretary has already involved herself, demanding results. It's not going to be long before the force is under the full focus of media glare. The case requires a more senior investigating officer, someone like yourself, with the skills and subtleties Lewis lacks. Lewis, I'm afraid, just won't do.'

Kesey looked up, forcing an unconvincing smile as Janet waved to her from the water's edge.

'Surely, there must be somebody else who can take the case on. I'm not the only senior detective in the force.'

'You've dealt with similar high-profile investigations effectively in the past. Your reputation goes before you. Mr Williams has asked for your involvement by name.'

In any other circumstances, she would have been flattered, but not now. Halliday really was an insufferable prat.

'I'll be back home in a few days. If you want to allocate me the case then, that's fine. I'll give it my full attention. But I'm sure Ray's more than capable of covering until then.'

'You know the way things work in the force, Laura, and circumstances are exceptional. Your flight has already been booked for you at three forty tomorrow afternoon. You can pick the ticket up at the airline desk. There is only the one Wales flight. Be on it. You can report to me at seven sharp the following morning. I'll give you a full briefing before you meet with the team. The quicker you're up to speed, the better for everyone.'

She closed her eyes for a beat.

'No, this is ridiculous; you're being entirely unreasonable. I'm entitled to leave. I need this. It's a stressful job. You know I was struggling with some of the shit I dealt with. You have a duty of care.'

'Am I correct in thinking you're an ambitious young woman, Laura?'

'What's that got to do with anything?'

'I don't know if you've heard, but DCI Donovan is retiring in a few months' time after thirty years of exemplary service. I'm going to need an equally able replacement. I had you in mind to fill the post, but if I can't rely on you in a crisis, well... I'm sure you know where I'm going with this, I'd have to look elsewhere. There are other senior detectives in the force, as you said yourself. Some officers are destined for the top, and some are not. There are followers, and there are leaders. It would help if you decided which you are. What you say next will have a huge impact on your career path. I can be a facilitator or a barrier. Make your choice.'

Kesey looked up as her wife and son strolled up the beach towards her.

They were only a two- or three-minute slow walk away. She had to be quick.

'Do you guarantee me that promotion?'

'I've made my position clear. I've told you the score. Now it's up to you.'

'I'll be on that plane.'

Kesey hurriedly ended her call, rushing to put her mobile back in the beach bag as Janet and Ed approached. Janet had a curious look on her face as she sat down on the sand, drying her long hair with a large yellow towel.

'Who was on the phone?'

'Oh, it was nothing important. I'll tell you about it later. We'll talk when Ed's in bed – now's not the time.'

'Come on, Laura, what is it? You couldn't get that phone back in the bag quickly enough. I know there's something up. Is it my father? Is he ill again?'

Kesey put a comforting arm around Ed's shoulder as he started to cry. 'It's not your father, Janet.'

'Then what is it?'

'Do we really have to do this now?'

'Yes, yes, we do. Otherwise, I'm going to be worrying about it all damn day. I know you're hiding something. I can read you like a large-print book.'

'It was Halliday.'

Janet made a face. 'We're on holiday. What the hell did he want? Can't the man leave you alone for three frigging weeks?'

'I've, er, I've got to go back to Wales.'

Janet's voice rose in pitch and tone. 'You've got to *what*?'

'You can, um, you can stay, but I'll be catching a plane home earlier than planned. It's an order. I wasn't given a choice. There's nothing I can do about it. I either do what I'm told, or I'm out of a job.'

'You have got to be kidding me.'

Kesey reached out to touch her partner's arm, but she withdrew her hand quickly when Janet pulled away.

'I'm so sorry, Jan. You and Ed can stay – the villa's booked and paid for – but I've got to go.'

'You can bet your sweet life we'll be staying. I can't believe you're doing this. I thought we were more important to you than that.'

'You are, of course, you are. You both mean everything to me.'

'It doesn't seem that way to me.'

Kesey felt conflicted in the extreme, letting her family down was always difficult, and staying on holiday certainly had its attractions. But work came first, career and promotion were important to her, however challenging. She searched for the right words. Anything that might placate Janet even slightly, even if it wasn't entirely true.

'I've told you I'm sorry. I don't know what more I can say. Like I said, if I don't go, I'll be sacked. I'm the main breadwinner. What else am I supposed to do?'

Jan blew the air from her mouth.

'When are you going?'

Kesey mumbled her response. 'I'm flying tomorrow afternoon.'

'*Tomorrow afternoon?!*'

'Yeah, yeah, sorry. The, er, the ticket is already paid for.'

Janet jumped to her feet, picked Ed up in her arms and began striding towards the steps leading back to the car park. She called out without looking back.

'Right, come on, let's go. You can carry the bag. Leave the umbrella if you can't manage it. I wouldn't want you putting yourself out on our behalf. Police work is far more important than we are.'

Kesey carried the sun umbrella in one hand and the beach bag in the other as she jogged after her family, keen to catch up but dreading the inevitable further conflict she knew was coming her way.

'I've said I'm sorry. And I am, really I am.'

'Just be quiet, Laura. I don't want to hear it.'

Kesey knew she was in the wrong, and no amount of apologies on her part would make the rest of the day anything less than awful. She searched for something else to say, anything to slightly alleviate Janet's anger and disappointment. But she gave up on the idea as they climbed the steps. Sometimes silence was best. Ambition had got the better of her. That was the truth of it. Here was hoping it would all be worth it in the end.

31

Kesey first saw Lewis in the notoriously terrible police canteen on the morning of 17 June, the day after her return from Lanzarote. He was sitting alone at a table at the back of the room, enthusiastically tucking into a full English breakfast of bacon, sausages, fried eggs, beans and black pudding, the greasy fare piled high on his plate, all covered in copious amounts of brown sauce, as was his custom. Kesey wasn't in the least bit surprised to see he had a second smaller plate of fried potatoes to accompany his main order. There was at least a day's recommended calories in one unhealthy meal. No wonder he was piling on the pounds.

Kesey called out to Lewis on approaching the serving counter. She waved when he looked up from his food, ordered a black coffee and two rounds of brown toast with jam, a treat she thought justified in the circumstances, and then joined him at the table. Lewis slurped his frothy coffee, leaving a milky moustache above his top lip before speaking with his strong West Wales lilt. He looked tired, the bags under his eyes even more prominent than usual.

'Good holiday?'

Kesey shrugged. 'Well, it was until I heard from Halliday.'

'The man's a tosser.'

Kesey sipped her hot black coffee and smiled. 'That's one word for him. I can think of a few more, most of them worse.'

'Ordering you back was a bit much.'

'You won't hear me arguing.'

'How did Jan take it?'

'How do you think?' Kesey momentarily covered her eyes with an open hand.

'That bad, eh?'

'Worse. You can't imagine. I'm not exactly flavour of the month. It's going to take us some time to get over this one.'

Lewis shovelled a loaded fork of bacon and egg yolk into his mouth and chewed. A dribble of brown sauce ran down his unshaven chin. He wiped it away, talking with his mouth full as Kesey shook her head.

'I wish Halliday would fuck off back to London. He bangs on about the place often enough, you'd think he'd be on the next bus out of here.'

Kesey nibbled at her toast and nodded. 'I'd happily pay for his train ticket and run him to the station. I'd even kiss him goodbye if it meant he'd sod off.'

Lewis laughed before eating half a pork sausage in one greedy mouthful. It didn't stop him from talking. Almost nothing ever did.

'Wouldn't we all? We'd have to form an orderly queue.'

Kesey nodded towards the remains of Lewis's breakfast, shaking her head slowly with a disapproving look.

'I can see the diet's going well.'

He tilted his head back, draining his mug. 'Don't even start,' he said after.

'What was it your doctor said? You need to lose at least two, maybe three stones. You're not getting any younger. You need to start looking after yourself.'

'Who are you, my mother?'

'I worry about you, Ray, that's all. You're a good friend as well as a colleague. If I don't tell you, who's going to? You've had one heart attack. You don't want another one. You very nearly died. You might not survive the next time.'

'Yeah, yeah, I know, you never stop telling me. My wife used to nag the hell out of me, and now you've started. I've heard it all before.'

'Well, start listening to me then. Take some responsibility for your health. Look at the size of that meal you're devouring – it's ridiculous. And it's swimming in fat. What's wrong with some fresh fruit and a slice of wholemeal toast? Some fibre would do you good.'

'Oh, come on, give me a break, Laura. A man's got to eat. It's one of the few pleasures I've got left.'

'Okay, I'll be quiet. I've said my piece.'

'Thank fuck for that. I was beginning to think you were never going to shut up. Now, do you want to hear about the Williams case or not? I hear you're taking over.'

Kesey took another sip of fast-cooling coffee, nodding twice. She hoped her facial expression communicated regret.

'Sorry about that, Ray – it's a top-down thing. Halliday didn't give me a choice. You know what he's like.'

'I was handling it. We were making good progress. A few more days, and I'd have cracked it wide open.'

She didn't feel entirely persuaded but there was no value in sharing her true thoughts.

'I don't doubt it, not for a second. I know you're a good copper, one of the best. It's a rank thing, that's all. The case is starting to get a lot of media attention, and, well, you know, the brass want a DI as the SIO. The force needs to be seen to be following procedure. You'll be my right-hand man – I couldn't do anything without you.'

He smiled, obviously pleased with the direction the conversation had taken. He munched on his last piece of sausage, only chewing twice before swallowing.

'Yeah, and don't you forget it. We're a team, you and me.'

Kesey checked the time on the wall clock to her right. Enough of pleasantries; it was time to get down to business.

'Halliday's given me a summary of the investigation, curtsey, doff my cap, and all that. Now I want to hear it from you. The white van seems like an obvious line of enquiry. How far have you got with tracking it down?'

'There's 116 vehicles of the right make, model, age and colour in the force area. Only twelve of those are owned by someone with a criminal history, all men. We've interviewed seven so far, none of whom seem likely suspects. There's five to go. I'm planning on a visit to Fisher's Scrapyard this afternoon. It's a case of working through the list one at a time. Hopefully, we'll get the break we need.'

Kesey screwed up her face. 'What, Carl Fisher? I can't see it myself. A bit of burglary, theft, receiving stolen goods, yeah, but abduction? No way, he's not the type.'

Lewis pushed his empty plate aside before wiping his mouth clean with a tweed jacket sleeve. 'Yeah, I know what you're saying. Fisher's a bit of a wide boy, but he's not one of the world's evil bastards. I've known him since he was a kid and his father before him. It's just a case of ruling him out, covering all the bases. It's not him in the driver's seat, that's obvious from looking at the CCTV – Fisher and the driver are completely different builds – but it could be his van driven by someone else. And if not, you never know; he may have heard something on the grapevine. He's well connected in the criminal community. People must be talking.'

'The perp may not even live within the force area. The van could have come here from anywhere.'

'I do realise that, but I had to start somewhere. I planned to cover our patch and then move on from there.'

'I'll come with you to see Fisher if you like. We could talk tactics on the way. It would be an opportunity for a proper catch-up.'

He looked far from persuaded.

'I'll do this one myself, if that's all right, Laura. I know you like to stick to the rules. I wouldn't want to offend your sensibilities.'

'Oh, here we go again. Take it easy and don't push it. You can't afford another complaint. Put some pressure on Fisher by all means, but don't go too far.'

'I had a word with that criminology professor you used for the Miller case, the bloke in the wheelchair. He reckons it's likely our man's offending in an area he knows well.'

Kesey swallowed the last of her toast, a small piece of crust, washing it down with a mouthful of bitter coffee.

'Yeah, I appreciate that's likely, but what about the Bristol case?'

'That may have nothing to do with ours. The van could be a different one entirely. There's a lot of white vans on the road, thousands of them.'

Kesey wasn't wholly convinced, but she silently acknowledged that Lewis had a valid point. The link was a possibility, no more than that.

'What do you make of that name, Moloch?'

'It's got to be a Welsh thing.'

'How can you be so certain?'

'It's the *ch*. The Welsh alphabet is different from the English. It's one letter, commonly used, like *chwarae* for "play" or *diolch* for "thanks". It's pronounced as if you've got phlegm in your throat. Cerys reckons the bloke had an English accent. But I'd say he's either Welsh or knows the language. Maybe he's a learner. That could be another point of enquiry if we get nothing else.'

Kesey pressed her lips together. She'd tried to learn a few essential Welsh words and phrases, but it proved challenging.

'How certain can we be that the man who met Lucy at the café is the same man who abducted her? Halliday says it's a slam dunk. But I want to hear it from you.'

'I had some stills blown up from the CCTV. I showed them to Cerys – it's him. And anyway, the fingerprints are right. We've got them on the letter he sent her and the package sent to her mother.'

'But they're not on record?' She'd known the answer before asking the question.

'No such luck.'

Kesey nodded, deep in analytical thought, considering her options. Lewis had said much the same as Halliday. She'd simply wanted to allow her second in command to say it for himself.

'That is good enough for me. Did you talk to Halliday about a potential press conference? We've got a good amount of information. Asking for the public's help seems a logical next step. Someone must know the bastard. Someone must have seen him. I don't think we've got anything to lose.'

Lewis made a grumbling sound deep in his throat before speaking. 'I had a word with Clive Larkin at the *Herald*. We used to play rugby together back in the day. He ran an article mentioning the van and the driver's description. It was picked up by one of the nationals. We got a couple of calls after that, but nothing useful. I'd have sorted out a full press confer-ence soon enough if you hadn't come back, but now it's over to you.'

Kesey knew such things were well out of her sergeant's comfort zone, but she chose not to comment. Her question had been more a means of a confirmation than anything else. His reply had come as no surprise. She thought Ray should have acted more quickly, and Halliday too. The press conference was well overdue. The investigation had progressed far too slowly. But there seemed little purpose in saying it. What was done, was done.

'I'll have another word with Halliday today to get it sorted. Speak to the mother for me to tell her what we're planning. I'll give the father a ring. Let's aim for tomorrow afternoon at three. We can use the conference room. The media are already interested. It shouldn't be any problem getting them here.'

Lewis rose stiffly to his feet, a slight groan accompanying the effort of it all.

'Nice to see you, Laura. Is there anything else, or can I sod off and leave you in peace?'

'I want the entire team together for a briefing at four this afternoon. Sort it out for me and make sure you're there. I want everyone crystal clear what's expected of them.'

Lewis gave a little curtsey and saluted. 'Yes, ma'am, anything you say. Your wish is my command.'

Kesey tried her best not to laugh. The last thing she wanted was to encourage him. It didn't take much, and everyone in the canteen was watching. For some reason, she felt more self-conscious than usual. She wasn't sure why.

'Yeah, thanks very much, Ray, hilarious as always. I'll sign you up for the Christmas concert.'

He saluted for a second time.

'I'll let you know if I find out anything useful at Fisher's place.'

She lifted her coffee cup close to her mouth, speaking before drinking. 'You do that – I'm here all day. Now piss off and do something useful.'

He looked at her with a lopsided grin. 'So I'm still on the case?'

Kesey was unsure if his response was sarcasm or a genuine query. She decided to opt for the latter; better safe than sorry. The big man sometimes needed reassurance for all of his alpha-male bluster. The occasional pat on the back could work wonders.

'Of course you are. You've told me you're going to see Fisher. Now get it done. We'll chat about what comes next when you come back.'

32

Lewis was glad, at least in part, that Kesey was back in charge. As he drove towards Fisher's Scrapyard in the nearby industrial town of Llanelli, he realised he was happy in his first-line management role. He'd sat and passed his inspectors' exam many years before, but he'd never really wanted promotion. The extra cash would have been nice, but he didn't need the additional responsibility or paperwork that went with it. Being a sergeant was like wearing an old pair of comfortable slippers. He was a front-line investigative copper, no more and no less, and there was nothing wrong with that.

Lewis popped the last chunk of a family-sized fruit-and-nut chocolate bar into his open mouth as he drove through the yard's gates, bringing the CID car to a sudden skidding halt for no other reason than he enjoyed doing it. He exited the vehicle on virtual autopilot as Carl Fisher appeared from his corrugated-iron office building. Lewis had been in the job a long time. He knew what he was going to do and how he would do it. His actions were instinctive, born of experience, requiring little thought. He strode straight towards Fisher, staring at the younger man with unblinking eyes, never looking away.

'Where's your fucking van, Carl?'

'And a good morning to you as well, Sergeant Lewis, it's been too long.'

'Don't take the piss. Answer the fucking question.'

Fisher held his hands wide.

'I've got three vans. Which one are we talking about?'

'The white Luton, the heap of crap that's more rust than metal. A vehicle matching its description was used for the abduction of two young women, one in Bristol and one local. Neither woman has been seen since. We could be talking murder.'

All of a sudden, Fisher didn't look quite so cocky.

'No fucking way, that's got nothing to do with me.'

'Where's the van?'

Fisher took a backward step. 'It's, err, it's in the shed having the bodywork sorted.'

'What's that supposed to mean, exactly?'

'We're patching the rust and giving it a paint job.'

'You have got to be kidding me. Don't even try telling me this is a coincidence.'

Fisher frowned hard.

'I don't know what you're talking about.'

Lewis's expression hardened. 'Show me.'

Fisher led the way, with Lewis walking close behind. The detective's instincts were telling him something wasn't right. Fisher was twitchy.

Lewis walked around the van, closely studying the bodywork, which now looked immaculate, almost like new. If it was the van he was looking for, the number plates had been changed again. Lewis opened the rear doors, peering inside, using his phone's torch function to increase the available light. The smell of bleach couldn't have been more obvious, assaulting his nostrils as he looked around. He couldn't get his head out of there quickly enough as his eyes began to sting. He looked in the driver's cab, finding much the same.

'Why is this thing so clean, Carl? What the hell are you hiding?'

'Fuck all. Honestly, I haven't been anywhere near Bristol. And I wouldn't grab a woman even if I had. You know me, you know that's not my thing.'

Lewis knew he had a point.

'Then why the bleach?'

'It's not bleach, it's the stuff we use to get rid of oil stains.'

'Who else has driven it?'

'No one, it's been here in the yard for months, waiting for the work to be done. It's only now I've got round to it. It's been a busy time. I'm doing the Luton up to sell. I wasn't even sure where the keys were until I found them this morning. If you'd come this time yesterday, it would still have been outside in the yard. If I need a van, I use my Transit.'

Lewis looked Fisher in the eye, looking for any sign he was lying. It all seemed too much of a coincidence. He pointed towards the van, now even more sure that the scrap dealer was hiding something.

'I'm going to get the scenes-of-crime officers to go over every inch of that thing. And if there's anything to find, they'll find it. If anyone else has driven it, now's the time to say. You don't want to go down for being an accessory. Anything to tell me before I make the call?'

'You've got this one wrong. None of this has got anything to do with me. I can't tell you any more than I already have.'

'How do you fancy the tax people having a good look at your books?'

Fisher dropped his head. 'I've never hurt a woman in my life, never have, never fucking would. I've got no time for the scum who do that sort of shit. If I knew anything, I'd tell you. But I can't because I don't know nothing.'

'Give me the keys.'

'For fuck's sake, give me a break.'

'The keys.'

Fisher reluctantly handed them over.

'Is this the only set?'

Fisher nodded. 'Yeah.'

'If it turns out you're lying, I *will* nick you.'

'I lost the others years back. You've got the only ones.'

Lewis locked all the van's doors with a gloved hand, preparing to leave. He tried each in turn, ensuring they were secure.

'It'll be collected and taken to headquarters later today for a full inspection. I will find out if you've got any involvement in these crimes, so I'm giving you one final chance. It will be a lot easier on you if you cooperate. Don't make me come back here to drag you off in cuffs.'

'You've known me since I was a kid. I'm not a violent man. I think you know that. If two women are missing, I'm sorry, really I am. But you're wasting your time. I don't know how many times I've got to say it. It's got fuck all to do with me.'

33

Halliday and Lewis were already seated behind three adjoining tables covered with pristine white tablecloths when Kesey led Graham and Myra Williams into the West Wales Police Headquarters conference room at five to three in the afternoon on Thursday 18 June. The three stopped briefly when met by a barrage of flashing cameras and lively journalistic chatter, but they were soon seated alongside Halliday, who was resplendent in his best dress uniform despite his plainclothes CID role. Anything to be the centre of attention.

Kesey sat next to the chief super with Mr and Mrs Williams next to her. She noticed that Graham was holding his wife's hand the entire time, gripping it tightly, offering what support he could in the difficult circumstances, not letting go. Both parents looked somewhat shell-shocked, even the father, despite his years working in the public eye. The mother looked exhausted in spite of expertly applied make-up and a brown shoulder-length wig with a low fringe that came close to her eyes. It was blatantly evident that events were taking their toll.

Halliday seemed keen to ingratiate himself with Graham Williams. Kesey thought it typical of the man as he stood to shake the MP's free hand with a nod and suitably welcoming words. It was almost as if Myra Williams wasn't there at all. Kesey gave Lewis a knowing sideways look.

Both officers understood exactly what Halliday was up to and why he was doing it. The slimeball never missed a trick; anything to climb the greasy pole to the top of his profession. It was all about making a good impression, self-serving ambition, no more and no less. The man really was a toad.

Halliday rose to his feet at precisely three o'clock, standing directly under a large West Wales Police logo on the white wall behind him. He waited for the chatter to slowly subside to virtual silence before addressing the twenty or so representatives of the media. He raised a hand in the air as if stopping traffic, silencing one last whispered conversation between two journalists in the back row of four, and then spoke, clearly enunciating each carefully chosen word in his privately educated Southern accent. He seemed in his element, taking obvious pleasure in his high-profile role.

'I'd like to start by welcoming you all to West Wales Police Headquarters. For those of you who don't know me, I am Detective Chief Superintendent Nigel Halliday, the head of the force's Criminal Investigation Department. Also present is Detective Inspector Laura Kesey, the senior investigating officer for the case, Detective Sergeant Raymond Lewis, her second in command, and Mr and Mrs Williams, the parents of Lucy Williams, the missing girl. I'm going to start by asking DI Kesey to outline events as we know them. I'll then ask Mr and Mrs Williams to add anything they'd like to say. And finally, there'll be the opportunity for questions. I would ask that you keep those questions until the end to make this process as smooth and helpful as possible.'

He turned to look at Kesey, who was dressed in the smart black trouser suit and white blouse she reserved for such occasions.

'Without any further delay, Laura, I'll hand over to you. Please try to be as concise as possible.'

Halliday returned to his seat as Kesey walked around to the front of the three tables, standing a few short feet from the lens of a BBC Wales television camera operated by a middle-aged male journalist she'd met before. She looked first at him and then at the seated crowd. She cleared her throat.

'Ray, if you could put up the first slide, please.'

Lewis pressed a button on a table-mounted projector, displaying a large ten-by-six-foot colour photo of Lucy's smiling face on the white wall to the right side of the force's logo. Kesey looked back at the image for a brief moment before speaking again.

'Lucy Williams has now been missing for fifteen days. We have very good reason to believe she has been abducted.'

She waited for the resulting chatter to die down before continuing, glad her initial statement had grabbed the room's attention.

'Lucy was seen leaving the Lammas Street Gallery here in town at approximately one o'clock on the afternoon of the fourth of this month.'

She turned to Lewis, who was already reaching for the projector.

'If you could put the second slide on now, please, Ray.'

A large image of Fisher's van was displayed on the wall where Lucy's pretty face had appeared only a short time before. Gove, complete with wig and beard, could be seen in the driver's seat, although the image remained grainy despite Digital Forensics' best efforts. Lucy was slumped in the passenger seat next to him. Kesey pointed towards the photo.

'This is the last time we know of Lucy's whereabouts. The image was taken from CCTV here in town exactly eight minutes after she left the Lammas Street Gallery and got into the van, parked on the opposite side of the road, close to the Taste Of Rome Italian restaurant. Lucy was seen speaking to the van's driver before she got in. We know he refers to himself as Moloch – that's M-o-l-o-c-h – although that may well not be the name by which he's commonly known. Enquiries with the various government agencies haven't identified the name in any official records. It translates from the Welsh as *please praise*. The van had false number plates, so we know the man actively sought to hide his identity. If you could show the next slide now, please, Ray.'

A blown-up image of Gove's face taken from CCTV now appeared on the wall in black and white.

'This is the clearest image we have of our suspect. You can see that he's slim, wearing glasses, and he appears to have short grey hair and a neatly trimmed matching beard, although, and this is important, statements suggest these *may* be false. I would stress that's only a hypothesis at this time, but I have good reason to believe it's a strong possibility. The same van, possibly driven by the same driver, is also implicated in the abduction of a young female Bristol sex worker, who, like Lucy, is still missing. I'm certain you can all appreciate the seriousness of the situation.'

Kesey took two steps towards the TV camera, looking directly into the lens.

'Someone must know who Moloch is. And someone must know where the van is. Someone may even know where Lucy is. It is imperative that any member of the public with information contacts the police as a matter of the utmost urgency.'

Kesey waited a brief moment for Lewis to display a telephone number on the wall behind her. She pointed towards it before returning her attention to the room.

'My team is ready and waiting for the public's calls. Anyone wishing to contact us can ring this number twenty-four hours a day or contact their local police station. If you have any information, anything at all, please don't hesitate to ring. Let the police decide if it's relevant. You could be saving Lucy's life. Now, I'd like to invite Mr Williams to speak.'

Very unusually for a press conference, no one said a word as Graham Williams stood, letting go of his wife's hand for the first time. Kesey could see that he was making every effort to compose himself. The man was struggling with the strain of it all. He raised a hand to his mouth, coughing twice.

'Thank you, DI Kesey, your help is very much appreciated. As Laura said, my wonderful daughter has now been missing for fifteen days days. She's an intelligent, talented, hard-working girl, employed as a lecturer at the local art college here in town. She's beautiful, she's kind, she's generous and she's loyal. My wife and I are blessed to have her as a daughter.' He stalled, wiping a tear from his eye. 'The idea that someone has harmed, or may harm her, is truly too much to bear. I'd willingly take her place if I could. I want to make a personal appeal to anyone with information to come forward. If you're a parent, I'm sure you can understand just how desperate my wife and I are feeling. Any help would be hugely appreciated. And finally, I'd like to speak directly to the man who took Lucy. I'm asking you not to harm her and to free her from wherever you're keeping her.' He stalled again, sucking in the air. 'If our lovely daughter is alive, please let her go.'

Graham Williams returned to his seat, once again gripping his wife's hand in his. Halliday turned to her with a thin smile that seemed entirely inappropriate in the circumstances.

'Did you want to add anything, Mrs Williams? Or shall I ask for questions?'

Myra struggled to stand, placing her hands on the tabletop to assist herself from her chair. She was only on her feet for a matter of seconds before her legs gave way, causing her to fall backwards, hitting the floor hard, her head bouncing off the thin blue carpet. Kesey was already dialling 999, calling for an ambulance by the time Graham Williams knelt at his wife's side, loosening the top two buttons of her blouse to aid her shallow breathing. Kesey noticed he adjusted her wig, no doubt in the interests of her dignity. He whispered words of reassurance until two paramedics in dark-grey uniforms arrived in the conference room about ten minutes later. Halliday sent the news reporters on their way, making his apologies while the paramedics did their job, completing vital checks, assessing the risks of serious harm. Lewis headed back to his office as Kesey accompanied Mr and Mrs Williams through the police station in the direction of the ambulance. Myra was carried on a stretcher, breathing more strongly now but still unable to speak.

As Kesey waved the ambulance away, she thought things really couldn't have gone any worse. Three journalists were taking photographs of the ambulance as it left the car park, travelling in the direction of town. Kesey pondered that it wasn't exactly the news report she'd had in mind. Hopefully, the publicity would still come to something. All she could do was wait for the evening news.

34

Cerys was feeling the pressure as she stood in her parents' kitchen on 19 June. It seemed almost every aspect of her life was falling apart. Lucy was a major concern, and now her mum too, back in hospital with anxiety, as if the cancer wasn't enough. Cerys feared that as bad as things were, they were about to get worse. She told herself that she somehow had to cope as she had as a child. She had to find that same courage. Something it was becoming increasingly harder to do with each day that passed.

Myra Williams had been kept in hospital overnight due to the adverse effects of severe stress. She was prescribed tranquillisers for the first time but allowed home the following day on the condition she rested. Graham provided the transport, and Cerys was already waiting at the house when her parents arrived. Cerys was in two minds about telling her parents about the parcel sitting on the kitchen table for the past five minutes. The parcel with the same blood-red ink and flowing script she knew so very well. She'd considered ringing the police herself rather than wait for her father, but now it was too late. She hurriedly hid the package in a saucepan cupboard when she heard her parents' car coming up the drive towards the house. Her mother had more than enough to deal with without the shock of the delivery.

Cerys forced a less than convincing smile when she met her parents at the front door, holding it wide for them to enter. She already had the kettle on as she ushered them in. Cerys led her mother to the comfortable lounge as her father began sorting through a pile of letters she'd left sitting on a small hall table next to a Victorian coat stand.

'Sit yourself down, Mum. It would be best if you rested today. Dad told me what the doctor said. You look exhausted.'

Myra removed her wig, placing it to one side, hiding it under a cushion.

'Is there any news? Have the police phoned the house?'

'Not while I've been here, I'm sorry, no.'

'Dad spoke to Laura Kesey late last night. They'd had a lot of calls after the news report but nothing truly significant.'

'Someone must know something.'

Myra averted her eyes to the wall.

'A cup of tea would be nice.'

'The kettle's already boiling.'

'Put a spot of brandy in it for me, but don't tell your father – he'd disapprove. And fetch me my painkillers, the new ones. There's a packet on the shelf next to the fridge.'

Graham Williams appeared at the lounge door, carrying his paperwork in one hand as Cerys was about to head to the kitchen. She took the opportunity to gesture to him with her eyes. She suspected her mother would realise something was up, but she felt it was the best option she had.

'Can you give me a hand in the kitchen for a minute, Dad?'

Cerys closed the kitchen door after them and opened the cupboard, pointing to the brown parcel on the middle shelf of three. 'That thing arrived a few minutes before you did.'

Graham's face became ashen. 'Oh, God, no, not again – what's the maniac sent this time? Fetch me a bag, a carrier bag, and some gloves, any sort of gloves. I don't want to touch the damn thing. I'll get it straight to the police station and let DI Kesey deal with it there. You did right not involving your mum; she's at breaking point. Tell her I've had an urgent work call, and I'll go out through the back door.'

* * *

Graham Williams handed Kesey an orange supermarket carrier bag, explaining its contents about fifteen minutes later while they stood in her office. She looked at the parcel with a concern she couldn't hope to hide as a sudden coldness hit her core. She examined the postmark, Swansea, and then opened the package carefully, ensuring to preserve evidence, as Graham watched from a few feet away. Kesey cut the clear tape securing the parcel with sharp scissors, lifted the box lid, gasping slightly as she looked inside. She turned to face Williams as the sour smell of decay filled the room despite a half-open window letting in the morning air. She could see the fear in his eyes.

'I'm sorry, Mr Williams, there's no easy way of saying this; it's a partially decayed human hand. I'd say, either an older child's or a woman's. One of the fingers appears to have bite marks on the tip. An animal's possibly, or human, it's hard to say.'

The MP took a tentative step towards her. 'Show me.'

'I'm not sure that's a good idea.'

'Show me! I need to see. If that's Lucy's hand, I've got to know. Nothing can be worse than the pictures in my head.'

Kesey nodded; she knew he was right. Were she in his place, she'd need to see too. She held the box open for him to peer in.

Graham lifted his eyes, looking heavenward. He pressed one hand to his stomach.

'Thank God, it's not my daughter's hand.'

Kesey tilted her head and paused.

'Are you certain? Do you need to look again?'

'That won't be necessary. It's too small to be Lucy's. Her hands are significantly bigger, and her nails aren't that long. She keeps hers trimmed short, always has – she used to bite them as a child.'

Kesey closed the box, pursing her lips in thought. She pushed the window wider open, sucking in the fresh Welsh air.

'I'll get it to the lab for tests.'

Williams slumped into the nearest chair.

'I think you may have found your Bristol prostitute.'

'There's every chance you're right. We'll know with certainty within a few hours.'

'Some other poor father will get the news he's dreading.'

Kesey closed the box, sealing it in a clear plastic evidence bag. 'If it is the Bristol girl, she was a nineteen-year-old who grew up in care.'

Graham looked across the room with an empty stare, speaking to the air rather than making eye contact. His face was expressionless. 'If the same man has Lucy, it could be her hand next. Or it could be even worse.'

'We're doing all we can to catch the bastard.'

'Let's hope it's soon enough to save my daughter's life.'

'How's Mrs Williams?'

His voice was deadpan. 'She's home from the hospital.'

'Does she know about the package?'

He shook his head; his movements precise and functional. 'No.'

'Do you plan to tell her?'

'No, or at least, not yet. Myra's not a well woman; I don't know how much more she can take.'

35

It took Carl Fisher almost half an hour to find the private road leading to Gove's luxury Georgian home on Saturday 20 June, despite using his satnav. He passed the heavily wooded entrance off the quiet B-road three times before finally spotting it on the fourth attempt. It was almost as if Gove had allowed the foliage to become overgrown to hide the entrance from any passing traffic. Fisher drove the newly painted Luton slowly down the stone-strewn track until he had his first view of the imposing house. Gove's German SUV was parked a few yards from the front door on an area of even gravel bordered by lawn.

Fisher parked the Luton next to the SUV, exited his vehicle without bothering to lock it, and began banging on the front door, becoming increasingly frustrated when he didn't receive an answer as quickly as he'd hoped. He peered through the brass letterbox into the grand hall and could hear country music coming from somewhere inside. He walked away to his right, looking into one six-paned sash window after another until he spotted Gove sitting alone on a brown Chesterfield leather sofa in what looked like a cinema room. He was eating popcorn from a red cardboard container while watching what looked like an X-rated horror film on the large wall-mounted screen, featuring a naked, bruised and battered girl captive in what looked like a cellar. Just for a moment, Fisher considered walking away, leaving the property as if he'd never been there at all. But the lure of potentially easy money was enough to override his reticence. If Gove wanted to watch that repulsive shit, it was up to him, each to their own. The bloke was obviously loaded. That's what mattered. He wasn't there to be Gove's friend. He was there for cash.

Gove looked up, meeting Fisher's eyes when he rapped on the glass with the knuckles of his right hand. Fisher watched as Gove hurriedly switched off the film and stood, glaring at him with angry eyes. Gove walked across the room, disappearing from Fisher's view, and then appeared at the front door less than a minute later. Gove's hands were behind his back as he stood there in the entrance.

'What the hell are you doing here, Carl?'

Fisher stood directly in front of Gove, about six feet apart.

'What the fuck have you been doing? Did you see the Welsh news? I've already had the police at the yard sniffing around. I don't need that sort of attention. I want ten-thousand quid cash in used notes if I'm going to keep my mouth shut. And I want it quickly, as soon as the bank's open. You've put me in a difficult position, and I want paying. It's the cash, or I'm grassing you up.'

Gove was holding a yellow taser when he took his arm from behind his back. Fisher froze for a fraction of a second and then turned to run, but he wasn't nearly quick enough, collapsing, shaking to the ground when Gove fired, the metal barb striking the approximate centre of Fisher's back between his shoulder blades.

Fisher had never felt such pain. He urgently tried to roll away without success as Gove threw the taser aside, lifting a large, heavy stone from a nearby rockery and holding it high above his head. Fisher closed his eyes as Gove brought the stone crashing down for the first time. Fisher felt an explosion in his head, but nothing after that.

36

Gove shoved Lucy up the cellar steps, through the house, down the hall and out through the front door, to where Fisher's body was lying a few feet from his Luton van. Fisher's head and face were a bruised and battered, bloody mess, unrecognisable as the man who'd arrived at the house only twenty minutes before. Gove raised a blood-spattered hand, pointing at his victim.

'Look at him, Lucy, look at that filthy, rotten cunt. That's what happens to people who betray me. And now, as if his disloyalty wasn't enough to ruin my day, I've got to get rid of the rat's body. That's where you come in. You're going to help me with the disposal of rubbish.'

It was the first time Lucy had been to the front of the house since her unconscious arrival. Gove could see she was looking around, at the trees, the fields, the track leading away.

'Don't think you're getting away from here, Lucy. There's not another house for miles. Don't even think about betraying me as he did. You'd end up sharing the same grave.'

'The thought d-didn't, it didn't c-c-cross my mind.'

Gove kicked one of Fisher's booted feet hard.

'Look at this pile of steaming shit. I have no desire to cut up a man; the thought repulses me. There's no beauty in him. And so, you're going to earn your keep. You're going to do it for me. Another test you have to pass. All part of your evolution. If you're going to be my soulmate, there are hurdles to jump.'

Lucy's tears began to flow.

'I'm, I'm, I'm not s-strong enough.'

He drew his arm back, slapping her face with an open hand. She regained her footing after staggering backwards.

'Do you think I haven't considered that, you ridiculous girl? I'm going to help you drag that worthless pile of meat as far as the back garden, and then I'm going to allow you to use my electric chainsaw. I'll even teach you how to operate it. Once he's dismembered, you can burn him and bury what's left. There's petrol and a spade in the shed. Once you're done and back in the cellar, I'll get rid of the van. We're a team, you and me. This is your chance to prove your worth. Succeed at this, and I'll know you're worth keeping alive.'

37

Lucy looked at Moloch and then around her the following day. The room was impressive, with its large screen, surround-sound speakers, cinema seating, and all that went with it. In very different circumstances, in her previous life, she'd have been looking forward to enjoying a convivial evening of entertainment in such a place. Moloch was smiling, a grin lighting up his features as she stood waiting for his next instruction. He turned in a small circle, spinning on the ball of one foot and pointing in every direction.

'What do you think? Wonderful, eh? I like to think it must be one of the most magnificent private cinema rooms in the entire country – not just in Wales, but in the whole of the UK! It might even be number one – it wouldn't surprise me. It's worthy of my film. Only the best will do.'

She wondered what to say. Something positive would be best, anything to avoid another slap, punch, kick or worse. She glanced towards a shuttered window and tried to forget what she'd done to the body, but the congealed blood left on the stony ground close to the front door flashed in her mind. Dark red. Brutal, offering hope. Someone might see it; someone might call for help.

Say something, she had to say something.

'The, the, room's very, it's very n-nice.'

Moloch's smile became a hateful glare. His eyes were wide, showing the whites.

'Nice? *Nice?* Is that really the best you can do? I would have thought it's a *lot* better than *nice*.'

She rushed her response. 'It's wonderful, truly w-wonderful.'

He relaxed slightly. 'Now, that is so much better – what a good girl you are. Don't just stand there, take a seat, sit at the front. Welcome to the world premiere of my masterpiece. The film is about to start.'

Lucy sat as instructed, and Moloch joined her on the next seat along. She reached down to where the shackles were cutting into her left leg, trying to find some relief from where her skin bled just above the ankle. Red raw, cut down to the bone.

Moloch turned in his seat to face her. Not for the first time, she could feel his hot breath on her face. She loathed that feeling. She despised everything about him. He was the first man she'd ever encountered with no redeeming qualities whatsoever. She hadn't known such people existed until now.

'Would you like some popcorn and a drink before we start? It's an extraordinary event. I want to make sure you're comfortable.'

The irony wasn't lost on Lucy, even in her weakened state. She thought it best to say yes. Anything to please him even slightly until the chance of escape finally came, if, indeed, it ever did.

'That, that would be l-lovely, thank you, sir.'

He handed her both items with a frown that made her shiver. It was so very difficult to decide on the best course of action or appropriate choice of words. Placating him, alleviating his explosive rages to any great extent, seemed to be getting harder by the day. She'd become only too aware that he took sadistic pleasure in hurting her. Inflicting suffering turned him on. She couldn't rationalise with the man like you would a normal human being, because he wasn't normal. She couldn't appeal to his better nature because he didn't have one. All she could do was follow his instructions and hope for rescue, surviving long enough to get out of there. She'd even looked for the possibility of a weapon, a sharp knife with which to stab him, or a heavy hammer with which to cave in his skull. But he was always careful, keeping a close eye on her at all times, feeding her only limited nutrition, ensuring her weakened state. Even walking up the cellar steps was becoming more challenging. She was out of breath and panting when she reached the top. In the unlikely event she somehow persuaded him to remove the metal shackles, the idea of running seemed a lost cause. She was still clinging to hope as she sat in her cinema seat, dreading what she was about to see on screen. But holding onto that hope was getting more difficult. Occasionally, as she worked to complete her cellar mural, she thought death might offer a welcome release. If it wasn't for her pregnancy, she'd likely have embraced it.

Moloch performed a ten-second drum roll with his voice, eyes sparkling, his body in constant motion. Everything about him communicated excitement, as if the prospect of showing the film was one of the greatest moments of his life.

Lucy dropped her popcorn to the floor as he reached out, grabbing her by the throat, digging in the tips of his fingers, making her cough and splutter. He looked directly into her eyes and retained eye contact as he spoke.

'Watching this film is your penultimate test. Pass today, and we move onto the main course, the one final test to come. You may find some of what you're about to see shocking – there'll be a lot of screaming, blood, and a great deal of gore. I'm well aware of your regrettable sensibilities. You haven't yet overcome those entirely despite my best efforts. But if you look away from the screen or close your eyes even for a single second, I will use a razor-sharp blade to slice off your eyelids. You'll never close your eyes again.' He released his hand, allowing her to breathe more easily as she gasped for air. 'That's the deal. I hope I've made myself clear. Say yes if you understand.'

Lucy whispered her confirmation in a croaky voice.

'I didn't quite hear you.'

She said yes again, louder this time, her bruised throat hurting with the effort.

'Yes, what?'

'Yes, sir.'

He sat back in his seat, unfastening the zip of his trousers with his legs stretched out in front of him. He was looking at the screen now rather than her.

'Okay, that's good to hear – we got there in the end. Let's make a start.'

38

Kesey pushed her overtime budget report aside on Monday 22 June, answering her office phone almost as soon it rang. She was doing her best to ignore a persistent headache as she held it to her face.

'DI Kesey.'

'Hello, ma'am. It's PC Nicholl on the front desk.'

'How many times have I got to tell you? Call me *boss* or *guv* – I'm not the frigging Queen. *Ma'am* makes me feel about a hundred and ten.'

'Sorry, ma'am, I'll try to remember.'

Kesey swore under her breath.

'How can I help you, Ben?'

'I've got a Dr Sally Barton here with me who wants to talk to the officer in charge of the Lucy Williams case. She has some information to share. She thinks she may be able to help.'

Kesey sat upright in her seat as a wave of adrenalin caused her heartbeat to race.

'Are any of the interview rooms free?'

'All three.'

Kesey was already on her feet.

'Put her in Room One and make certain she doesn't leave before I get there. This could be important. I'm on my way.'

* * *

Kesey entered the interview room to be met by a dark-haired woman who looked to be in her mid to late forties. She was casually dressed in fitted blue jeans, a chequered shirt with a grandad collar, walking boots, and long red socks almost to the knee over her trousers. Her face was lightly made up and well-tanned by the early-summer sun. Above all, Kesey quickly decided her potential witness looked comfortable in her own skin. She reached out to shake the doctor's hand.

'Detective Inspector Laura Kesey, nice to meet you. I'm the senior investigating officer for the Lucy Williams case. I'm told you may have some information for me. Please take a seat.'

The two women sat on either side of the small interview-room table.

'What I've got to tell you may be relevant, or may not. To be honest, I was in two minds about coming at all.'

Kesey took a notepad and pen from a table drawer. She handed them to Dr Barton with a reassuring smile. 'If you could write your full name, address and best contact number down for me, that'll save us a bit of time.'

The doctor followed instructions, writing in bold capitals before pushing the notepad back across the table. Kesey accepted it gratefully, together with the biro.

'Okay, that's the formalities out of the way. What have you got to tell me?'

Dr Barton rubbed her jaw. 'I'm not sure where to start.'

'How about at the beginning? I usually find that's best.'

The doctor nodded. 'I'm on holiday in the area with my partner. We've got a shared interest in historic buildings, castles and the like, and there's more per square mile in Wales than anywhere else on Earth. We've rented a lovely cottage with a view of the estuary in Ferryside. Llansteffan Castle is right across the water. We've been here for ten days with another four to go.'

There was a tightness to Kesey's face as she responded, moving the interview along, keen to get to the point. 'That's all very interesting, but what's the relevance to Lucy Williams?'

'Yes, I was just coming to that. I work as a senior forensic psychologist at the Ashdean Hospital, a high-security facility in Kent. I saw a report of Lucy's abduction on the Welsh evening news. I couldn't help but notice that the details of the case, the MO, are remarkably similar to that used by a serial killer I've worked with, a paranoid schizophrenic named Fredrick Harrison. He drove a white van, abducting his victims off the streets, sometimes in broad daylight.'

Kesey's eyes narrowed, her head cocked to one side.

'Are you suggesting this Harrison may be the man we're looking for?'

'No, that's not what I'm saying – he's still locked up, has been for years. I suspect he will be for the rest of his life.'

Kesey drew a breath, releasing it before speaking. 'I'm sorry then, but I don't understand the relevance.'

'About five years back, I interviewed a male nurse several times as part of a disciplinary process, a man named Marcus Gove. Gove had become overfamiliar with Harrison, developing an excessive interest in his crimes, which went far beyond the professional.'

Kesey leaned forward, sitting on the edge of her chair. 'Can you expand on that for me?'

'It got to the point where Gove actually *admired* Harrison. He began to justify Harrison's murders, seeing them as a triumph over society's restrictive moral framework. Those are his words, not mine. He really did start to worry me. By the time Gove left the hospital, I was beginning to question his mental health. I was starting to think he may pose a danger himself.'

'You said Gove left. When was that, and in what circumstances?'

'He resigned about five years ago – he won the lottery. He walked out on me at his final appointment and never came back. He was a particularly unpleasant man by that time, disturbed. He actually assaulted me, licked my face, grabbed my arm.'

'Were the police involved?'

'He was leaving. I knew a conviction was highly unlikely, and it didn't seem worth the hassle. I decided to let it go.'

'Did Gove ever mention the name *Moloch*? M-o-l-o-c-h?'

'No, I'm sure I'd remember if he had.'

Kesey's shoulders slumped slightly. She made a written note in her pocketbook, writing quickly, keen to ask her next question. It was a question that really mattered. She jittered a foot against the floor.

'Okay, let's move on. You said you saw the report on the Welsh evening news. It included an image of the suspect taken from CCTV. Could that man be Marcus Gove?'

Dr Barton pressed her lips together in a slight grimace.

'Gove didn't immediately come to mind at the time. The build was right, but Gove was cleanly shaven with an entirely bald head. And he didn't wear glasses, at least not then, never that I saw. There was something familiar about the man on screen, though, his eyes possibly, but I couldn't think why at the time. But then, this morning, about an hour ago, I was sitting at a café window here in town with my partner when Gove walked past, looking just as he did when I last saw him at the hospital.'

'Are you certain it was him?'

Dr Barton touched her fingertips together. 'Yes, definitely, 100 per cent it was Gove – I haven't got a doubt in my mind. I'm not saying he abducted that poor young woman, but he may have – it's a possibility I can't rule out. I felt obliged to raise my observations with you. His being here in town could be a coincidence, or on the other hand, maybe it's not. I won't be at all surprised if he's the man you're looking for; I think it very likely he has the capacity to commit a crime of that nature.'

Kesey felt a lightness in her chest, her senses heightened.

'I'd like you to take another look at the CCTV image. I had a still photo of the suspect's face blown from the original. I'll just fetch it from my office – I'll be back with you in two minutes. There's a kitchen two doors down on the left if you fancy making yourself a cup of tea. Feel free to help yourself.'

'I'm fine, thanks. I haven't long had lunch.'

Kesey returned a short time later with the picture in her hand. She placed it on the desk in front of Barton without sitting herself.

'Take a good look, take your time, study it closely and tell me what you think.'

'Is it okay if I pick it up?'

'Yes, absolutely, please go ahead.'

Dr Barton held the grainy black-and-white image a few inches from her face, squinting, her forehead wrinkling.

'I can't say it's definitely Gove. But it could be, it certainly could be. There's something about his face, even as grainy as it is, a coldness that stuck in my mind.'

Kesey felt like jumping up, punching the air in relieved triumph, but she just smiled, retaining a professional persona. She could quite easily have hugged Barton, had it been appropriate. She took a statement form from the desk drawer before returning to her seat.

'Give me a second. I'll just make a quick call to get someone looking for Gove's address. And then we'll get something down on paper.'

Within a short time, Kesey had issued her order, focusing back on her witness.

'Okay, let's get on with that statement. If I write an outline of what you've told me, are you happy to read it and sign, confirming it as a true record?'

'Yes, that's not a problem, and if Gove did abduct that girl, I'd be happy to appear in court as a prosecution witness if required. I have expert-witness status. It's something I've done many times before.'

Kesey smiled more warmly this time as she prepared to start writing. The quicker the statement was complete and she could act on the information, the happier she'd be. Moments like this made the job worthwhile.

39

Kesey found Lewis tucking into a late lunch in the police canteen, a substantial meal of a crusty pie, eggs and chips, which didn't surprise her at all. She was too excited about the developments in the Williams case to bother commenting, not that Lewis would have listened, anyway. He looked up at her with a dribble of soft yolk running from the corner of his mouth, again talking with his mouth full.

'What are you looking so pleased with yourself about? Don't tell me Halliday's pissed off back to London.'

Kesey smiled at the familiar joke. She'd heard it many times but it amused her nonetheless.

'It's even better than that. I interviewed a witness in the Williams case about fifteen minutes ago, a Dr Barton. It's big, Ray, she works at a secure hospital in Kent. She's here on holiday. She saw the news report and she thinks she recognised our suspect. She named a man called Marcus Gove. I've run some checks – he's got no criminal record, just like our man, but he does live in this area. He's got a large place out in the wilds near Brechfa about twelve miles from town.'

'Do we know what vehicle he drives?'

Kesey lent her neck forward, paling slightly. 'I checked with the DVLA, and there's no Luton van registered in his name.'

Lewis chewed and swallowed.

'He could have borrowed it, I guess.'

'That's what I thought. She seems pretty certain it was him.'

Lewis forked four greasy chips into his mouth, washing them down with the last of his tea.

'Right then, let's visit this Gove character. Let's see what he's got to say for himself.'

'Get hold of one of the local magistrates and arrange a search warrant. Get it done now, quickly. Bethan Evans is always helpful – get on the phone, arrange to see her and get it signed yourself. I want everything done by the book.'

'Don't you always?'

Kesey pushed up her sleeve, checking her watch. 'You can drop the sarcasm, Ray. I don't want some clever barrister challenging any evidence on a technicality. And we're taking two uniform officers as backup. If Gove is our man, which seems likely, he could be dangerous. I don't want us taking any chances.'

Lewis pushed his empty plate aside before standing.

'Okay, looks like I better get on with it then.'

She checked her watch for a second time. 'It's twenty past two now. I'll meet you in reception at three. Fingers crossed, we'll have Lucy found and the bastard in custody by four o'clock.'

40

Lucy was teetering on the second step of the aluminium ladder, putting the finishing touches to her painting of a giant bull's head with four-foot horns, when Moloch entered the cellar. He was naked except for the black nylon belt and holster holding the yellow taser around his slim waist. He stood with his hands on his hips, leaning back slightly, watching from about ten feet away as she continued to work. Almost the entire cellar was painted now; the muscular man with the bovine head, the bronze cauldron, the blazing orange-yellow fire, the terrified children, they were all there. A few more hours of work and the project would be completed in line with Moloch's instructions. Lucy had no idea what would happen after that. She thought of the life inside her, the unborn child she wondered if she'd ever get the chance to meet. Her every effort to develop a relationship with her captor that could be manipulated in her favour had failed dismally. However challenging, however repulsive, nothing she did seemed to please him for very long. He was so unpredictable, so prone to violence. Was her end near? She wasn't sure, and a part of her no longer cared. She wanted to live, she wanted to be a mother, but as a free woman, not in the hands of a raving monster. Every day was a living nightmare that seemed to never end. And what life would any child have in Moloch's version of hell?

'Come on down, lovely Lucy. Off the ladder, that's it, that's enough painting for today. I require your undivided attention. This is an important day.'

She climbed down slowly, the weakness in her shackled legs making every movement difficult.

'Are you pleased with my work, sir?'

'I am, Lucy – it's to your credit. Now sit down on the floor, keep your mouth shut, not another word, and listen to what I've got to say.'

Lucy sat as instructed with her legs out in front of her, not knowing whether to look him in the face or avoid his eyes. There was no telling, and either option could result in threats, a beating or worse. In the end, she decided to focus on the painted wall just behind his head. It was as good a choice as any. She pressed her lips together, listening, not uttering a sound.

'I don't think it will come as any great surprise to you when I say I've been evaluating your performance since your arrival. Are you my soul-mate, or are you not? Are you the one, or do I need to keep searching? Your life, of course, depends on the answer.'

He began touching himself now as he paused between sentences, slowly massaging the swollen pink tip of his penis between thumb and fingers.

'I've been pleased by some aspects of your performance, naturally – the mural, as I mentioned before, and your disposal of Fisher's corpse was done with reasonable confidence and efficiency once you mastered the use of the chainsaw. Your tears were somewhat regrettable, and being sick as often as you were wasn't ideal, not with so little food in your belly, but over-all, you got the job done. And then we come to my film, my dark master-piece, my work of destructive genius. Had you looked away even once, I would have killed you. I would have torn you limb from limb. But in fair-ness, you didn't – you stared at the screen until my co-star breathed her last agonised breath. I don't think you enjoyed the film as much as I'd hoped or anticipated, but overall, despite that, I've decided to award you a pass. You'll undoubtedly learn to take greater pleasure in such things as time goes on. I never expected you to fully flower at this early stage. Such things take time. They did even for me.'

He walked towards her, now fully erect, his penis standing to attention, a beaming smile on his cleanly shaven face. There was a sheen of sweat on his brow. He was panting very slightly.

'I am delighted to inform you that you've now passed all but one of the tests I devised before your arrival. Pass the final trial, and you get to live. And not just live, but to live here with me as we explore the darkest of my fantasies, making them real. I hope you find that prospect as exciting as I do.'

He was only three feet from her now, his genitals in line with her face. She slowly pulled her head back, trying to move subtly so as not to anger him.

'I cannot wait to tell you this. I've been building up to it for days. Your final test will be your most challenging by far. I'm going to capture your bitch sister as I have others. She's going to join you here in your beautiful cellar home. And that's when things get *really* interesting. She'll be shackled to the wall, and then, if you want to survive, you'll cut her throat on film. Fail, and you both die together. I think that's reasonable. You get the one chance. I can't be any fairer than that.'

He moved forward, closing the gap between them. Lucy flinched as he reached down, grabbing her ears, sinking in his nails, making her squirm. She tried to turn her head without success, gagging, coughing, spluttering as he forced his erect penis into her mouth and down her throat. She pictured Cerys shackled, helpless and bleeding, as she suddenly jerked her head back, leaving only the top two inches of his phallus in her mouth as he began to move his hips. And then she bit down hard, using all the strength of her jaw, sinking in her teeth and shaking her head violently from side to side, first one way and then the other, as he screamed out, landing one hooking punch after another to her head and face. Moloch didn't reach for his taser, he kept punching, landing blow after vicious blow, but Lucy didn't let go. She clung on with everything she had, clamped onto his penis like a dog with a bone as his blood poured from her mouth, soaking her naked body, running down his legs. She heard a siren sounding somewhere in the distance, getting gradually louder as she bit down. The siren sounded much closer now as her teeth met, and she tore the head of his penis from its shaft. She spat it to the concrete floor as he staggered backwards, clutching his genitals in a hopeless attempt to stem the blood gushing from his body in an explosion of red. Lucy had never felt so relieved, never so resilient, never so powerful as she rose to her feet, watching as he slowly sank to the floor.

She pointed at him, jabbing out a finger, shouting her words, deliberately mimicking his own.

'Now it's your turn to listen to *me*, you crazy *bastard*. If you don't get help, you *will* die. Now, where is the key to the security doors? This is your one and only chance. If you give it to me, you live, and if you don't, you'll die. Make your choice.'

He looked up at her with a confused expression. Everything had changed, his survival hanging by a thread.

'It's, it's in a pouch on my belt. There's, there's a small zip on my left side, quickly, please. It's fucking agony, I'm losing a lot of blood.'

She heard voices calling out upstairs as she slowly approached Moloch, kneeling at his side. There were two voices, a man and a woman, both calling her name, both shouting, police. They must have seen the blood outside the front door.

Moloch lay back groaning in an ever-expanding pool of blood, still clutching what was left of his genitals as she reached out, undoing the zip, taking the key to freedom in her hand. She slipped in his blood as she got back to her feet but quickly regained her footing.

Lucy approached the cellar door, but she didn't open it. She formed one hand into a tight fist, banging on the metal surface while yelling loudly.

'Help, please help! I'm here; I'm down here. He's bleeding. Call an ambulance. Please get me out. I can't find the key.'

Lucy quickly returned to Moloch's side, kneeling by his head. His breathing was shallower now, his bare chest moving only slightly as the blood flow from his mutilated penis finally began to slow. He was close to unconsciousness, the light fading from his eyes as Lucy placed the key aside, squeezing his nostrils shut with one hand while covering his mouth with the open palm of the other. He struggled only slightly as she held her hand there, pressing down firmly enough to be effective but not hard enough to leave bruising, counting in her head until she was sure he was dead. She rolled away from his corpse with a newfound energy a short time later, the relief overwhelming.

Lucy unlocked the cellar's steel door just as the second door at the top of the stairs crashed open. She flinched, looking up, covering her naked, bloody body as best she could as two male uniformed police officers descended the steps towards her. She burst into a flood of tears, sinking to her knees as the taller of the two men handed her his softshell fleece.

The sight of the police was enough to make Lucy giddy. She was weak, cold and shaking as the officers led her upstairs towards the waiting detectives, still in shackles. Each step was a challenge but one she conquered gratefully.

She'd lost a good deal of weight and strength but she felt like dancing when she reached the living room. She smiled and then laughed as they approached the front door. Happy tears streamed from her eyes as she looked at the blood she'd left on a large stone, then stepped over it, leaving the house behind.

Outside, the sun was shining, the birds were singing, everything looked brighter, the sky, the flowers, the trees, more colourful than ever before. Her legs gave out as she tried to walk across the ground, but it didn't matter now. It was over; it really was over. She was free, her baby was safe, and the monster was no more.

EPILOGUE
ONE YEAR LATER

Lucy's baby daughter Ava was fast asleep, reclined in her pink pushchair, oblivious to events, as her mother entered Carmarthen's Lammas Street Gallery at seven o'clock on a warm Welsh summer evening. Even the sudden claps and camera flashes from the attendant guests and journalists failed to wake the young child, still lost to her dreams.

It was Lucy's first exhibition since escaping her tormentor's clutches and she silently acknowledged her nerves; even leaving home had sometimes been challenging since her trauma. But she told herself the exhibition had a purpose beyond mere entertainment. It mattered to her and others, too, in a way her art never had before.

As Lucy stood just inside the gallery door, she observed that her work now had more depth and meaning, reflecting the dark world she'd experienced at Moloch's hand. She took a deep breath, settling herself. She wanted to run, hide and be alone with her daughter. But there were things she needed to say, things she needed to do. Her life had a new purpose now. She now had over a million social media followers, was an influencer with a voice people listened to, particularly women and girls. She reminded herself of her determination to make that voice heard. *Come on, Lucy, you can do this – it'll be over soon. It would be best if you got it done.*

She glanced around the room with anxious eyes, searching for reassur-

ance. Her mother, father and sister were there, and the art college principal, close friends and DI Kesey and Ray. Lucy smiled as her mother
approached and lifted the baby from her pushchair, holding her close. She
looked so much better now that her cancer was in remission.

'Are you doing okay, Lucy?'

'Yeah, good, thanks. I'm delighted you've come.'

The proud grandmother rested Ava over one shoulder, gently patting
her back.

'Of course, I've come – I wouldn't have missed it for the world.'

'I'd better start saying hello to everyone. I can't put it off forever.'

'You're doing brilliantly, Lucy. Well done, you.'

Lucy smiled again, appreciating her mother's kind words.

'Are you okay holding Ava?'

'I'm just fine. Do what you need to do. I can always give her to Cerys if I
need to rest.'

Lucy took one last deep breath and then turned away, slowly circling
the room, saying hello, greeting everyone, accepting compliments with
good grace, making small talk, anything that helped create the right
atmosphere for success. She made her way to the far end of the room at
precisely seven-thirty, to where a small raised platform and polished steel
microphone on a matching stand were located against the white-painted
wall. The mic was plugged into an electric socket with a length of black
wire Lucy was careful not to trip over. In some strange way, it reminded her
of her time in the cellar; many things did, but she drove the intrusive
thoughts from her mind. This was her moment, all her efforts had led to
this, and she had to get it right.

Lucy trembled as she stepped onto the platform, her entire body shud-
dering as if frozen with cold. She tapped the mic three times to gain the
room's attention and then spoke in a sometimes faltering voice but one
strong with passion and emotion. She looked out on the small crowd.

'Welcome, and thank you all for coming. It's wonderful to see so many
of you here. And I'd like to say a special thank you to Katherine Garvey,
our local domestic violence refuge manager here in town. She does
wonderful work and collaborated closely with me as I prepared for this
evening.'

Lucy paused momentarily, took a breath, cleared her throat, and then continued.

'This exhibition isn't like any other I've ever worked on.' She raised a hand, pointing from one side of the room to another. 'And as you can see, there are twelve paintings in total, and each portrays the portrait of a real-life woman who died due to male violence. Some have said the paintings are shocking, and I admit, they are graphic, but I make no apology for that. Two women a week are killed by men in the UK, most by a current or former partner. Killings by strangers like the monster I encountered are thankfully rare by comparison, but they happen. I know that better than most. Make no mistake; there is a plague of male violence and toxic masculinity that urgently needs to change. That's why I'm here talking to you now.' She paused for a beat, meeting the eyes of each reporter in turn, searching them out. 'So, I'm sure you can all appreciate that much more needs to be done to change attitudes, support vulnerable females and bring abusers to justice. Therefore, this exhibition aims to increase public awareness of this very real issue and raise as much money as possible for the women's charities involved, not just here in Wales but in the rest of Britain, and ultimately, if we raise enough, throughout the world. That's my ambition. I want this to be the start of something that truly matters, a revolution, something big. Even the greatest of oak trees starts with an acorn. Tonight is my acorn, and it's going to grow.'

Lucy waited for the resulting applause to slowly subside before speaking again. She wiped a single tear from her face.

'I'm delighted to announce that the paintings will spend the next six months touring some of the UK's most prestigious galleries. And at the end of that process, they'll be publicly auctioned, with all the resulting funds going to relevant charities. Several high-profile female celebrities have already kindly offered their support, two of whom have experienced male violence themselves. I won't share their names now – that's for them – but they'll be making social media announcements tomorrow morning with radio and TV appearances to follow. That should bring enough people on board to make this a catalyst for genuine change. Not all men are toxic, but many are, and that needs to change. The female voice needs to be heard a lot louder than it has been up to now.'

Lucy heard her baby cry despite the enthusiastic applause. She thanked all those in attendance for one final time, placed the mic back on its stand, and then stepped off the platform, pleased with what she'd achieved. Ava stopped crying when Lucy held her, which made her smile. Maybe today was the first step in a better world for Ava.

MORE FROM JOHN NICHOLL

We hope you enjoyed reading *The Cellar*. If you did, please leave a review.

If you'd like to gift a copy, this book is also available as a paperback, digital audio download and audiobook CD.

The Sisters, another gripping psychological thriller by John Nicholl, is available to order now.

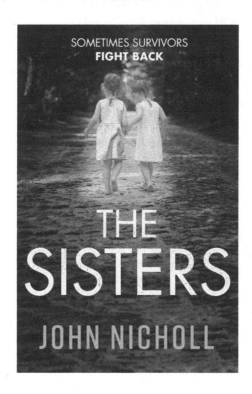

ABOUT THE AUTHOR

John Nicholl is an award-winning, bestselling author of numerous darkly psychological suspense thrillers, previously published by Bloodhound. These books have a gritty realism born of his real-life experience as an ex-police officer and child protection social worker.

Visit John's website: https://www.johnnicholl.com

Follow John on social media:

 twitter.com/nicholl06

 facebook.com/JohnNichollAuthor

 instagram.com/johnnichollauthor

Boldwood

Boldwood Books is an award-winning fiction publishing company seeking out the best stories from around the world.

Find out more at www.boldwoodbooks.com

Join our reader community for brilliant books, competitions and offers!

Follow us
@BoldwoodBooks
@BookandTonic

Sign up to our weekly
deals newsletter

https://bit.ly/BoldwoodBNewsletter

9 781804 263709